THE RELUCTANT VAMPIRE QUEEN BITES BACK

JO SIMMONS

HOT KEY BOOKS

First published in Great Britain in 2023 by
HOT KEY BOOKS
4th Floor, Victoria House, Bloomsbury Square
London WC1B 4DA
Owned by Bonnier Books
Sveavägen 56, Stockholm, Sweden
bonnierbooks.co.uk/HotKeyBooks

This is a work of fiction. Names, places, events and incidents are
either the products of the author's imagination or used fictitiously.
Any resemblance to actual persons, living or dead, is purely
coincidental.

A CIP catalogue record for this book is available from the British
Library.

ISBN: 978-1-4714-1183-0
Also available as an ebook and in audio

1

Typeset by DataConnection Ltd
Printed and bound in Great Britain by Clays Ltd, Elcograf S.p.A.

Hot Key Books is an imprint of Bonnier Books UK
bonnierbooks.co.uk

THE RELUCTANT VAMPIRE QUEEN BITES BACK

1

Mo Merrydrew bounced up the stairs in her dressing gown, a piece of buttered toast gripped between her teeth. She thumped her bedroom door shut, put her breakfast down on a pile of books – physics, maths and *Macbeth* – and began towelling off her wet hair.

It was a gloomy December day. The bare branches of the tree beyond her window were silhouetted against the sky like skeleton fingers. The sun, recently risen, had made no dent in the thick grey cloud. Mo, though, was humming.

'You're cheerful,' her mum said, coming into her room with a hot chocolate. Mo quickly threw the towel over the fake vampire teeth that were sitting on her desk – a specially commissioned new set, made with a custom-fitted plate and shiny fangs hand-crafted in bright white acrylic.

'Would it kill you to knock?'

'Sorry. I forgot teenagers like privacy,' her mum said. 'I can't believe you're almost sixteen. Seems just days ago you were a baby.'

'Don't get comfy!' Mo said, seeing her mum sit down. 'And please remember you can't just wander in here any more. No point looking all sad about it, Mum. I'm just putting up some healthy boundaries.'

'Absolutely,' her mum said. 'I've heard boundaries are all the rage now, aren't they? Of course when I was young –'

'Mum!' Mo said forcefully. 'I don't have time for this. I've got to get ready or I'll be late.'

'Not like you, sweetheart. You always used to be so punctual.'

Mo raised her eyebrows and stared hard at her mum.

'Going. I'm going,' she said. 'Have a great day. Enjoy your studying.'

Once the door was shut again Mo picked up the fake fangs and slipped them into her mouth. She looked into the mirror, her pale oval face serious and tough. Then she pulled back her lips in a huge hiss, her dagger-like teeth shining and her eyes glinting with malice. She took a selfie and sent it to her best friend.

Scary, no?

Lou messaged back almost immediately.

Looking fierce! But why are you cosplaying vampires when you should be getting ready for school? You better be on the bus in a minute.

Quickly Mo texted back.

This isn't fancy dress. I'm the Vampire Queen and you'd better show me respect or else I'll rip your head off and drain your blood!

Lou pinged back.

Whatever.

Mo laughed. Tucking the fangs away in a locked box in her wardrobe, she grabbed her school uniform, her hand grazing the soft velvet of the black regal robe hanging next to her white school shirt. She dressed quickly and scooped her school books into her backpack. She hid the letter that she was working on in her desk drawer, written in thick black ink, inviting all the undead of Great Britain to their first reception with the newly appointed Vampire Queen, just as her phone trilled into life. It was Luca, video-calling.

'Morning, girlfriend.'

Mo grabbed her backpack and headed for the door. 'Hey! Your timing's terrible,' she said through the last bit of toast she'd just stuffed into her mouth. 'I'm going to be late for the bus and it will be *your* fault!'

The face on the screen smiled back.

'I just wanted to say hi before you disappear into school and leave me all alone again.'

Mo slammed the front door and broke into a jog.

'Luca, give up!' she half shrieked, half panted, the cold turning her breath into clouds. 'You've got the easiest gig going. You're a vampire's familiar to a fake vampire. It's not a real job. You get to relax all day, all expenses paid.'

'I know, but it's a bit boring. I almost miss being Bogdan's familiar.'

'Miss clearing up vampire vomit and dead bodies?'

'Yeah, that wasn't great, but Bogdan was very cultured and at least he needed me.'

'I need you,' Mo said, then blushed at her words.

'Are you finally going to tell your parents about us?' he asked. 'It's been three weeks now.'

Three weeks since Mo had convinced the Vampire King of the East – aka Matislav Rosstistavich, aka Steve – the mightiest vampire in all of Europe, that she was the Vampire Queen, the Chosen One, destined to rule, ruthless, fearless, good at ripping heads off. Only she wasn't. A vampire, or a head-ripper-offer. She was a human schoolgirl from a small rural village, focused on her studies and ambitious for her future career but also, it turned out, super good at facing down vampire overlords.

'Are you ashamed of me?'

'What? Luca! No!' Mo gasped. 'Really no. It's just that keeping that side of my life secret is what I'm used to. You know, the vampire side.'

'But I'm not a vampire.'

'I know, and neither am I,' Mo said. 'I just want to keep my parents out of it. There's so much they don't know about me. Suddenly I've got a whole other life. I've got *you*.' She blushed again.

'I get that,' Luca said, 'but your parents will always be your parents, and you do still live at home.'

'I know, I know. It's me that's changed, I suppose. Squaring up to the Vampire King, protecting you and Lou from him . . .'

'Saving us,' Luca said. 'He was *so* going to eat us. Me first, all hypnotised and floppy, and then Lou for dessert.'

'I don't like to think about it,' Mo said, 'the way he ran his fingernail down the vein in your throat, eyeing it up . . .' She shuddered. 'But, him not eating you is definitely my biggest-ever achievement. Mum and Dad have always been proud of my good grades and prizes, but standing up to the Vampire King feels like the most real thing I've ever done, and they know nothing about it.'

'Are you going to tell them?'

'God no!' Mo said. 'Never! My vampire life needs to stay secret forever.'

'At least tell them about me though. I'm sick of meeting outdoors,' Luca said. 'Anyway, your folks will be happy. You've got a boyfriend. Normal. Well done. Pop open the champagne.'

'I've always been normal, thanks very much.'

'Sure, but you studied a lot and they worried about you, and then I came along and changed everything!'

'Shut up!' Mo puffed. 'I don't need a man or a woman or anyone to complete me.'

'Yeah, but it's fun, right? Having a boyfriend, having *this* boyfriend.' He jabbed his thumb into his chest. 'It's pretty good, isn't it?'

'Luca, where did you get all this confidence from? You used to be so polite.'

He laughed.

'Look, OK, I'll tell them,' Mo said.

'When?' Luca asked.

'Soon,' Mo replied. 'I've got to go. The bus is pulling in.'

'Try not to miss me too much.'

'Shut up *again*,' Mo said, climbing aboard.

'I know it's hard to be apart from me, but you need to concentrate on your schoolwork, OK?'

'Bye, Luca,' Mo said firmly, and quit the call.

2

Mo walked halfway up the bus and stood next to her regular seat. Lou was looking up at her, her blonde fringe almost covering her blue eyes.

'Talking to Luca? Ahhh, young love. So beautiful!' she said.

'Any room for me?' Mo pointed at Lou's broken leg, still encased in plaster after she had been run over by Bogdan in the lane outside Mo's house. It was resting on the seat. She squeezed in next to it.

'How much longer?' she said, tapping the plaster with her knuckles.

'Another three weeks. They're taking it off just before Christmas.' Lou sighed. 'It's doing my head in. It's so itchy. I have to poke a knitting needle under the cast to scratch. What was lovely Luca saying?'

'He was moaning about getting bored while I'm at school.'

'Sweet,' said Lou. 'He's into you. That's great.'

'Do you think so?'

'I know he is,' Lou said, and paused. 'You do too. There – you're smiling and blushing.'

'I still can't quite believe I've got a boyfriend,' Mo said shyly.

'I'm shocked too,' Lou said, and didn't look like she was joking.

'A few months ago, when I wasn't at school I was always at home with Mum and Dad, focusing on The Plan for my life. I mean, I do still really want a job in politics or the UN, in the future, but right now I've got a boyfriend, I'm the Chosen One and I've convinced the Vampire King of the East that I am the rightful Vampire Queen of Great Britain. Everything's changed. *I've* changed.'

'Now you've just got to do it.'

'Do what?'

'Be the queen. Rule. What does that even involve?'

Mo shrugged. 'I'm not sure, but I'm aiming to keep it quite minimal. I've seen what the real human king does on royal visits. A short speech, shake a few hands, then he's off. I can do that.'

'I'm pretty sure he does other stuff too, when he's back in his palace. Paperwork and letter writing and dinners. It's a full-time job.'

'Yes, but he rules over millions of people and I rule over just twenty.'

'But they are vampires,' Lou pointed out. 'This isn't the debating society any more.'

'Yes, but they're not power-crazed psychopathic vampires like the Vampire King. These guys have been hiding away for the last couple of decades, since vampire hunters killed loads of them during the purges. They have been ignored and frightened. They'll just be glad someone has noticed them.'

'You sound confident,' Lou said.

'What's wrong with that?' Mo snapped. 'You're not going to pull me down, are you? Women should support each other.'

'Of course I support you, I just want you to be OK.'

'Sorry, yes, I know, and thanks for caring, Lou, but I've got this.'

Lou nodded. 'Loving the new fangs, by the way,' she said. 'So much better than Tracey Caldwell's gumshield with teeth painted on.'

Mo glanced over her shoulder to where Tracey was sitting on the back seat, staring sullenly at her phone. Tracey, who used to call her a neek as soon as she got on the bus each day, but was now silent.

'I know,' she said. 'I can even speak with them in, they fit so perfectly. They were really expensive.'

'That's not all you've been buying though. New coat, am I right?' Lou said. She pushed Mo's long hair back a little. 'And earrings. Been hammering your vampire charge card again?'

'I only got a few things. Bogdan is always on at me to spend more. "Queen Mo, go splish-splashing the vampire cash, yes? You have Dark Card now. No limits! Enjoy plenty shopping."'

'Can I see it, the Dark Card?' Lou asked.

Mo pulled it out of her wallet and passed it to Lou. It was shiny black and at first appeared to be completely plain, but then silver numbers appeared like a hologram when she moved it in the light.

'Cool,' Lou said. 'How much could you spend on this then?'

Mo shrugged. 'I don't think there's a limit.'

'What? You're kidding. I am *so* jealous!'

The bus swung through the school gates.

'We're here,' Mo said, putting the card back in her wallet. She stepped into the aisle and crashed straight into Tracey Caldwell. Tracey moved backwards a bit, but said nothing. Mo still couldn't get used to this. Tracey Caldwell not shouting at her, calling her names, belittling her. Since that night when Mo stood up to her, just before Lou got run over by Bogdan, Tracey had stopped all of it. Just like that. Three-plus years of picking on Mo were over.

'Hi, Tracey,' Mo said.

Tracey didn't reply. She was looking beyond Mo at a couple of younger kids who were standing in the aisle. 'Move it, you two!' she shouted. 'Lou needs space.'

'Yeah, can't you see she's on crotches?' piped up Danny Harrington, her regular sidekick. Danny, who never used capital letters because he didn't 'believe in them'. Who said ketchup sandwiches counted as one of his five a day. Who once gave mouth-to-mouth resuscitation to a duckling (it survived).

Mo gripped her backpack strap hard, trying not to grin – at Danny's 'crotches' and Tracey's personality transplant. She glanced behind them at Jez Pocock, the school alpha male. He hadn't looked so alpha when Bogdan had hurled him to the ground in the lane near Mo's house, intending to suck his blood. He'd knocked Jez unconscious, which meant Jez never saw Mo hit Bogdan with a chemistry textbook. Fine, Mo thought. My little secret. Or, rather, one of my little secrets . . . She smiled quickly at him. He flicked his eyebrows up at her in response.

'Thank you, Tracey,' Lou said cautiously as she slowly manoeuvred herself upright and hopped down the bus.

Tracey nodded sternly.

'Wow,' said Mo when they were outside. 'Tracey still isn't hassling us.'

'It's guilt. She thinks she's to blame for this.' Lou indicated her broken leg.

'Maybe she actually cares about you,' Mo suggested.

'Say what now?' Lou's manga eyes pinged wide in disbelief. 'Tracey only cares about herself.'

'People can change,' Mo said. 'I have. I've got a boyfriend now.'

'Oh really? I had no idea. You didn't mention him for about, like, two minutes.'

'You're the one that likes talking about him.'

'Prefer looking at him.'

'Lou!' Mo said. 'Back off! Anyway, it's wrong to objectify a man.'

'Doesn't feel wrong,' Lou muttered, then changed tack. 'What does your mum think of him?'

'Ummm . . .'

'Your dad? Oh, you're kidding! He hasn't met your parents yet, has he?'

'Not exactly,' Mo said, wincing. 'He met Dad once, before we were together, but Dad was weird and wouldn't shake his hand.'

'Mo! Come on. What are you doing? You can't keep Luca a secret forever. Anyway, your parents are great.'

'My mum can be touchy-feely.' Mo said, wincing.

'Your dad's nice.'

'He's obsessed with carpets.'

'It's his job.'

'It's his job to fit carpets, not to be obsessed with them. Plus, he can be really judgmental.'

'Not about Luca though, surely? They'll love him. He's great. Big shoulders, even bigger smile, kind, intelligent, smells like apple crumble.'

'Well, more like a cinnamon bun really.'

'They'll love him because they love you,' Lou said.

'I suppose so,' said Mo.

'And because you love him.'

'Yeah, I guess.'

'Ha! Got you,' Lou shrieked, whacking Mo with one of her crutches.

'Wait, no, I didn't mean I, you know, feel *that* way about him. I don't love him, of course I don't.'

'You do, you love him. You *luuurve* him. Mo loves Luca. Forever!'

'You're being childish now.'

'You're the one who hasn't let her boyfriend meet her parents. If I had a boyfriend, I'd introduce him to my rellies right away, but you've always liked to keep things boxed up. I've seen your desk. Weirdly tidy. Sticky notes colour-coded. Pencils sharpened. You're doing that now. Luca over here. Vampire Queen over there.' Lou moved her hand from place to place. 'Schoolwork here, parents over there. All neat and organised.'

'Lou! I'm going to tell my parents about Luca. I am. I promised him just now.'

'Cool,' Lou said. 'Now what do you say?'

'Erm . . .'

'Not *erm*. You say, thank you, Lou, you're the total best. How would I cope without you?'

'I'm not saying that,' said Mo, starting to smile.

'Say it!'

'Never!'

'Say the words!'

'I will not say the words!' Mo shouted.

Lou shrugged. 'It's OK, I don't care. You're thinking it, I can tell.'

Then she planted the end of one crutch in the small of Mo's back and shoved her through the school door.

3

When Mo got home she found an envelope on the mat, addressed to her in a familiar swirling hand. Inside was a postcard, showing palm trees lolling above a turquoise sea, white sand and a setting sun. She flipped it over.

Dearest Mo,

How are you liking this sunset? Pretty nice, eh? This is new beach I discovered. I swim here every night. I have made friends with turtle. I am calling him Atilla. Looks like paradise, no? But I am not going to lie to you Mo, I am feeling a tiny bit boring. There is nothing much to do here. No cinema, no art galleries, hardly any shops. At least plenty tourists coming and going so I'm having nice international menu. When are you meeting your subjects? Do not delay. Are you exciting for this? I wish I could see you ruling. And Luca. Is he plenty well? Send me your news! I hope to read from you soon.

Bogdan

Mo smiled and tucked the postcard away in her desk drawer, alongside the six others Bogdan had sent since he had retired to the Caribbean. In each one he moaned about retirement not being as much as fun as he'd hoped. They were oddly emotional too, for a six-hundred-year-old vampire, often referring to Mo as family. I'm not, she thought. I could never be related to a vampire. I can only pretend to be one, and that's as far as it goes. Bogdan must be going soft in his old age.

The front door slammed. Dad. Fifty years old, and still no idea how to close a door quietly.

I have to tell him I have a boyfriend, Mo thought. I'll wait until Mum gets home. Then I'll do it. And there she is now. Oh great. Fine, right, let's get this over with. Mum, Dad, I've got a boyfriend. Gah!

Mo felt bubbles of resistance rising up and popping at the surface of her thoughts. Is it any of their business though? They don't know I'm the Vampire Queen, so why do they have to know about Luca? And what if they start asking difficult questions about how we met?

Mo was thinking all this as she left her room and trotted down the stairs and into the kitchen.

'Are you all right?' her mum asked. 'You look worried.'

'I've got a boyfriend,' Mo blurted.

'You've got what?' her dad said. He was rummaging for snacks deep inside the fridge, like a fox in an overturned bin. He turned to face her, a slice of ham pincered between finger and thumb.

'A, erm, boyfriend?'

'A boyfriend,' he said, staring at Mo like she'd just confessed to shoplifting or getting a full sleeve tattoo. The ham hung motionless.

'Yes. One of those. That.'

Silence from dad, but Mo's mum rushed over and hugged her.

'That's so lovely, darling,' she said. 'Is it Jez?'

'Jez? No, it's Luca. Remember him?'

Dad's eyebrows climbed slowly up his forehead. 'Hmmm,' he said.

'Hmmm?' Mo replied.

'Yes, hmmmm.' He stuffed the ham messily into his mouth.

'We'd love to meet him, properly. How about dinner tonight?' suggested her mum.

'Tonight?' Mo said.

'All right. Get him over,' said her dad. 'Let's find out what he's made of.'

Back in her room, Mo messaged Luca.

Dinner, here, tonight at 7.

Luca messaged back:

You told your parents about us then?

Mo quickly replied:

Yup. Dad wants to find out what you're made of, apparently. Mum wants to feed you. You asked for this! Don't be late.

Luca wasn't late. In fact, he arrived early. Mo gave him a hasty kiss on the doorstep.

'Remember, you're here studying at Donny College, OK? Just say any kind of techie course. They're both clueless about stuff like that.'

Luca nodded. Mo led him into the kitchen.

'Mum, Luca's here,' she said. 'Where did Dad go? Oh, Dad, there you are and . . . oh, you're filming this, are you?'

He had appeared behind them in the doorway.

'Some of it,' he said, panning his phone across their confused faces. 'For my records.'

'You've put on a suit too. That's nice. Possibly. It's a Tuesday though. We're just having some dinner. Like we do every Tuesday. Every evening, in fact. Plus, you hardly ever wear a suit anyway. Except to funerals.'

'Hopefully that's not what this is,' Luca joked.

'Well, we'll see, won't we?' Mo's dad replied.

'I think your father looks very smart,' Mo's mum said, smoothing her hands across his shoulders and straightening his tie. 'It reminds me of when we were first dating, and you always looked so dapper and handsome and I used to think –'

'OK, moving on,' Mo said in a voice that was a little too loud. 'Luca, why don't you sit here next to me?'

'And I'll sit here, at the head of the table,' Dad said.

'The table's circular,' Mo pointed out. 'There is no head of it.'

'I'll carve too,' he went on.

'Carve what?' Mo asked. 'We're having veggie lasagne, not a roasted boar.'

He picked up a large, sharp knife and pointed it straight at Luca. 'Now, young man, what are your intentions towards my daughter?'

Mo sprayed the mouthful of water she'd just sipped across the table. 'Come off it, Dad! It's not the Victorian age. He doesn't have "intentions".'

Her dad didn't even look at her. He simply raised a hand in a stop sign, then nodded at Luca to speak.

'Well, Mr Merrydrew, we're just dating and enjoying each other's company for now.'

'Define dating, please.'

'Dad, please stop,' Mo said.

Luca swallowed nervously. 'Just, you know, spending time together and, er, that's it really.'

'Is this how you go about things wherever you're from? You have a hint of an accent.'

'Dad!' Mo shouted, sharp and loud. 'I'm so sorry, Luca, my dad's turned into some sort of racist patriarch from the Dark Ages.'

'Mo, you have to understand that, from my position, this young man has just turned up here, in your life, in our family, from who knows where. I wouldn't be doing my job as your father if I didn't ask a few tough questions.'

Mo's mum put a huge dish down on the table. 'Come on, Mike,' she said. 'Lighten up. Sorry, Luca. He can be a tiny bit protective of his daughter.'

'Of course I'm protective,' he said. 'I want the best for Mo. She's special. Precious. She will always be my priority. Family is everything.'

'What about friends and a career and travel?' Mo said. 'And carpets, eh, Dad? Sometimes they definitely seem to be your priority.'

He didn't laugh. He plunged the knife into the lasagne and swiped through it.

'Family first, always,' he said. 'Understand, Luca?'

'Yup,' said Luca, nodding.

Mo's face creased into an apologetic grimace. Family first at being super embarrassing. I knew this was a bad idea, she thought as she squeezed Luca's hand under the table.

They ate in silence for a few seconds, then Luca smiled at Mo's mum.

'This is delicious, Mrs Merrydrew.'

'Call me Kate, please,' she replied.

'Or stick to Mrs Merrydrew,' Dad said.

'More salad, Luca?' Mo's mum pushed the bowl towards him, smiling encouragingly. Mo's dad shoved it away.

'Now for those tough questions,' he said.

'Haven't we done those already, Dad?' Mo asked.

'Nope. We're doing them now. Ready, Luca?'

Luca nodded uncertainly.

'Why are you here?'

'Well, that's a big question. Why is anyone here?' Luca replied. 'I guess I believe people are here to do good, help their fellow man and –'

'No, why are you *here*?' Mo's dad stabbed the table with his finger. 'In Lower Donny.'

'Oh, I see. I'm studying at Donny College.'

'Course?'

'Technological studies. With digital software interface relations.'

Mo's dad blinked a few times and continued.

'Favourite day of the week?'

'Saturday.'

'Favourite smell?'

'Lemons,' Luca said.

Mo's dad made a tutting sound. 'It's freshly mown grass. Best season?'

'Spring?'

'Really?'

'Autumn's nice too.'

'Better,' said Mo's dad. 'TV or radio?'

'Ummmm.'

'Don't think, just answer!'

'Both!' Luca yelped.

'Who would win in a fight between a bear and a lion?'

'Would it be the –'

'Too slow. Favourite part of a museum?'

'The gift shop?'

'No!' said Mo's dad, slamming his palm down and making everyone jump. 'It's any Bronze Age artefacts. Last time you cried?'

'Oh, er, not sure,' Luca said. 'Maybe later on this evening.'

'Don't be clever with me, young man. What's better, jazz flute or jazz recorder?'

'Sorry?'

'Dad, stop this,' Mo pleaded.

'Just a few more. Do you have any plans to grow a moustache? What was your nickname as a child? Have you ever sworn at a senior citizen? Ever been stung by a jellyfish? Can you tell the difference between a frog and a toad? Any survival skills? What's the correct way to address the Pope? Can you curl your tongue? Do you have any piercings? Ever gone to prison? What do you consider your greatest achievement? How many kilos can you bench-press?'

'Dad!' Mo said.

'I've started so I'll finish. What's the longest you've gone without talking? Can you whittle? Have you ever eaten eel? What would your superpower be – flying or reading minds? How often do you say thank you and not mean it? What's the best time to –'

'DAD!' Mo shot up, shoving her chair back noisily.

Her dad blinked up at his daughter.

'This is stupid. It's unfair. You're not even giving Luca a chance to answer. Please can you stop?'

'Mo's right, Mike,' her mum said. 'Perhaps that's enough questions for now.'

'I'm just finding out about him,' he said. 'You can tell a lot about a person by firing questions at them.'

'What can you possibly find out from all that? Apart from he likes spring and isn't sure who'd win in a bear-on-lion fight?'

'I have ascertained that he seems . . .' he searched for the word, 'acceptable.'

Luca smiled like he'd just been given a prize. Mo was less impressed.

'Acceptable?'

'Yes, but here's the thing, Luca, and the thing is this. And it's here. You may be acceptable, but that doesn't mean I have to like you. I do, though, have to trust you. Can I trust you?'

'Yes,' said Luca.

'Trust is vital. It's essential. Do you understand?'

'Yes,' said Luca.

'Great!' said Mo. 'So, now that all this patriarchal sparring is over and Luca is officially "acceptable", we're going upstairs, OK?'

'Thanks for the meal, Mrs Merrydrew. I mean, Kate,' Luca said. 'Great to chat, Mr Merrydrew.'

'You can put your camera down and stop filming now, Dad,' Mo said.

'Leave your bedroom door open a bit,' he called after her.

'I won't!' Mo called back cheerfully.

4

Mo and Luca ran upstairs. Once inside her room, Mo slammed the door shut so hard her signed photograph of the Mayoress of Middle Donny fell off the wall.

'Oh god, oh god, oh god, sorry. That was too weird,' she said, flopping on the bed. 'That's why I didn't want you to meet them! That's why I should have kept you separate from my unbelievable parents. What the hell was up with my dad? Those questions? I'm so embarrassed. He's normally all right, but that was awful.'

'Have you ever slapped a senior citizen?' Luca said, doing an impression of Mo's dad. 'Would you eat bacon on a Tuesday? When was the last time you wrestled a child? Any plans to rob a post office?' .

'Stop, stop!' Mo squealed, pressing her teddy, Mr Bakewell, into her blushing face.

'It's OK,' Luca laughed. 'He's just protective of you. Funny though, because if he had any idea about who you have been hanging out with lately, he'd realise *I'm* not the problem.'

'Bogdan, the Vampire King . . . Can you imagine, if he knew about *them* . . .'

Mo shuddered.

'Anyway, nice room. Much more comfortable than the shed,' Luca said.

He began inspecting Mo's shelves. 'You have a lot of books. Not much fiction though. So many political biographies.'

Luca studied all the framed certificates and medals hanging up – for spelling and debating competitions and outstanding achievements in maths and science and English, then he sat down on the bed next to Mo.

'Who's this guy?' he asked, pointing at Mr Bakewell. 'I need to ask him some questions, find out if I can trust him. Don't think, teddy, just answer. When was the last time you ate custard? Have you ever said good morning and not meant it? Do you believe in ants?'

Mo whacked Luca with Mr Bakewell several times.

'Oh no, he's got anger issues,' Luca said. 'That's not acceptable at all. Is it OK to kiss him?'

He leaned towards Mr Bakewell and planted a kiss on his furry head, then moved to do the same to Mo. He was aiming for her smiling lips when the door opened and Mrs Merrydrew walked in with two hot chocolates.

'Don't mind me,' she said. 'You two get cosy.'

Mo leaped up. 'Mum, you're supposed to knock. We talked about it this morning!'

'I couldn't! I'm holding these.'

'But you must have put them down to open the door, so you could have knocked then.'

'You can tell she's president of the debating society,' Mo's mum said, winking at Luca.

Mo took the mugs and began ushering her mum towards the door.

'Goodbye, and thanks for those drinks we didn't ask for.'

'It's lovely to see you two so happy,' her mum said, hovering. 'It's very special, your first real romance. Mine was Gary Ritter. We all called him Sponge. No idea why. He worked in the brick factory. Very strong arms. I remember once –'

'Mum,' Mo said firmly, 'it's time for you to leave my room.'

'No, don't go, I want to hear more about Gary Ritter,' Luca said.

'Shut up, Luca. Mum, out. Now.'

Mo began to close the door.

'Never mind, Luca, I'll tell you another time,' Mo's mum said through the narrowing gap. 'Oh, and you must come to my birthday party.'

'That's not until after Christmas,' Mo said.

'You'll come, won't you, Luca?' Mum went on. 'It's an annual tradition. All of Lower Donny is there.'

'Sounds great!' Luca said, as Mo closed the door firmly.

'It's not great,' she said. 'Everyone drinks a lot and then Mum and Dad do a slow dance. Once you've seen it, you can't unsee it. You don't have to come. I would skip it if I could, but apparently being related to these people means I have to go.'

'I will definitely be there,' he said. 'I guess you will have met the vampires by then too. Have you set the date yet?'

Mo shook her head.

'You're not putting it off, are you?'

'No, just building up to it. I've been working on a speech.'

'You made it up as you went along with the Vampire King, and that worked out brilliantly.'

'I know, but this is my "friends, vampires, countrymen" moment.'

'What will you say?'

'Something empowering. Sort of like, come on, guys, put the past behind you, this is a new era for vampires, you've got a queen now, me, in my posh robes, so get out there, walk tall and I'll see you again in six months. Or a year. Yes, a year would be better.'

Luca nodded.

'I'll reassure them that I'm looking out for them now, but also make it clear I'm not their mum, you know? I can't be answering letters from them all day or sorting out their arguments. It will get in the way of school and, you know, us.'

'Sounds good,' said Luca, smiling. 'Park the vampires and make time for some Luca loving.'

Mo pointed her finger at Luca sternly. 'If you ever talk like that again, we're instantly over.'

'Yeah, it didn't sound great, did it?'

He laughed, but Mo held up a hand. 'What was that?' she whispered.

'Is it your mum again?' Luca asked, looking at the door.

'No, at the window. Shhh.'

They both heard it this time. Tapping at the glass. Mo tensed. Luca put his finger to his lips, then edged silently across the room, moved the curtain back a little and peered out.

'It's OK, just a bat,' he said. 'Probably a message from one of the vampires.'

Before Mo could remind him that she really, really disliked bats, Luca had swung the window open and let it in. It flapped around the room before settling on Mo's desk and folding its wings until it seemed to have two hand-less arms by its side.

'Weird kind of bat though,' Luca said, looking at it. 'It's not an Express Bat. Far too small. Doesn't look like it's carrying any kind of message, there's nothing in its claws and –'

'*Greetings, Queen Mo.*'

Mo yelped in shock. It was the Vampire King's voice. Unmistakably. She leaped up and scanned the room anxiously.

'Where is he?' she hissed. 'Did he fly in through the window? Is he under the bed?'

'You're wondering where I am,' the Vampire King's voice came again, filling the room.

Mo grabbed Luca's arm and pulled him close, her fingers digging in like claws.

'I'm in the bat!' said the Vampire King, with a shriek of high-pitched laughter. 'Well, not in him exactly. He's speaking my words. He's a mimic. I tell him the message; he says it to you in exactly my voice. I call him a Chat Bat. Neat, eh? And he can find anyone, anywhere in the world, thanks to his super deluxe sense of smell. Modern vampire technology is so sophisticated! Now I don't have to write to you with actual ink which can be so, you know, boring! Who's got the time, right?'

Mo and Luca stared in stunned silence at the bat. It opened its tiny mouth again, revealing a shockingly pink interior, and more of the Vampire King's words tumbled out.

'Anyway, Queen Mo, I was in the bath the other day, relaxing after a heavy night, listening to my favourite rapper Lil Snack, when you suddenly popped into my head. Pop!'

The last word was so loud Mo jumped.

'I thought to myself, how is that delightful, eccentric little queenie of mine getting on over in damp Great Britain? It's been a few weeks – is she kicking ass? I thought I'd better check. So – are you? Being ruthless? Ruling in a manner suitable for a Vampire Queen? I hope so or . . . How can I put this?'

The bat fell silent. Had it forgotten its lines? Then there he was again, his voice a menacing growl.

'If you are not ruling well, if you're not making your subjects kiss your robes, swear their loyalty and offer their undead lives for you, then you're not doing it right. And not doing it right is not good. Understand?'

Mo nodded weakly, her eyes big and panicked. How could the Vampire King be so terrifying when he wasn't even there?

'I don't really care if you're the Chosen One, Mo. That was enough to get you the job, but as I myself know, once on the throne you've got to hold onto the throne, and sometimes it's other vampires, not humans, who are the biggest threat to success. Capeesh?'

Mo thought she probably did capeesh.

'Excellent! I'll leave you with that then. I'm going to get a bite to eat. All this talking has made me ravenous. So, Queen Mo, do your job well. Don't disappoint me! King Stevie hates to be disappointed. Don't make me come over there! No, seriously, don't. Such a dismal place. All right, that's enough, see you around, Mo. Can't wait to hear how you're getting on. Sayonara, sweet cheeks! Ciao, ciao, ciao!'

The bat shut its mouth and didn't move.

Mo stared at it, breathing fast.

'Can you shoo it out?' she eventually whispered to Luca.

'Don't speak,' he whispered back, 'in case it's recording what we say.'

Mo clamped her mouth shut and nodded.

'Please thank your master for his message,' Luca said in a loud, polite voice, stepping closer to the bat. 'I'm Luca, by the way. The queen's familiar. The one you wanted to eat? Anyway, thank you for getting in touch. It was good to hear from you.'

Mo was glaring at Luca, urging him to shut up.

'Right, yes, bye then,' he said. Then he pushed the window as wide open as it would go and beckoned the bat to leave. Its tiny black eyes flickered between the two of them and its hairless ears twitched, but at last it took off and flapped quickly and silently out. Luca slammed the window shut, pulled the curtains across and went over to Mo, who had slid down the wall and was now hugging her knees to her chest.

5

Luca sat down next to Mo.

'Always lovely to hear from Steve,' he said.

'He had to show up in a *bat*. Two of my least favourite things combined.'

Luca reached for her hand. 'You're shaking,' he said.

'I haven't even met the vampires yet and already I've got the Vampire King threatening me from miles away. I had hoped I'd never see him again. He said he didn't think he'd have to come back for a couple of hundred years. He said that, in Lower Donny Village Hall.'

'I know, I heard him,' Luca said.

'So what did he mean by, "Don't make me come over there"?'

'It's mind games. He's just putting pressure on, that's all. He's good at that.'

Mo wasn't convinced. 'Maybe just meeting the vampires and making a speech isn't enough?' she said, looking desperately at Luca. 'Perhaps I do need to be ruthless, like the Vampire King said, at least at the start.

Do something really tough straight away. Stun them with a big, scary gesture – I don't know, rip the head off a dove or set fire to something maybe – then they won't doubt I'm the real thing. Maybe the Vampire King is right – I need to make them fear me.'

'By decapitating a pigeon?'

'I don't know!' Mo snapped, standing up suddenly. Luca watched her pace the room, hugging her sides and chewing her lip. 'I can't though, can I? I can't rip anyone's head off. It's not who I am. I can hardly get the lid off the jam some mornings.'

She stared at her hands for a few seconds.

'I just have to rule as me, as I planned. An inspiring figurehead. That's all the vampires need. Forget about the Vampire King. He's miles away, in his big bath, listening to Lil Fang or whoever . . . He won't even know how I'm doing. He'll lose interest. He's *always* busy squashing uprisings. You're right, Luca. This is just another classic vampire threat. I need to ignore it. I'll make a success of being Vampire Queen on my terms. My rule, my way. He doesn't need to know the details. So long as the vampires are happy he'll stay away.'

'Right,' said Luca, 'but you should probably meet them soon, before Steve sends another Chat Bat, or worse.'

'Yes.' Mo nodded. 'I can't put it off any longer. I mean, build up to it any longer.'

'So you were putting it off?'

'I was enjoying the break, between meeting Steve and ruling, if you must know,' Mo said. 'But the Vampire Queen honeymoon is over, I guess. I need to stand before my vampire subjects and rule. Let the queening commence.'

'Queening?'

'You know what I mean,' Mo said, with an irritated flap of her hand. She grabbed her laptop and handed it to Luca. 'Could you look for a venue? Somewhere with a big enough space for all of us. I can't do a tour to visit all of them separately. They're all over the UK and it would take too long, plus Mum and Dad would never let me go away overnight with you. So I think we'll need to meet somewhere central – try around Birmingham. Look for a hotel with meeting rooms. We'll have to risk them all gathering together in one place. Twenty vampires in a room, out in human society, what could possibly go wrong?'

Luca opened his mouth to speak.

'Don't answer that,' Mo said. 'I'll write to them,' she went on. She pulled out the letter she'd already began drafting and filled in the blanks. When? She wrote out the date. Today was Wednesday, so the next Saturday would be too soon, but the one after? Yes. A week and a half to get ready. Perfect. She filled in the date and then added other crucial details.

'I'm making it very clear that this is a fangs-free event. No draining, no complaining,' Mo said to Luca as she wrote. 'They will need to keep a really low profile. Dress code: casual (and as un-vampiric as possible). Oh, and I'll tell them it's BYOB – Bring Your Own Blood.'

'Great,' he said. 'Here's a possible location.'

He showed Mo the website of a hotel with fancy grounds and meeting rooms.

'It's got a spa too,' Luca added.

'Are you thinking we could all go for a sauna?' Mo asked. 'Or maybe a facial. Do vampires do skincare?'

He clicked on the images of the meeting rooms.

'Nice fancy chairs with gold padded arms. The vampires will love those,' Mo said. 'The carpet pattern is a bit migrainey though, and what colour do you call those curtains? Mustard? Korma?'

'Baby poo?' Luca added. 'Look, it says this room has space "for up to 24 delegates" and also great views.'

'Even at night?' Mo asked.

'It's called the Sunshine Boardroom.'

'Ironic,' said Mo. 'Let's book it, for a week on Saturday. That's the twelfth of December.'

Luca typed in the details. 'It's expensive.'

'Doesn't matter,' Mo said. 'Put it on my Dark Card. Here.'

She passed her vampire charge card to him and then added the address details to her letter to the vampires. A knock at the door broke her concentration.

'Dad says you're awfully quiet in there,' came Mum's voice from the other side.

'He didn't want to come and say that himself?' Mo shouted back.

'No, he's a bit busy,' she replied, and then pushed the door open a crack.

'As you can see, Mum, I'm doing some homework and Luca's just logging onto the website of his favourite donkey charity to make another donation.'

Luca looked up and grinned. 'Got to support the donkeys,' he said.

'Lovely,' Mo's mum said, looking confused. 'Well, I'll let Dad know. All very wholesome.'

'That's us,' said Mo. The door clicked shut and they heard her padding back downstairs.

'You're *so* not wholesome,' Luca muttered.

Mo snorted but didn't stop writing, her fountain pen skidding over the thick cream paper, summoning the vampires to the Sunshine Boardroom for her first-ever meeting as their queen.

6

Over the next few evenings replies from the vampires flooded in by Express Bat. Pat and Richard in Wales – yes. Derek – yes. Natasha and the girls – yes. The Tartan Fangs – aye. A vampire called Sven the Viking – tak. Luca brought the letters to Mo each evening and she ticked names off a list. By Monday everyone had accepted.

'They all sound excited,' Mo said to Luca in her room that evening. 'They can't wait to meet the Vampire Queen of Great Britain.'

'Good. You should get a warm welcome. Unlike what I got from your dad. He's still quizzing me, you know. He just asked me if I've ever had major surgery, ever eaten a whole watermelon or ever looked into the eyes of a dolphin.'

'Sorry,' said Mo, pulling a pained face.

An uneven thudding on the stairs told them Lou was on her way up.

'All right, losers, how's it going?' she said.

'Not bad – we've got twenty yeses to the royal reception,' said Mo.

'Great. As your official stylist, I've put together some fierce hair and make-up ideas for you.'

'I thought I looked OK like this,' Mo said, pointing at her pale, make-up-free face.

'Ha ha,' Lou laughed. 'Oh sorry, you weren't joking. I've curated some looks too.'

'Curated?'

'Yes. It's what stylists do. We curate.'

'If you say so.'

'How would you know anyway? Right, so I'm thinking when you finally meet all the suckers as their queen, you need to go all out. You know, really bring it. High drama, big impact. Something like this . . .'

Lou started swiping through images on her phone of celebs at premiers and parties. She talked Mo through the looks, with Mo frowning and commenting – 'too bling . . . too much thigh . . . you know I won't agree to heels.'

'What are you going to wear then?' Lou huffed finally.

Mo went to her wardrobe and pulled out her velvet robe encrusted with pearls, her jewelled hair slide, her bangles.

'What do you think of this?'

'Put it all on,' Lou said, so Mo did.

'You look great, Mo. Really elegant. Like a queen in fact. It's very gothic chic,' Lou said. 'Did the vampires give you the jewellery?'

'Yes, all presents.'

'How about your hair?' Lou asked. 'I can help with that at least. A ponytail doesn't shout regal leader.'

'Great. And can you find a really strong perfume for me to wear too, to mask my human smell? Vampires can sniff humans from a long way away.'

'No more *eau de carpet cleaner*,' Luca said.

'Oh yeah, that was nasty,' said Lou. 'I can find something better than that. On it.'

'Thanks, Lou, you're the best,' said Mo, hugging her.

By Thursday, Lou had sourced a new perfume. Mo tried it out after school.

'It's very citrussy,' Lou said, spraying it on her.

'Wow, yeah, like having a grapefruit peeled inside your nostrils,' Mo spluttered. 'Does it repel mosquitos too?'

'No, only vampires.'

Then Lou sat her in front of the mirror and styled her hair, explaining each stage. 'Weave a plait like this, then pin it just here . . .'

Mo felt soothed, gazing in soft focus at her face in the mirror and at Lou's hands, gently combing and moving her hair.

'Do you want me to come with you when you meet the vampires?'

'I can't believe you'd offer, Lou, after you were nearly the catering for the Vampire King,' Mo said.

Lou shrugged. 'Just want to support you. I could stake them with my crutches if things got eggy.'

'Or at least bruise their shins, right?' Mo said. 'Things won't get eggy. It's going to be fine.'

'Where do your parents think you're going?'

'To a Christmas market.'

'Oh cute. Sounds nice.'

'Yeah, but I'm not actually going to a Christmas market, am I?'

'No, I know, but you should do that too, if you've got time. Make a real outing of it.'

Mo wasn't sure if Lou was joking.

'There you go, finished,' Lou said.

Mo leaned in to the mirror. Her hair was still free-flowing, but thin plaits ran through it and Lou had cleverly woven some on top in a ring that looked almost like a crown.

'It's brilliant, Lou,' Mo said, turning to hug her friend tightly round the waist. 'Come on, let's go get a snack. I've got Mini Battenbergs in the kitchen.'

Mo was making tea, Lou sitting with her broken leg resting on a kitchen chair, when Dad came in from work, slamming the door as usual.

'Afternoon you two,' he said. 'Oh, your hair looks nice, Mo.'

'Lou did it.'

'Rather elaborate for you though, isn't it?'

'I fancied a new look.'

'I see,' said her dad, sounding like he didn't.

'What are you getting at, Dad?' Mo asked.

'Nothing. No. Not much. It's just, Luca shows up and now you're doing your hair all posh and, you know, you're changing, that's all.'

'The hair isn't for Luca,' Mo said firmly.

'It's OK to feel a bit threatened by Mo growing up, Mr Merrydrew,' Lou said, smiling sweetly. 'She's not your little girl any more, is she? She's looking older, doing her hair differently, got a boyfriend. It must be difficult for you.'

She took a bite of her Mini Battenberg and seemed unaware of the shock rippling across Mo's dad's face.

'It's not quite like that, Lou,' he said.

Lou smiled again. 'Except it is. Loving is letting go, Mr Merrydrew.'

He frowned. 'Yes, well, I'll leave you two to it,' he said, and left quickly.

'Lou!' Mo said.

'What?'

'I thought you wanted to work in fashion, not as a therapist.'

'Oh, that,' Lou said, stuffing the last mouthful in. 'I was speaking truth to power. Well, speaking truth to your dad.'

'It was brilliant and also *really* embarrassing,' Mo said.

'The truth can do that,' Lou said, reaching across the table for another cake.

7

A dark December Saturday, drizzle falling. Mo had carefully packed all her Vampire Queen clothes, her jewellery and stinky perfume and now, at 3 p.m. with the light almost gone, she and Luca were on a train, speeding through the murky landscape.

'Want one?' Luca said, offering Mo a crisp. She shook her head and bit her lip.

'Nervous?' he asked.

'Excited,' Mo said.

'Really?'

Mo rolled her eyes. 'You can be super annoying when you try.'

'I don't have to try,' Luca said, smiling with delight. 'And sorry, Your Majesty.'

'Please don't call me Your Majesty. You know I hate it.'

'I'm practising,' Luca said. 'I have to put on an act too, don't I? Loyal vampire familiar to the queen. I need to get into the role.'

'Fine, but can we just be quiet for now,' Mo said, a little firmly. 'You focus on being a servant, I'll focus on being the boss.'

They sat in silence for a while. Mo felt nerves hopping in her stomach like fleas in a jam jar. This is it, she thought, no more just *saying* I'm Vampire Queen, I've got to go and do it, for real now. She gazed blankly out of the window, trying to focus on the scenery going past, but could only see her own face reflected back at her. Lou had styled her hair again and given her a slick of cat-like black eyeliner. It was a mask, to cover her humanness and plunge her firmly into the role of Vampire Queen.

Once off the train, Mo and Luca walked for twenty minutes. He held her hand. She said nothing.

'Ooh, fancy,' Luca said, as they walked up the drive of the hotel.

It was an old, handsome red-brick building with lots of fat brick chimneys and a pointy-roofed clock tower rising over the entrance.

'Look, they've got one of those rotating front doors,' Luca said, but Mo was busy taking in the expensive cars parked outside, the clipped yew trees in massive planters and the immaculate lawn sweeping off past the tennis courts. They hurried inside.

'I booked you a room, so you can change in comfort and get yourself prepared,' Luca said, zipping over to the check-in desk.

He returned with a key card and gave it to Mo. 'What's wrong?'

'Sorry, it's just that that's so thoughtful of you,' Mo said, her bottom lip quivering. 'I thought I'd have to hide in the loos until they arrived.'

Luca glanced around hastily and then planted a quick kiss on Mo's cheek.

'You're welcome. Room 204,' he said quietly. 'I'll come and get you once they're here.'

Mo dashed upstairs and into her room. She yanked off her jeans and jumper and pulled on her black dress. On went the robe studded with pearls, the golden bangles, the hairslide with strings of gems hanging from it. Next she doused herself in the strong citrus perfume to mask any human aroma. 'Pulse points, a little on my hair, lots on my throat and definitely a splash under the arms. I am *sweating*,' she muttered.

Then she checked the clock. Almost 6 p.m. The vampires should be arriving now. What would they look like? Would they be excited and chatty or morose and withdrawn? Wearing capes? Surely there had to be some capes? Black velvet with red satin lining?

Mo went over to the mirror and stared at herself.

'You've got this, Queen,' she said and then leaped at two loud knocks on the door.

She opened it and Luca rushed in.

'Why are you panting? Is everything OK?'

'Yes, fine, I just took the stairs,' he said. 'They're all down there now.'

'Oh god,' said Mo. 'I mean, oh good. Great! Yay! How do I look?'

'Beautiful,' he said. 'You stink, but you look great.'

'How do they look?'

'Mixed. Some look like they've been kept in a cupboard for decades, others look more excited and assertive.'

'Assertive?'

'Pat from Wales,' Luca said. 'You'll spot her, don't worry.'

Mo gulped, nerves tsunami-ing through her. 'Everything's set up? Did they write their names on sticky labels?'

'The ones that can write did, yes,' said Luca. 'Ready?'

He held open the door, but Mo paused and looked over her shoulder back into the bedroom, as if she must have forgotten something. Luca reached for her hand and coaxed her over the threshold. Together, they went downstairs.

Outside the Sunshine Boardroom, Luca pointed at the sign on the door.

'I moved it to OCCUPIED. Hopefully that will keep the humans out,' he said. Then he pushed the door open and shouted, 'Vampires of Great Britain, please stand to greet your leader, the mighty, the majestic, the one and only, Queen Mo.'

Really, Luca? Mo thought, wincing. Is that the right tone? But there was nothing else for it but to take a deep breath, slip in her shiny new fangs, hold her head high and stride into the room.

Immediately Mo sensed twenty sets of vampire eyes locking onto her. She heard several vampires gasp and one or two clap. She stared coolly into the middle distance, chin slightly raised, lips pulled back in a slight sneer that revealed her fangs and made for the large table at the front of the room. Only once she got there did she look around, slowly sweeping her gaze across the assembled creatures, keeping her facial expression strong and calm, despite her belly flickering like a dying light bulb.

They were all standing silently. As Luca had said, some looked grey and stooped, in clothes that were faded and worn – jackets with greasy elbows, gowns with grimy collars. Some held themselves proudly and looked Mo squarely in the eye. One of them was Pat, who seemed to take in every millimetre of Mo with her cool, curious gaze. Mo quickly glanced away. Another vampire – Mo checked her name label, Natasha – beamed a warm, maternal smile that made her heart skip a beat. There were two young-looking vampires next to her – presumably 'the girls' that Natasha always referred to – wearing expressions that were a blend of shy and sulky. They wore simple collar-less black dresses in a heavy cotton, the sort of fabric you might upholster a stool in. Bands of woven ivy and holly encircled their tangled dull brown hair. Nice of them to make an effort, Mo thought. Festive too. Their names read Olga and Lenka.

Next to the girls stood a vampire built like a barn door. Sven the Viking. On the table in front of him was a hardback Danish–English phrasebook with a red leather cover. And an axe.

One vampire stood out. He looked groomed and fresh, and was dressed like a 1980s pop star, in a sapphire-blue silk suit and white shirt, his long pale hair tied back in a ponytail. Mo read his name with surprise. So that's Derek, she thought. He doesn't look much older than me. He waved at her, bobbed a sort of bow and clapped his hands with delight.

Mo cleared her throat to speak. She spread her arms wide, took a deep breath and . . .

BOOM!

Mo stumbled backwards, dazed, her ears ringing. An explosion had rocked the room and smoke plumed into the air. Her hand flew up to her head. Was there blood?

Luca rushed to her side. 'Are you hurt?'

'I'm OK, I'm OK,' Mo gasped. 'Was that a bomb?'

The room was grey with smoke now and smelled like fireworks. All the vampires were coughing and panicking.

'It's the vampire hunters! We're under attack!' one shouted, which made others scream and shout, 'Run for it' and 'Where's the exit?'

Mo tried to speak, to prevent a vampire stampede, but she could only cough. Someone else spoke though, in a shrill, withering voice that cut through the kerfuffle.

'Richard, you crispy piece of turd. I told you a hundred thousand times not to bring that cannon.'

8

A figure appeared from the smoke. It was Pat. Now it was Mo's turn to take her in. She was wearing a red velvet jacket and matching long skirt. There was a huge froth of lace at her throat. She wore a top hat too, which she now took off as she swept into a deep bow.

'Majesty,' she said, stretching her crimson-painted lips into a smile, 'I am honoured to meet you. I am Pat, from Wales, and this gigantic ninny biscuit is my husband, Richard.'

Richard moved forwards through the smoke, a great mountain of a vampire, with a bald head and an expressionless face. He bowed silently.

'He insisted that a cannon salute is the only way to greet our new Vampire Queen,' Pat said. 'I told him it was a stupid idea, like the kind only a ridiculous little walnut has, but what do you know, he didn't listen to me. Said nothing, ignored his wife, and brought the bloody cannon.'

Mo raised her hand, but before she could speak a high-pitched *WEE-OO, WEE-OO* ripped through the Sunshine Boardroom.

'It's the vampire hunters again, confusing us with their siren of death,' Natasha wailed.

'It's not,' Mo shouted, finding her voice at last, 'it's the smoke alarm. We need to go outside. Follow me.'

Wow, they're super paranoid about vampire hunters, she thought, before she pulled the meeting room door open and paused. People were filing down the corridor towards the exit. People wearing Christmas hats, laughing and weaving about despite the ear-splitting alarm. Human people in party mood, with lowered inhibitions and delicious warm blood in their veins. Lots of them. Uh-oh!

'Luca,' she said, beckoning him over, 'make sure no one decides these guys are dinner, yes? I'll lead, you follow at the back.'

Mo swept down the corridor and into the hotel lobby. The light was strong here. She glanced back over her shoulder and winced. The vampires following her looked like, well, vampires. Dull skin, dark eyes, long hair on all the women and some of the men. Forget lustrous healthy locks though – theirs looked as if it had been styled with porridge and cobwebs. She noticed two reception staff whispering and glancing their way.

'It's fancy dress,' she shouted at them, above the noise of the fire alarm. They nodded, but looked unconvinced.

'Fancy dress?' said a man in a suit, pivoting towards Mo on wobbly legs. He was clutching a bottle of vodka. His tie was undone and he wore silver tinsel like a sparkly scarf. 'What have you come as? Ooh, gothy vibe, pale faces, you look like . . .'

'No, we don't,' said Mo. She ushered the other vampires past him, encouraging them to keep moving and head for the exit.

'Yeah, like vampires,' said the man.

Some of the vampires cringed, uncomfortable with being noticed, and scuttled quickly past. Pat on the other hand looked irritated, her top lip twitching.

'I'm Greg by the way. Want a drink?' He held out the bottle.

'We don't drink,' said Mo.

'That's not true,' said Pat, reaching into her skirt pocket. 'I do.'

She pulled out a silver hip flask, flipped open the lid, threw a big mouthful back and then wiped her lips on the back of her hand.

'What you got in there?' Greg asked, spotting the crimson smears on Pat's mouth and frowning. 'Some kind of red wine?'

'The reddest of red wine,' said Pat, rolling all the Rs and licking her lips.

'Very nice,' said Greg, nodding and backing away. 'Well, I'll leave you to it.'

'Yes, Gregory darling, I suggest you absolutely do that,' Pat said, in a purring-but-snarling voice.

Mo hurried Pat towards the exit. Natasha had got her long skirt caught in the revolving door, jamming it, and Derek was trying to yank it free while Olga and Lenka were tutting and rolling their eyes.

Mo watched, jaw tense and fists clenched, aware that Pat was simmering menacingly. *Please don't kill anyone, please don't kill anyone*, she found herself chanting in her head, sensing Pat's tiger-on-a-leash energy. Finally, with a rip, Derek pulled Natasha's skirt free, leaving a strip of dark green crushed velvet behind, and the doors began turning again. Mo swept out.

'Stupid utter fool,' Pat fumed, once they were outside and striding across the car park towards the grounds.

'Who?' Mo asked.

'That drunk gibbon in his ugly suit. Greg.' Pat hissed. 'Staring like that. Hasn't he seen a vampire before? I should have punctured his veins and drunk him dry. He would have looked like a sun-dried tomato once I finished with him.'

'Oh, that would have worked,' Derek said, rolling his eyes.

'I beg your pardon, Derek,' Pat said, her voice getting louder with each word. She marched over to him.

'Murder isn't the solution to all life's problems,' Derek said. 'It's time to grow up, Pat. I mean, how old are you? Four hundred? Five hundred?'

'How absolutely dare you, you little –'

'ENOUGH!' Mo shouted. 'Derek is right.'

'Thank you, Your Majesty,' he said, beaming, 'and can I just say it is *such* an honour to meet you. I've got so many ideas for our future with you as queen. I cannot wait to share.'

I bet, thought Mo, remembering how Derek had given her a ruby ring, then sent his familiar to ask if he could be her deputy, clearly hoping the jewel would act as a bribe to soften Mo up. It hadn't.

They assembled under a tree on the edge of the hotel's lawn.

'Remember, everyone, we are trying to keep a low profile,' Mo said. 'We do not want to attract the attention of humans, let alone vampire hunters, so that means no hissing, no fangs and murder is absolutely out of the question, OK?'

Nodding. General look of having been told off.

'But are we safe?' Natasha asked. 'What if those humans follow us over here? They could be vampire hunters.'

'They're too drunk to drive a stake into anything,' Mo said.

'But there might be vampire hunters hiding behind this tree,' she said. 'Or that bush over there – what is it?'

'I think it's a rhododendron,' Mo said, and then shook her head impatiently. 'Luca – check for vampire hunters.'

He looked behind the tree then jogged around all the bushes, peering between their leafy branches. The vampires watched in tense silence.

'It's safe,' he said.

The vampires sighed with relief. Mo noticed a fire engine pulling up by the hotel entrance and the crew streaming inside.

'It's clear we could be stuck outside for some time, so let us begin our meeting here,' Mo said, hoping to drag things back on track. She spread her arms wide, her heavy robe draping down. She had memorised her speech. She had practised in the mirror. She was ready. She took a deep breath and began.

9

'Vampires of Great Britain, I stand before you as your queen. I am the Chosen One. Chosen to lead you, chosen to inspire you, chosen to give you back your confidence. I know you have suffered since the purges.'

The vampires hissed and covered their ears. Some turned away from her.

Mo paused. 'I realise that –'

'Speak up,' said Pat. 'We can't hear you.'

'Because you've got your hands over your ears,' Mo said.

Slowly the vampires dropped their hands.

Mo gathered herself again. 'I realise that the purges were –'

Hissing, hands on ears and wounded, angry glances again.

'Oh for goodness sake,' said Mo. 'This is ridiculous. "Purges" is only a word.'

Yet more hissing.

'Look, what do you want me to do?'

'Kindly desist from such proclamations,' said Sven, reading from his phrasebook.

'Yes, just stop saying it, please,' Pat barked.

'It's very triggering,' Derek wailed.

'OK, OK!' Mo shouted. 'I promise I won't say the P-word. Now please take your hands away from your ears so you can hear me properly.'

Slowly they lowered their hands. When all the vampires were paying attention, Mo spoke.

'I can see how damaged you've been by the . . . by the you-know-whats, but when was the last time a vampire in Great Britain was killed by a vampire hunter?'

The vampires murmured between themselves.

'Pretty sure that was Uncle Stewie, staked on the fifth of February 2002,' said a vampire with a wild white beard, fiery dark eyes and a kilt. His name label read Malcolm. 'He was a kind soul. A poet.'

'Aye, aye,' agreed two vampires standing alongside him – Duncan and Donald. The Tartan Fangs. The three of them looked identical and, in addition to the matching kilts, they all had black painted fingernails and numerous ear and nose piercings.

'That's over twenty years ago,' Mo said. 'Isn't it time you put it all behind you?'

The vampires shrugged and looked sulky.

Mo tried again. 'I understand that you were badly burned by what went on.'

'This is so,' said Sven, reading from his phrasebook again. 'Human men enforced my cherished compatriot Ludo to step from his domicile, and thence to be burned egregiously in the solar luminosity and smouldered away to nothing.'

'His phrasebook's a bit out of date, Your Majesty,' Derek explained. 'Basically, he said his best friend Ludo was dragged into the sun by vampire hunters and fried to a sizzle in seconds.'

'I'm sorry for your loss,' said Mo.

'We've all lost someone to vampire hunters,' Malcolm said sternly. 'Every one of us.'

'Mum and Dad.'

It was Olga and Lenka.

'Your parents?'

They nodded.

Mo saw the hurt in their eyes. 'I'm so sorry,' she said, then tried to move the conversation on. 'As I understand it, there have always been vampire hunters, right? There has always been some risk?'

'Of course,' Pat said. 'There would always be some foolish little twerp who thought he could kill a mighty vampire, and occasionally they did, but the vampire hunters behind the you-know-whats were different.'

'They were organised and brutal,' said Malcolm. 'This wasn't the usual break-open-the-coffin-and-stake-you-while-you-sleep routine. They were devious. They tricked us and lured hundreds to their death across the land.'

'Remember how Alexei died?' Pat asked the group. 'They rang his doorbell one night and shouted through the letterbox, "Special delivery – French human!"'

Everyone nodded solemnly.

'Alexei could never resist French cuisine so he opened the door, the stupid silly half-baked birdbrain, and got staked in his own home.'

The vampires shook their heads sadly.

'The you-know-whats were a carefully calculated drive to remove all vampires from Great Britain,' Malcolm said grimly. 'A war, but we didn't want to be at war. We wanted to live alongside humans, as much as possible.'

'We did not deserve to be hunted like that,' said Pat. 'Yes, I know we kill humans and the humans take that very, very personally, but we only do it to survive. What choice do we have?'

'I actually can't stand the sight of blood,' said Natasha, smiling apologetically. 'I'm terribly squeamish. Funny really.'

No one laughed.

'We wrote to the Vampire King of the East for help, but he never sent any, did he?' Pat added. 'He's always so busy fighting other vampires for territory and money and castles that he's forgotten about the age-old conflict, the biggest one of all – vampires versus vampire hunters.'

'He is a gross and putrid sore on the visage of the vampire cosmos,' said Sven.

'That's right,' said Pat. 'I don't know who I hate more. The vampire hunters or that giant toxic man-boy clown, the Vampire King. He failed to support us, to come to our aid. He ignored us, the dirty little ear mess, and pretended it wasn't happening. Can you imagine a leader doing this? I can never forgive him for that. Never. It's like he didn't care.'

'I care,' Mo said, surprised by the power in her voice. The vampires looked keenly at her. 'I care. You have been persecuted, hunted and attacked in your own homes.'

She paused for effect.

'You have been forced to flee and hide out.'

Another pause. Damn, being the debating-society president was paying off!

'You have been made to fear for your lives, isolated and unsupported, without backup from those who could have helped you. That's wrong, but it changes today. Right now. This second.'

The vampires were leaning in now, listening intently.

'I am your queen and I am here for you.'

'But what can you do?' Pat said, a sneer in her voice. 'We will never be safe until every vampire hunter is annihilated.'

'How are you going to take out every vampire hunter?' Mo asked. 'Do you know who they are? Or where they live? Do you have names?'

No one answered.

'See?'

'So what's the solution?' Pat flung her hands up angrily. 'Keep hiding, like snivelling scared little teaspoons? If that's all I can look forward to for the rest of my life, stake me now!'

'You have to live in spite of the hunters,' Mo said. 'Live your best life, understanding that every day could be your last. That's what humans have to do, after all.'

Pat's lip curled.

'It's time you felt proud of who you are,' Mo said. 'You deserve a voice and respect.'

'Aye.' The Tartan Fangs nodded.

'You have the right to celebrate your identity, to freely express yourselves and be accepted for who you are. You didn't ask to be turned, right?'

'I did,' Derek said.

'*Most* of you didn't ask to be turned,' Mo went on. 'But you're all vampires now. *We're* all vampires now. Let's own it, freely and bravely, without fear of oppression.'

'Yes!' the vampires shouted.

'Without apology.'

'Yes!'

'Without excuses!'

'Yes!'

'Seize your destiny, connect with your ancient story. You are mighty vampires, feared and admired for centuries.'

'Yes, yes.'

Then Mo paused, silently eyeing them all.

'Vampires of Great Britain, now is the time to step forward into your future,' she said, her voice low and urgent. 'Pledge your allegiance to me and I will serve you as your queen.'

'I pledge allegiance,' Derek shouted, and dropped to his knees, one hand over his heart.

'We pledge allegiance,' the Tartan Fangs shouted, kneeling too.

'Oh yes, definitely,' said Natasha, who had to lean on Donald's shoulder but got down on one knee eventually. 'Arthritis, sorry,' she murmured.

One by one, all the vampires knelt in front of Mo, declaring their loyalty and staring up at her, eyes shimmering.

Mo felt flushed with adrenaline and pride. She let it pulse through her for a few moments, taking in the scene, feeling strong, powerful and brave.

Then Luca whispered in her ear. 'Majesty, the fire crew has left now. We can go back in.'

Mo glanced over at the hotel entrance and watched as the fire engine pulled out of the drive.

'Rise, loyal subjects,' she said, sounding super regal. 'To your feet at once. Let us return to the meeting room. There is much to discuss.'

Derek sprung up first and bounded over.

'Can we get a snack too?' he asked, hopping about next to her like an excited puppy. 'I'm famished.'

'It's Bring Your Own Blood, Derek, keep up,' said Pat, waving her hip flask at him and then taking a big swig.

'No feeding until you're far from here,' Mo said.

'How far?'

'Quite far.'

'Three miles?'

'Just, you know, *far*,' Mo snapped back. 'Snacking on the hotel premises is forbidden. Understand?'

'Oops, too late, sorry.'

Everyone spun round to see who'd spoken. A figure emerged from the shadows. She was young, with thick straw-coloured hair tumbling over her huge hoop earrings and black leather jacket. Her nails were painted scarlet, clearly visible as she wiped the last trace of blood from the corner of her mouth with one finger. She walked towards the group and dropped her motorbike helmet on the ground.

'Long ride,' she said, 'and when I got here I was so hungry, and there was this super cute waitress that I met by the bins and . . . Is there a problem?'

'Who are you?' Pat asked, flashing her fangs.

'I am new here.' She had a silky deep voice and Mo caught a hint of an accent similar to Bogdan's. 'I arrived few days ago. Thought I'd come and introduce myself, not that any of you look very pleased to see me . . . I'm Vanya.'

'You're late,' Pat said.

'I'm sorry,' Vanya said, but her grey eyes looked amused rather than apologetic. 'As I mentioned, long ride.'

Vanya approached Mo now and studied her face closely. Her eyes narrowed slightly as she took Mo in and her full lips twitched just a little.

'Your Majesty,' Vanya said quietly, then she bowed and kissed Mo's fingers.

Mo had to fight not to snatch her hand away. She felt herself blushing. Her mouth went dry. Vanya eventually let her hand fall, but continued to gaze at Mo, hardly blinking. A ripple of goosebumps travelled across Mo's skin.

She turned back to the other vampires. 'Go,' she said almost angrily. 'Return to the hotel. I will follow.'

They made their way across the grass and Mo watched them go, her eyes glued to Vanya's back, and then Luca appeared at her side.

'What are you doing?' he said.

Staring at Vanya, Mo realised.

'I thought the plan was to give the vampires a confidence boost and leave them to get on with it,' Luca whispered. 'Now you're promising to help them.'

'You heard them describing the purges. They've been systematically persecuted. The vampire hunters have made their lives a living hell.'

'Well, a hell,' Luca said. 'They're not technically living.'

'You know what I mean,' Mo said. 'It's like ethnic cleansing or something.'

'OK . . .' he said slowly, sounding not OK.

'Luca, sorry, of course you're my priority, but I'm also their queen, and if you think I'm going to turn my back on them, you can think again.'

'Fine. All right. I get that you feel sorry for them.'

'A persecuted minority with no rights, recognition or dignity – you bet I feel sorry for them. They have been absolutely terrorised by the purges. How would you like to live in fear for twenty long years? I've got to do what I can for them, put right the wrongs of the past. This is a project I can really sink my teeth into.'

She turned and marched off, her robe swinging out behind her, leaving Luca standing alone on the lawn. He let out a long, slow breath as he watched Mo stride away, then followed her inside.

10

Back in the Sunshine Boardroom, Richard was thumping about, lifting up tables and shoving chairs aside.

'Is he looking for vampire hunters?' Mo asked.

'No, he's looking for his ridiculous and completely pointless cannon,' Pat fumed.

'It's obviously not here, is it?' Derek said, tutting. 'It's not like you can lose a cannon. It's not your keys or a pen or something.'

Pat hissed quietly at him.

'Luca will ask the hotel manager where the cannon is later, but for now, be seated,' Mo said firmly. 'The meeting of the vampires of Great Britain will resume.'

They all sat down at the long table, smoothed their robes and pushed the glasses of water and plates of biscuits away from them.

'Now, you have sworn allegiance to me, and I, in return, promise to help you reclaim your vampire lives,' Mo said. 'You must be cautious though. Come out of hiding, but do it carefully. So, let's start by looking at how you dress.'

'What's wrong with how we dress?' Pat erupted.

Mo blinked, blindsided by Pat's ever-present aggression.

'No, seriously, tell me great Queen, what is actually totally not OK about how I dress? This riding suit is made from the finest Milanese velvet, just so you know, tailored to my exact proportions.'

'It's beautiful, Pat,' Mo said, 'but it absolutely shouts vampire.'

'But we *are* vampires,' Pat snapped back. 'First you say, own your vampire identity; now you say, change your vampire clothes. I don't even get what on actual ruddy earth you're talking about.'

'I just mean, tone your outfits down a bit,' Mo replied. 'That man in the lobby reckoned you looked like vampires, and he had been drinking since lunchtime. If he can spot it, a vampire hunter certainly can.'

'OK, Your Specialness, keep your flaming hair on,' Pat muttered.

'Look at my robes,' Mo went on. 'Classy, but not too showy. A simple black dress underneath. Then a few accessories. Maybe dress down but try accessorising instead.'

'I absolutely do accessorise,' Pat said, waggling her fingers, which were weighed down with heavy silver rings set with black and red gems. 'Listen, Queen Mo, maybe you don't really get it because you've only been a vampire for a few weeks, but I am several centuries old and I have been dressing like this my whole entire vampire life. Some of these lace neckerchiefs are over three-hundred years old!'

She yanked at the lace around her throat. Mo thought she saw a moth fluttering in there.

'If I wanted to be insulted, I could go and see my mother, you know?' she grumbled to Natasha sitting next to her. Natasha smiled awkwardly.

'I understand what you're saying. I just think you need to find a way to look and feel good that doesn't make you a vampire-hunter magnet,' Mo said.

'Lose the velvet and lace, right?' Vanya said. 'I think that's what the queen means.'

Mo glanced at her. 'Thank you, Vanya, yes that is what I mean,' she said. 'How about I get my personal stylist to work on some new looks for all of you?' She was thinking of Lou and her curating – time to put that to use.

'I think it's a good idea,' said Derek. 'It will help everyone fit in. Plus, it's a change, isn't it? A rebranding. Get us away from the traditional clothes and all those negative connotations, you know? People think of vampires and they instantly imagine veins being sucked and blood up the walls.'

'But that's what we do. That's exactly what we do!' Pat said. 'Really, Derek, what planet are you on?'

'Yes, but to feel more twenty-first century and live alongside humans like we all want to, we need to market ourselves with broader appeal,' Derek said. 'So instead of it all being about the blood we drink, how about focusing on what we *don't* consume? I mean, we're gluten-free and dairy-free, which is totally now.'

'What is this absurd little dimwit talking about?' Pat said, curling her lip. 'We're food-free, you colossal nincompoop!'

'Look, I made these badges,' Derek said, handing some around. 'I picked traditional vampire colours – black and red – then added fun slogans. You can have "GLUTEN-FREE AND GORGEOUS", or "DAIRY'S "SCARY" or "IMMORTALITY IS FOR LIFE, NOT JUST FOR CHRISTMAS".'

The vampires stared blankly at them.

'Feel free to wear them.'

'Thank you, Derek,' Mo said.

Derek smiled and sat down.

'Now, that's dressing covered. Let's turn our attention to your hopes for the future.'

Mo grabbed a marker pen and went over to the whiteboard. 'Tell me what you want from your vampire lives. I will do my best to make it happen.'

Unsurprisingly, Pat spoke first.

'I want my old husband back,' she said, jabbing a thumb towards Richard. 'He used to be a mighty vampire, feared by humans and the undead alike. He wore gleaming robes. His hair streamed down his back like silk. That all changed with the you-know-what.'

The vampires shuddered.

'The life we loved was ripped from us. We hid ourselves away in Wales, and Richard changed. All his confidence was gone, like a fart in a hurricane. He used to be a warrior, not a worrier. Now look at him. No better than a slack-cheeked turnip nibbler. He wears a cardigan over his robes. He says it's "comfy". Vampires don't use words like comfy. Please! Whoever heard of a vampire with no hair? It's against nature. And yet, here he is. Completely bald, his head shining like a Christmas bauble.'

She folded her arms across her chest and glared into space.

'Thank you, Pat. I will do my best to restore confidence and self-esteem to all of you, not just Richard,' Mo said. 'What else?'

'I'd love to visit my home country,' said one vampire called Jimmy. 'I came here by boat in the 1950s from Jamaica, hoping for a career in England, but there was a vampire on board too, so . . .'

Mo wrote 'TRAVEL' on the whiteboard.

'I would love some new crampons,' said a short wiry vampire with a moustache. For a weird second Mo thought he said tampons, but then read his name label: 'Francis the Mountaineer – Turned at 4,000 feet!' She wrote 'CLIMBING EQUIPMENT' on the board.

'Any other suggestions?'

'We are super excited for a new look,' the girls said, at exactly the same time. Then Olga went on. 'I want long straight hair like yours, Queen Mo. I want to dye it jet black too.'

'And we want eyelashes,' Lenka added.

Mo frowned. 'Did yours fall out?'

'False ones. Can we have them? And smartphones.'

'Vampires can't use mobile phones,' Mo said. 'We can't work the touch screens. No electrical current in our undead fingers.'

'We still want them,' the girls replied.

Unsure how to categorise all this, Mo wrote 'HAIR THINGS' and 'MOBILES' on the whiteboard and then turned back to the vampires. She noticed Vanya leaning close to Luca's ear and whispering something, and Luca laughing.

'Anything else?' she said sternly.

'I would love my own place,' said Natasha. 'I'm too old to share a house. I'm three hundred and six! The girls were spooked by the you-know-what, especially since they lost their parents, so they moved in with me. Olga, Lenka, you're lovely, you really are, but if I've said it once, I've said it a thousand times – you are just so messy.'

The girls gave Natasha the side-eye.

Natasha appealed to Mo. 'They don't respect the house. It's like they were brought up in a hovel. Which they were, but still. They never clear up after themselves. Blood on the walls, all over the furniture, and the other day I came out of my room and tripped up on a spleen.'

'Oh,' was all Mo could manage, as she tried to picture a spleen and failed. She wrote 'ACCOMMODATION' on the board.

'I want to go out in the evenings, to a club or a party,' Derek said. 'Mix with humans a bit, in the real world.'

'Us too,' said the girls in unison.

'It doesn't have to mean eating them, right?' Derek added.

'Not all of them,' Pat muttered.

Mo wrote 'SOCIALISING' on the list.

'OK, great,' Mo said. 'Anything else?'

'Kill the Vampire King,' Pat said in a cold, hard voice.

'Pardon?'

'Are you deaf or something, Majesty? Do you have hamsters in your hearing holes? I said, kill the Vampire King. It's what all of them are thinking, but they won't speak out. I'd like him dead, and so would everyone else here.'

A hiss rose up.

'I want my husband back and I want the Vampire King dead. Two things. Only two.'

Mo paused, took a breath. 'I cannot agree to that.'

'Why not? It's how *he* came to power. Killed the Vampire King at the time, when he was serving as his deputy. Then you can rule here and all of Europe too. Excellent.'

More hissing. Mo used both hands to pat the air downwards for silence.

'I don't think anyone should be planning murder.'

'But murdering is excellent!' Pat said.

'No further talk of killing the Vampire King. Forget about him and direct your energy into a brave new life, with me as your leader. OK?'

A few nods. Some shrugs.

'Now, is there anything else I can do for you?' Mo said, feeling a little shaken by this treacherous curveball. The vampires shook their heads. Mo clicked the cap back on her marker pen.

'Good. With more confidence, a little planning and better outfits, I'm certain you can lead fulfilling lives again, alongside humans and free of the constant dread of being murdered violently by vampire hunters.'

'Well, that *would* be nice,' said Derek. 'Sign me up!'

'I want you all to get laptops too,' Mo said.

Sven began flicking quickly through his phrasebook, frowning.

'What is *laptops*?' he asked.

'Personal computers. You can email me – it's a way of writing to me that's even quicker than Express Bat – and we can meet online too.'

'What's she talking about?' Pat asked. 'On what line? Which line?'

'I can organise a computer expert to visit your homes and get you set up,' Mo continued.

'A human in our house?' Malcolm said, licking his lips. 'Aye, now you're talking . . .'

'Maybe I should do it.' It was Vanya. 'Is not good idea to send humans into vampire residences, Your Majesty. I can help though. I was only turned a year ago, when I was twenty. I know computers. I can get everyone sorted with Wi-Fi, show them laptop.'

'All right, good, thank you Vanya,' Mo said. 'Once everyone is WiFi connected, I will schedule regular Zoom meetings for us all to connect, learn and grow together.'

Excited chatter rippled through the room. There was laughter too. A deep, rolling laugh. Mo turned to see it was Vanya, reacting to something Luca had said. He was grinning. He looked pleased.

'Anything I can help you with, Vanya?' Mo asked. It came out sharp as lemons.

Vanya looked up at Mo, a smile still playing on her lips.

'All good here, thanks,' she replied. 'Although I do need some help with motorbike. The throttle is bit sluggish, but Luca has agreed to take a look, once we're done here. Are we done?'

Mo felt her cheeks burn. She turned quickly back to the vampires.

'Let us draw this meeting to a close,' she said, reaching unsteadily for her regal voice. 'Await further communication from me. Until then, live well, immortal ones.'

The vampires bowed. Derek clapped. All three Tartan Fangs – Malcolm, Donald and Duncan – nodded at Mo.

Natasha beamed and Olga and Lenka gave Mo a shy wave. Luca held the Sunshine Boardroom door open and Mo swept out.

She found herself in the corridor, alone. What do I do now? Go back to the room, I suppose, and wait there until they have all left. She wandered a little uncertainly towards the lifts, but then heard footsteps and turned to see Luca running to catch up with her.

'OK?' he said, smiling.

'I think so,' said Mo, gripping his hand.

'That went really well. They're all super excited in there. I'll make sure they leave without eating anyone, then I'm going to help Vanya with her bike.'

'Really? Do you have to?'

'It won't take long. I'm handy with motorbikes. Me and my brothers were always fixing them up, back home. I'll see you in the room once I'm finished.'

The lift doors opened with a ping. Mo stepped inside and turned to wave at Luca, but he'd already gone.

11

Mo shut her bedroom door and flopped onto the bed, her eyes closed. Her hairslide slipped off and trickled onto the floor.

The meeting *had* gone well, Mo thought. No humans were murdered and no vampires got staked. The whole, 'let's kill the Vampire King' was a bit of an unwelcome suggestion. Can't have a coup. But I think I got on top of that. Plus no one mentioned me being human – thank you, Lou, for that excellent perfume – and, amazingly, I kind of liked them. Pat's a strong flavour and Derek's a bit in your face, but Natasha's sweet, the girls were friendly, and the Tartan Fangs seemed serious – and sensible, for vampires.

It's going to take work to get those guys back on track. It's the least I can do though, after all they've been through. Completely let down by the Vampire King. Ignored! While they were being massacred! It's a project. I love a project. Vampire advocacy. Something to get my teeth into, as I said to Luca. Ha! That's funny, although I don't remember him laughing . . .

Mo went over to the window. If she rested her head against the glass, she could peer down at the car park and see Luca crouched over Vanya's motorbike. Mo craned her neck more. There was Vanya, handing him a bottle of water. Mo studied her then stepped away. I'm sure she's fine once you get to know her, she thought. She's got that tough manner, which is a bit off-putting. I suppose she's quite cool, cooler than me anyway, which is also fine. Totally fine. I'm me, she's her. In a leather jacket. Yuck. I'm considering going vegan anyway, so that look wouldn't work for me *at all*.

A few minutes later, there was a tap on the door. 'It's me,' came Luca's voice. Mo opened it.

'I need to wash these,' he said, holding up his oily hands.

'I hadn't realised you could fix bikes,' Mo said.

'Oh yeah,' Luca called from the bathroom, over the sound of running water. 'Bikes, cars, tractors . . .'

'Have all the vampires left now?'

Luca appeared from the bathroom. He'd scraped his hair back with wet fingers and it dripped a little on his shoulders.

'Yes.'

'Vanya too?' Mo asked.

He nodded.

'Must have been quite tricky to fix her bike – you were gone a while.'

'We were chatting a bit. She's from a similar part of the world to me. Same sort of upbringing too. Rural, poor, you know?'

'Like me,' Mo said. 'Lower Donny is rural and kind of poor.'

'Yeah, but it is in western Europe. It's not quite the same.'

'Well, it's not a competition, is it?' Mo said, surprised at how sharp she sounded.

Luca didn't seem to notice. He sat down on the bed and carried on talking.

'Anyway, while I chose to be a vampire's familiar to get me out of my village and help me see the world, Vanya chose becoming a vampire.'

'Wow! What kind of life did she have, to want to be turned like that?'

'She said her parents had died, she was working two jobs and living in a tiny apartment with a shared bathroom, and then she got the option to become a vampire. It just made sense.'

'If she says so . . . Anyway, why has she come to Britain, where all the other vampires are traumatised by the purges? Bit of a dumb choice.'

'I don't think she's dumb,' Luca said. 'She seemed really smart and driven. She's a strong, independent woman. I mean vampire.'

She's also attractive and super confident and cool, Mo thought with a pinch of anxiety.

'She was asking about you too,' Luca said.

'Like what? Does she suspect I'm not a vampire?'

'No, it was more about what you're like, your personality.'

'Why does she want to know about my personality?'

'She was curious about you, the leader. You're kind of a celebrity to them.'

Mo sighed and frowned. She packed her vampire robes and jewels into her backpack and the two of them left the hotel and walked towards the station.

'You're quiet,' Luca said, after several minutes. 'What's wrong?'

'I'm tired,' Mo said.

'You might be even more tired in the months to come.'

'Meaning?'

'Meaning, you will be working for all those vampires. Attending to their every need. You'll be busy. It's not how you said you were going to rule.'

'Well, I didn't know – did I? – how much help they would need. Maybe being Vampire Queen is a bit more involved than I thought, but I can do it. I have to do it. I have to keep them loyal, that's what the Vampire King said, and if I succeed at that, hopefully he won't be forced to come over here and do something nasty to me.'

'I get it.'

'But . . . ? I sense a but. You're upset that I'm going to be helping the vampires out more than I said?'

'A little. I'm also worried it will be too much. You're not a real vampire, remember. You've got a whole human life to fit in.'

Mo shrugged and nibbled the side of her thumb.

'Anyway, you and Vanya seemed to hit it off.'

'So you're upset now, are you? Because I helped her out?'

'No,' Mo protested. 'I just didn't warm to her so much. There's something about her. She made me uneasy. The way she looked at me. Do you think she guessed we're together?'

'No way!'

'Maybe she likes you,' Mo said.

'You can't blame her for that.'

'Is everything funny to you?'

'Not everything, no.'

They walked the rest of the way in silence. The train was busy. Four lads were chanting Christmas songs and an excited three-year-old dressed like an elf was running up and down the aisle, but even with all that, Mo nodded off. When her head lolled uncomfortably in front of her, Luca gently eased it towards him. She slept like that the whole way home, resting against his shoulder.

12

Luca had been right when he predicted Mo would be busy caring for the vampires. She was. By nine o'clock on Sunday morning, barely twelve hours after the meeting, she was at her desk, working on their behalf. By ten she had drawn up a spreadsheet, by midday she had arranged for Natasha to view new accommodation in a retirement village – no stairs! – and by early afternoon she'd booked Jimmy onto a cruise to Jamaica that had space for his travel-coffin.

It was just getting dark when the doorbell rang and then Luca appeared in her room.

'Intercepted an Express Bat on my way over. More letters,' he said, depositing a pile of envelopes on her desk. Mo pounced on them. Luca kissed the top of her head and then lay on the bed, watching her reading through the mail, making notes, adding entries on the spreadsheet. The Tartan Fangs wanted the name of an upholsterer in the Glasgow area who could reline their coffins, no questions asked. Francis the Mountaineer asked for advice on frostbite treatment. Olga and Lenka wrote reminding Mo they still wanted super straight black hair like hers, false lashes and mobile phones, but had also thought of some other stuff. There was a list of questions too. Was it still good to pluck out your eyebrows and pencil them in? Could they get some face gems? (What the hell are those? Mo thought). Did Mo recommend a nude gloss or a statement lip? What music was hot right now? When they were human back in the early-nineteenth century, it was all about fiddles. Were fiddles still cool?

I can ask Lou about all this, Mo thought, as she picked up Derek's letter. He was running more positive vampire messaging past her, before getting T-shirts printed for everyone. Mo wrote back suggesting that T-shirts that advertised the wearer's vampire status were risky, but if he really wanted to go ahead, then 'NIGHT LIFE'S THE RIGHT LIFE' and 'LIVING MY BEST (UNDEAD) LIFE' were her favourites. 'ALWAYS SAY PLEASE AND FANG-YOU' was rubbish.

'How are you doing?' Luca asked. 'Fancy a walk?'

'I'd love to,' Mo said. 'I must get all this done though. The sooner I get the vamps up and running, the sooner we'll have more time.'

He came over to Mo and draped his arms around her shoulders. She gripped his hands and smiled.

'I'm *so* sorry. Just give me a few more days to sort out the vampires. I break up from school on Thursday too, and I'll be done with vampire work *and* schoolwork then.'

'I fly home on Saturday though, for Christmas. I won't be back until the thirtieth.'

Mo spun around.

'You'd forgotten?' Luca asked.

'Yes,' Mo admitted, 'but it's fine of course. I mean, we have Thursday evening and all of Friday to be together.'

'Sure.'

'The thirtieth is my mum's party too.'

'Wouldn't miss it for the world,' he said. 'See you on Thursday then.'

Just before dinner, Mo was in the living room warming herself by the fire and staring into the flames when the landline rang. The digital display showed a number she didn't recognise. Mo expected it to be a sales call, but the voice that spoke was deep and silky, with a lilting accent.

'Your Majesty? It's Vanya.'

'Hello,' Mo managed, shocked.

'I want to ask favour.' Nothing if not direct, Mo thought. 'I would like to borrow Luca. I've still got bike trouble and I think he can fix it.'

Mo was too surprised to speak.

'He can stay over in my house if he needs to. I live in Nether Slaughter, do you know it? Cool name but boring place. Luca said it's over an hour from his, so not easy commute. I'll take care of him,' Vanya said. 'As soon as my bike is repaired, I can head out and get all the other vampires online.'

More silence from Mo.

'Should I take that for a yes?'

'No,' Mo said finally.

'So it's a no?'

'No, I just meant don't take my silence for a yes.'

'Which is still a no, isn't it?'

'Maybe,' Mo said.

'I'm confused now. Can I borrow Luca or not?'

'You heard me,' Mo said, suddenly overwhelmed by a powerful need to be awkward.

'I'm sorry, I don't understand,' Vanya said.

'Oh dear,' said Mo. 'That's a shame.'

'What's going on?' Vanya asked.

'What *is* going on?' Mo repeated back at her.

'I just want to borrow Luca.'

'*I* just want to borrow Luca.'

'OK, this getting stupid now.' Vanya sighed.

'You're getting stupid now,' Mo replied.

'No, you are.'

'No, your *mum* is.'

Vanya made a sound that was a cross between a gasp and a laugh. They both fell silent. Mo was trying to work out where the last fifteen seconds of chat had come from. Perhaps Vanya was doing the same.

'How did you get this number?' she asked.

'Luca gave it to me.'

'Did he?' she said.

'That's what I just said.'

'So you want to borrow him, but what if I need him?'

'He thought you were very busy right now and also very independent,' Vanya said.

'I am,' Mo said firmly. 'I am a strong, independent woman. Female! A female vampire. Definitely.'

'Cool,' Vanya said.

'Yes. It is cool.'

'Look, if he comes over tonight, he'll be done soon. Can't say when exactly, might need to order in new parts,' Vanya continued. 'I could hire mechanic, but I'd have to explain why I can only see him after dark and that can get awkward and then I might have to kill him.'

'Do not kill Luca,' Mo blurted. 'And absolutely do not turn him.'

'I won't do either. I respect that he's yours.'

'My what?'

'Your familiar. What else?'

'Nothing else.'

'Good,' said Vanya. 'Well, thank you, Your Majesty. I am grateful. It's been good to talk to you.'

Has it, Mo thought? Weird more like. She had never spoken to anyone like she'd just spoken to Vanya, with a mix of trickiness and childishness. It was new. Even oddly fun. It also distracted her from the small detail that she'd agreed to Luca staying over at Vanya's.

Five minutes later her mobile rang. It was Luca.

'I'm off to Vanya's tonight then?'

'That's the plan,' said Mo.

'OK. We're still on for Thursday though, when you're going to start love-bombing me?'

'Yup,' said Mo, rejecting his joke with her flat tone. 'See you then. Oh, by the way, she's promised not to eat you or turn you.'

'Excellent.'

'If she quizzes you about me, don't tell her anything. Keep me sounding mysterious and mighty.'

'But she's already met you so she'll know that's a lie.'

'Ha ha,' Mo said. 'If she tries anything funny, anything at all, just get out of there.'

'OK, thanks, but nothing bad is going to happen. Trust me.'

13

The last days of term were a blur of festive activities. Danny Harrington fell off the stage during the Christmas show – this was considered a highlight by most people – and Tracey Caldwell got done for setting light to tinsel in the toilets. Mr Pascal, the head, played *Last Christmas* on the bagpipes as everyone streamed out through the main doors on the last day.

Mo and Lou could still hear his playing, which sounded like an asthmatic yak, as they climbed on the bus to go home.

'Got time to come over to mine?' Lou asked. 'I've put together some new looks for the vampires, like you asked me. I can show you. I'm thinking pure athleisure.'

'I have no idea what athleisure is,' Mo said.

'It's a style of clothing, you dinosaur.'

'I'm not a dinosaur. They're extinct. Do I look extinct?'

'Little bit,' Lou said. 'Anyway, are you coming?'

'Yes, but I can't stay long. Luca's back this evening and I haven't seen him since Sunday.'

'Wow, a whole four days. Why so long?'

'I've been really busy sorting out the vampires. Plus he's also been at Vanya's for a couple of nights, fixing her motorbike. Did I tell you about Vanya?'

'No, but I feel like I need to know right now.'

'She's this new vampire. She came to the meeting. Quite young – she was twenty when she was turned. Attractive, I suppose, if you like that rock-chick look.'

Lou's big blue eyes had grown bigger than usual.

'And you let your boyfriend spend time with this person?'

'Well, Vanya is my vampire subject. I'm her queen, doing her a favour by lending her my familiar. It's like a business agreement.'

'If you say so,' Lou said. 'Is Luca just business now? Mo, are you sure you're OK with this? He's just been hanging out with a hot vampire!'

'Which is completely fine. I've been busy anyway.'

'Yes, but he's hot and she's hot. That's a lot of hot.'

'Stop saying hot,' Mo said. 'And stop looking at me with your big, sad, questioning eyes. I'm *fine*, honestly. I'm Mo Merrydrew, a strong, independent woman, right? Anyway, I made Vanya promise not to turn Luca.'

'That wasn't what I was worried about. What if she, you know, steals him? Seduces him.'

'Don't say that word.'

'Seduce . . .' Lou said again, stretching out the word deliberately and making Mo wince. 'Can you trust her?'

Mo shrugged. 'I hardly know her. I sometimes think I hardly know Luca either. I didn't even know he can fix motorbikes. The other day I made him a cup of tea and he had milk in it, then the next time I made tea, he didn't. I'm like, who *are* you?'

'Yeah, weird,' Lou agreed. 'It's not been very long though. Not compared to us. We've known each other for absolutely ages, since we were three. You just need to spend a bit more time with him, that's all.'

'I want to, but now I've got all this work to do supporting the vampires. I have to get that right.'

Mo's phone rang.

'It's him,' she said, and answered the call. Lou studied Mo as she said 'yes' and 'no, that's fine' a lot, and then put her phone back in her pocket.

Lou raised her eyebrows. 'And . . . ?'

'He can't come home today – he's still waiting on a part for Vanya's motorbike. He'll be back tomorrow instead.'

'Oh,' Lou said.

'But Vanya has invited me over tonight, so we can all be together. I don't know if I should go. Royalty don't usually go round to their subjects' houses for the evening, do they?'

'Never mind that. You could do a bit of spying. Check out how they are together. If she laughs too long at his jokes, or she picks a bit of fluff off his shirt, or passes him a drink and he doesn't say thank you – that's a sign they've got too familiar with each other.'

'Too familiar?' Mo muttered. 'My familiar getting too familiar.'

'Or if she touches his arm, or they keep flashing little smiles at each other, or quick looks . . .'

'All right, Lou, this isn't some stupid Regency drama.'

The bus pulled into the stop and Mo jumped up gratefully.

Once inside Lou's house, Mo pointed at the Christmas tree in the living room.

'That looks pretty,' she said. 'Bit bare on the bottom branches though.'

'Nipper chewed everything he could reach,' Lou said. 'He's had three candy canes, a plastic bauble and a silver wooden star.'

'Oh, Nipper,' Mo said, dropping to her knees and rubbing his white fur. 'Are you a naughty dog? Are you a naughty chewy dog? Are you a naughty chewy Christmas dog? Or are you a good dog? You're a good dog, aren't you? Yes, you are, yes, you are.'

Nipper squiggled and snorted with delight, licking Mo's chin and headbutting her legs.

'Come on, enough of that,' Lou said, heaving her broken leg in its heavy cast up the stairs.

In her room, Lou opened her laptop and showed Mo images of leggings and bomber jackets and fluorescent trainers.

'See? Comfortable. Good for active day through to evening.'

'They only really need evening, to be honest,' Mo muttered.

'And it can also be dressed up if necessary – I know your vampires like a little bling.'

'It's certainly not lace or velvet, which is a plus,' Mo said. 'Great, let's try it. I can't wait to hear what they think. I hope they love it!'

'Sounds like you care about them, Queen Mo.'

'I do. At least, I definitely feel protective of them.'

She passed Lou a piece of paper with all the vampires' sizes on them.

'Sven the Viking and Richard are XXL.'

'Paying with your Dark Card?'

'Yup,' Mo said, taking it out of her wallet and handing it to Lou. 'Oh, and the girls want long straight black hair like mine. I never do anything to my hair except wash it and comb it, so I wasn't sure how to help there.'

Lou shook her head.

'Babe, have you never heard of hair straighteners?'

'Of course I have.'

'What do they look like then? Describe them to me.'

'Lou, I'm not going to do that.'

'That's right, you're not going to because you don't know what they look like.' Lou laughed. 'These are hair straighteners, look.' She pointed to the screen. 'I'll get them a cordless set and some hair dye. Deep Black looks good. Anything else?'

'They asked loads of questions about make-up looks. I don't even want to answer them.'

'Because you haven't got a clue?'

'Because obsessing about make-up doesn't feel very feminist. Oh, and they want false lashes. Why would anybody want false eyelashes?'

'Why would anybody want to be a human-rights lawyer?'

'I can think of tons of reasons, but the main one would probably be –'

'Don't,' Lou said, not looking up from the screen. 'Stop talking. Do not say any more words. Right, that's all done. Those vampire girls can thank me later.'

'I'll thank you now.' said Mo. 'Thanks.'

'No problem,' said Lou. 'Can I get some trainers? Whack them on the Dark Card?'

'I guess so,' Mo said. 'Think of it as payment for your fashion advice, not a freebie on vampire expenses, OK? I'm an ethical leader.'

Lou grinned, picked some out and then hit the BUY NOW button.

'I want to see selfies of the vampires wearing all this new gear too,' she said.

'They can't use mobile phones,' Mo said.

'Can't they get a friend to take photos of them?' Lou asked.

'They haven't got any friends,' Mo said. 'Well, human friends, although hopefully that's going to change. Derek wrote to me asking if he could join the local amateur dramatics group. They're doing *Wuthering Heights*.'

'*Wuthering* Bites, more like,' said Lou.

Mo laughed.

'He reckons he'd make an excellent Heathcliff,' she said.

'Or an excellent *Teeth*cliff?' Lou said and they both laughed now, a lot, and Mo hugged her friend and spluttered, 'Oh my god, I love you.'

'I've got a stash of Mini Battenbergs in the wardrobe too.'

'Now I love you even more.'

14

Vanya's home was a small cottage on the edge of Nether Slaughter. As she had said, it was an awkward journey. Mo had taken a bus to Middle Donny then picked up another bus there, eventually arriving at just after seven. She had changed into some simple black clothes that Lou lent her, doused herself in her stinky citrus vampire-fooling perfume that she always carried with her and submitted to a slick of eyeliner that Lou had insisted on applying, before heading off.

Mo opened the gate and walked up the path. She studied the house. It was built of honey-coloured stone, single-storey, small, old. The door was pink and flanked by a sash window on either side. There was a bench out front, plant pots that were empty now but perhaps full of flowers in summer. It all seemed rather sweet and idyllic, not at all like the home of a vampire.

Mo was about to lift the heavy brass knocker when the door swung open.

'Hey!'

It was Luca. Before she could warn him to address her more like a familiar should address the Queen, Vanya appeared behind him, casually laying a hand on his shoulder and smiling over at Mo.

'Greetings, Queen Mo,' she said. 'Will you come in, please?'

Mo nodded stiffly, struck by their easy intimacy, which was obvious before she'd even stepped inside. Mo wanted to turn and flee back to Lower Donny, but her body somehow carried her across the threshold and next thing she knew she was in the kitchen.

She noticed the smell first. It was clean, fresh and welcoming. The cupboards were painted in a soft sage colour and a huge range in the old fireplace was pumping out warmth.

'Nice place,' Mo managed to say, her voice tight and small.

'It works for me,' Vanya said.

'Here, let me take your coat,' Luca said. 'Then you two go and relax and I'll get the drinks.'

Vanya led Mo to the living room, where there was an open fire, handsome patterned rugs on the floor and a deep grey sofa that Mo now sank into. She realised that Vanya was asking her about her journey, but Mo was feeling so like a shy and sulky child ('didn't want to come, don't want to be here, this is stupid') that she couldn't reply.

Then Luca came in with a tray. There were bowls of nuts and crisps, some juice and two glass goblets, once

containing a greyish-pink liquid and one containing . . .
Well, it was obviously blood.

He passed the goblet of blood to Vanya who, Mo
noticed with a dry gulp, took it silently and without
thanking him – Lou had warned about that – and then
he held out the other glass to Mo.

'You often prefer blended worms, Mo, so I got these
ready for you,' he said.

He said it kindly. Mo sensed he was trying to make
eye contact, but she took the drink with shaky hands
without looking at him and put it on the coffee table in
front of her.

Silence now filled the room, until Vanya spoke.

'Luca tells me you were devoted student before you
got turned,' she said.

Her voice was softer than usual, less dry and amused
and more genuine, but the question made Mo cringe.
It felt like Vanya was the actual queen, asking Mo,
the young and star-struck subject, 'And what do
you do?'

'That's correct,' Mo replied, not taking her eyes off
the fire.

'I used to really like chemistry when I was at school,'
Vanya said. 'In fact, all the sciences. Although I do love
reading too. Always will.'

She gestured up at the bookshelves either side
of the fireplace. Mo glanced up at them, then back at
the fire.

Vanya the scientist. Vanya the reader. What next? Vanya the brain surgeon? Vanya the poet? Vanya the reiki healer?

'I couldn't have studied literature at university though,' Vanya went on. 'I just could never see point in dissecting the text, you know? I prefer to read it and feel it. I don't want to know about themes or narrative arc.'

'But understanding the social context in which the book was written can really help you appreciate the story,' Mo said, unable to resist.

'You think?'

'Of course,' she replied, becoming more enthusiastic. 'Read *Jane Eyre* knowing that Charlotte Brontë was an unmarried, super brainy woman, and that women didn't generally write fiction in the 1840s, let alone fiction featuring a determined, self-reliant, not even good-looking heroine, and it means so much more.'

Vanya was watching her closely, warmly. Mo suddenly felt self-conscious. She blushed a little and picked up her glass to take a swig, then remembered what was in it and put it back on the table.

'I thought you only read non-fiction, Mo,' Luca said. 'All those political biographies and history books and stuff.'

'You can like both,' Vanya said, flashing a smile at Mo. 'Anyway, how would you know? You're not much of a reader, are you, Luca? More practical. Good with hands.'

Mo darted a horrified glance at her.

'Not that you've actually fixed bike yet,' Vanya laughed.

Oh, she's talking about motorbike repair, Mo realised.

'Yeah, but I will,' Luca said. 'Once that part arrives. She thinks I can't do it,' Luca was talking to Mo now but pointing his thumb towards Vanya. 'No faith in my abilities.'

'That's not true,' Vanya protested, and she lobbed a cushion at him. It missed Luca but overturned Mo's glass, splashing her with blended worms. Mo shot up like she'd been sprayed with boiling water.

'Oh, Queen Mo, I'm so sorry, let me get cloth,' Vanya said, rushing towards her.

'I'll go,' Luca said.

'Get tea towel. There are clean ones in –'

'In the dresser drawer. I know,' he said, darting out to the kitchen.

Mo didn't wait for him to return. She began walking towards the door.

'Where are you going?' Vanya asked, following her.

Luca met her at the front door. She felt trapped, Luca in front, Vanya behind. It was like a humiliation sandwich.

'I need to leave. I shouldn't have come. It was a mistake,' Mo said, reaching for the handle. She yanked the door open and stumbled outside, oblivious to the cold, the blended worms soaking through her tights.

She had gone through the gate and onto the road by the time Luca caught up with her.

'Mo, stop,' he said. 'At least let me drive you back.'

'No, thanks,' she said, without turning round. 'I'll get the bus.'

'But you've only just got here. What shall I tell Vanya?'

Mo spun around, her face flushing red. 'Tell her to . . .' she shouted, but then, shocked at her own fury, she took a breath and started again. 'Tell her what you like.'

15

Mo let herself quietly into the house, not wanting to wake her parents, and tiptoed into her room. She felt wildly confused. To see Luca and Vanya so comfortable together – was it a test? Was she supposed to rip Vanya's head off, or maybe Luca's? Should she have screamed, 'How dare you insult the Vampire Queen?'

No, it wasn't that. It was all so natural, the way they were. Sweet and friendly. Too sweet and friendly? But Luca wouldn't do that, would he? He wouldn't get with Vanya and flaunt it in her face, would he?

Mo shook her head, shocked at her spiralling thoughts. A few weeks into a relationship and I'm having jealous fantasies. Get a grip.

But then again . . . Mo could see why Luca liked her. She couldn't deny that Vanya was cool and intelligent. Quite like me, Mo thought – the books, the love of science – but also not like me. It just made it all so confusing.

What was it about Vanya anyway? The other vampires just needed Mo to support them and help them modernise, but Vanya wanted to elbow her way into Mo's life. That stops now, Mo decided. I don't want to be friends with her. I *can't* be friends. She can't have any more special privileges either. No more time with Luca. I should never have let him go there. A real queen wouldn't loan out her staff or grant favours, I see that now. I shouldn't have visited either. So unprofessional! I lost focus. It won't happen again.

In the morning, Lou texted.

How did it go?

Not good, Mo texted back. **They seemed really sweet together.**

Lou replied **Like what???!!!!**

Everything you warned me about. Touching each other. Finishing each other's sentences.

Have you talked to him about it? Lou texted back.

He's still there! Don't want to think about it right now.

Do you want me to come over?

It's OK. I've got vampire work to do. But thanks. Love you.

Luckily, given how hungry for distraction Mo was, there was plenty to occupy her. More letters arrived that morning, bringing good news. The clothes had been delivered and everyone liked Lou's fresh look. Olga and Lenka loved their black, straight hair and adored the trainers – 'We haven't run so much since a rabid bear got into the village in 1814.' Natasha wrote saying she was 'wonderfully happy' in her new flat in a retirement village. 'I nibble the odd resident, but most of them are on their way out anyway, so I don't see the harm.' Derek said he'd got the part of Mr Lockwood in *Wuthering Heights*. 'I have to lie in bed and look ill. They thought my pale complexion made me perfect for the role. It's not the most exciting part, but I will make it my own!'

In place of selfies, Pat sent a sketch of Richard, and Richard sent a sketch of Pat, showing them in their new gear. Pat had accessorised with a cape, giving her a superhero vibe and Richard still wore his cardigan over his hoodie, but it was definitely a change for the better. Pat reported that Richard had 'got his ruddy damn-fool cannon back. He can let it off without worrying about any stupid silly smoke alarm. It's one of the good things about living here. Lots of open space.'

There was no more talk of overthrowing the Vampire King and, with things going well, no reason for him to steam over and 'remove her'. The vampires were happy, excited and loyal. Mo had things under control – and things being under control was usually her happy place – but her mind kept twisting back to Luca. Were they OK?

Late in the afternoon, one more Express Bat arrived and Mo's stomach jolted at the sight of the familiar jagged writing on the envelope it carried. Inside was a card. Mo gazed at the image on the front. It showed the Vampire King wearing white satin trousers with gold braid down the sides and black shiny boots with diamanté-encrusted heels. He was naked from the waist up, apart from some medallions of course, and riding a huge black horse. Part Napoleon, part stripper, Mo thought.

She flipped the card open anxiously, expecting more threats. Instead, she found a round-robin message, sent to all his subjects. It said:

Seasonal Greetings!

It's been a busy year. I quashed another uprising by the Vampires of the Real East. Very boring, but they understand who is the boss now. I also extended my palace, to include an underground crypt with fully integrated sound system – the guest accommodation – a nightclub designed by the celebrated vampire interior designer Svetlana Svetlanasvet, a mixed martial arts studio and a glasshouse which I will fill with orchids, peacocks and four specially commissioned life-size paintings of me.

There was no mention of his trip to Britain or Mo's new role as queen. The card was signed off like this:

I wish you an excellent new year. Drain humans, drink blood, dream big. I love you all – unless you rise up against me, in which case I will rain hot vengeance on your stinking heads. Kisses! The Vampire King of the East.

Mo tucked the card away in her wardrobe and was drawing her curtains when she noticed someone coming through the gate. Luca. She ran downstairs and outside.

'You're back,' she said, feeling a little self-conscious, not giving him a hug.

'Finally got the bike fixed,' he said. 'OK? You rushed off last night. What was that about?'

'Can't you guess?' she shot back, eyes flashing. Wasn't it obvious to Luca that his cosiness with Vanya would hurt Mo, his girlfriend?

'No, I really can't . . .' he said, but before Mo could say more, her mum appeared from the garage.

'Hello, Luca, lovely to see you,' she shouted.

'Hi, Kate,' he replied. 'How are you?'

'Well, thank you. Just looking for some paint. I need to redo the front door. Think it might be right up there.' She pointed at a high shelf in the garage behind her.

'I'll come and help you find it in a second,' Luca said, then turned back to Mo. She had folded her arms and was looking at the ground. 'Is there something you want to say, Mo?'

She shook her head, looked quickly at him and then something caught her eye. A single headlight in the lane, approaching. The sound of a motorbike engine. Through the gloom, Mo could make out a figure, an unmistakably slim female figure, getting off the bike, taking off her helmet, shaking out her hair.

'What is it?' Luca asked, clocking Mo's expression.

'I think it's Vanya.'

Luca pivoted round. 'What's she doing here?'

'You tell me. Wait, Mum's in the garage. Quick, go distract her. I'll try to get rid of Vanya.'

Mo took off across the gravel drive. Vanya was approaching the gate, walking in that slow, relaxed way that Mo found so irritating and wearing that leather jacket that Mo found completely . . . what was the word? There was no time for that. Mo had vaulted the gate and blocked Vanya's path.

'Your Majesty,' Vanya said, bowing and smiling. 'Love the casual dress. I didn't know queens were allowed to wear jeans.'

'I can wear what I like,' Mo shot back. 'What are you doing here?'

'Luca left some stuff in my bathroom. I was just dropping it round to your –'

'This isn't my home,' Mo blurted. 'Not my permanent home anyway. I'm just living here while I have my castle renovated.'

'Nice,' she said. 'Is Luca here?'

'Why do you care so much? Can't bear to be parted from him?'

Vanya raised her eyebrows.

'Anyway, he's not here, and he's definitely not in the garage.'

Vanya moved a little, trying to see round Mo.

'The lights are on though,' she said.

'Really?' said Mo.

'There's definitely someone in the garage – I can see through window. I don't know who it is but she's seen me. She's waving.'

Vanya waved back. Mo wanted to slap Vanya's hand down. She spun around to see her mum, with Luca trotting anxiously alongside, walking towards them.

'Oh look, there's Luca too,' Vanya said. 'He actually is here.'

'Mo, bring your friend in, if you like,' her mum called out. 'There are mince pies in the cupboard.'

'Go away!' Mo shouted, shooing her with her hand.

'What?' said her mum.

'I said, go away,' she shouted louder.

'Who is that?' Vanya asked.

'It's my chauffeur,' Mo said, then she turned back to her mum. 'We are OK out here, thanks, Mrs Chauffeur. Now run along back to the garage.'

'Mrs Chauffeur? What are you on about?' her mum called back.

'Come on, Kate,' Luca said, trying to lead her away.

'Is that how you think of me? Your chauffeur,' Mo's mum said, ignoring Luca. 'I do give you a few lifts here and there, but still.'

'Thank you, that will be all,' Mo shouted.

She turned back to Vanya.

'Sorry, she's not the sharpest pencil in the box,' she whispered.

'Are you all right, love?' her mum asked.

Oh my god, she's still here. Mo's hands clenched into fists by her side. She spun around angrily. 'Luca, please escort this woman back to the garage,' she barked.

'This woman?' Mum said. 'But I'm your –'

'I think Mo needs to talk in private with her friend,' Luca interrupted in an urgent voice. 'Girls' business, you know?'

'Oh,' said her mum, nodding. 'Oh right. Sorry. Boy trouble? I'll give you some privacy.'

Vanya looked amused. 'She called you love.'

'She does that. I shouldn't put up with it, but as I said, she's not very bright, so . . .'

'Then she was about to say something. I'm your . . . what?'

'No idea,' Mo said firmly.

'Your . . . ?' Vanya persisted.

Mo shook her head.

'Your what? Go on, tell me.'

Mo sighed. 'OK, well, you might as well know, but don't tell the other vampires, promise?'

'Yes.'

'It's a bit sad really, but here goes . . .' And she dropped her voice to a whisper. 'She thinks she's my mum. Or was my mum, you know, when I was a human.'

'Oh,' said Vanya.

'She's a bit confused, but she's an excellent driver so I let it go.'

'Right. That explains it.'

'Doesn't it?' said Mo. 'I mean, yes, it does.'

'So she's *not* your mum?'

'No, god, no,' Mo said, shaking her head. 'Her? No. As I said, she's just a woman I employed once I was turned. She's from Donny-on-the-Wold. That's a village near here. It's where the Museum of Agricultural Machinery is. You wouldn't know it. The village. Or the museum. But you should go actually, if you have time. To the museum, that is – the village is kind of dull.'

I'm blathering. I need to stop blathering now. Shut up!

'So anyway, if you just give me Luca's stuff, I'll make sure he gets it,' Mo said, holding out her hand and trying to sound in charge again. Just a bit. Just a teensy, weensy bit in charge. That would be good.

Vanya reached into her bag and passed Mo a bottle of shampoo.

'Thank you,' Mo said. 'You're supposed to be setting the vampires up with laptops. They should have arrived at your home by now. When are you getting started on that? It's a big job. A lot of travelling.'

'I am heading to Derek's tonight,' Vanya said.

'Good. Let me know when everyone is online.'

'Of course.'

'And don't mention to the others that I have a chauffeur. I don't want them to be jealous or think I've got unfair privileges. Don't mention either that I came to your house last night. That was a breach of royal protocol. It won't happen again.'

Vanya nodded.

'Understood, Your Majesty,' she said. 'Everything is totally understood.'

16

Vanya turned and walked back to her motorbike, put on her helmet and started the engine. Mo watched her speed away then she bent over, right there in the lane, her head in her hands, the tips of her long hair touching the Tarmac.

'No, no, no, no, no,' she moaned. 'Not good, not good, not good. So utterly not good.'

She felt a hand on her back and sprang up.

'It's just me,' Luca said. 'Are you OK?'

'Why didn't you keep Mum in the bloody garage?' Mo gasped, her eyes wild.

'I'm sorry. I was up on a ladder looking for the paint pot she wanted, and next thing I knew she'd escaped. Did she guess Vanya was a vampire?'

'I don't think so, but Vanya might have guessed that she's my mum. I had to tell her she's a confused woman that I gave a job to. Don't smile, Luca. It's not funny. How can you laugh now?' Mo threw her hands up. 'How?'

'I'm sure Vanya didn't guess.'

'Who knows with her?' Mo said. 'She had that smirking look on her face, like she finds everything so amusing. No wonder you two get on.'

'That's not fair. I don't smirk, I grin.'

'What if she guessed I'm human?' Mo asked. 'She's seen my house, not very vampiric, my clothes ditto and my mum-like chauffeur. Oh god . . .' Mo put her hands over her face and breathed heavily.

'And what was all that "leave them Kate, they're talking about girls' stuff"?' she resumed, suddenly dropping her hands. 'I was trying to run the vampire kingdom of Great Britain as a convincing Vampire Queen, in order to stop Steve the Psycho from coming over here and ripping everyone's head off, actually. I wasn't having some chat about sanitary towels.'

'Obviously I know that,' Luca said. 'Anyway, it worked. She went back into the garage.'

Then Luca pointed at the bottle Mo was clutching.

'Is that my shampoo? Brilliant.'

'Luca! I may have just blown my whole vampire cover, and all you can do is celebrate being reunited with your favourite hair product.'

She spun away from him, then almost immediately turned back.

'How did she find me here? Did you tell her where I live?'

'Of course not,' Luca said.

'Sure about that? I mean, you're such great mates. You love hanging out and chatting, find everything so massively funny all the time, maybe you did. You gave her my landline number after all.'

'I didn't give her your address, I swear.'

Then she must have followed you here. So in fact it *is* still your fault.'

'Don't blame me for this,' Luca shot back.

'No?' Mo said, her cheeks flushed red. 'Who should I blame? Those sheep over there? Nipper? Alexander the Great? Beyoncé? My mum? Your mum? Who?'

Luca sighed. 'Look, do you want me to speak to her? I can go over to her place now.'

'Oh, here we go, looking for more excuses to spend time with her, in her snug little cottage,' Mo said. 'Don't look so shocked. It's obvious you're more than just friends. Why don't you admit it? I watched how cosy the pair of you were at her house, her draping herself all over you, you two joking about bike repairs, ha ha ha . . .'

'So you are jealous,' he said, nodding and looking away.

'You knew exactly where the tea towels were,' Mo said, jabbing a finger at him.

'And that proves what?'

'That you're very close, maybe too close . . .'

Luca laughed, but it had a harsh sound. 'Oh my god, Mo, listen to yourself. Come on!'

'I knew I couldn't really trust Vanya. I don't even understand why she's here.'

'Well, she obviously came over to steal me off you,' Luca said.

'That's what Lou said! That she wants to steal you.'

Luca shook his head with disbelief. 'Mo, I was joking. Look, would it help if I told you she's gay?'

'She must think I'm so stupid. She must have been laughing at me last night, thinking ha ha, Mo, you don't realise *I'm* with Luca now and . . .'

'Mo!'

'. . . you thought he liked you and –'

'Mo!' Luca shouted now. 'She's gay.'

Mo looked at him and blinked. 'What?'

'Gay. Vanya. She is,' he said. 'Understand?'

Realisation scudded across Mo's face, her expression speeding from confusion to surprise to delight.

'Oh!' she said. 'Oh, I *see*. That's brilliant. I mean, great. Cool. But also, wow. Yes!'

She let out a long breath.

'So you two aren't . . . ?'

'No,' he said.

'And you probably won't ever be . . . ?'

'Correct.'

Mo nodded. 'Got it! Well, this is really, really interesting news. Great news, in fact. I totally didn't think of that. Vanya's gay. Excellent.'

'Yes, so everything is OK now. Vanya is not a threat because she doesn't date men,' said Luca. Mo missed his sarcastic tone.

'That's right!' she cheerfully agreed.

He sighed. 'Well, it's nice to know that you trusted me anyway,' he said, and the coldness in his voice finally snapped her attention back to him.

'Oh, but I did, I did, honestly,' Mo said, grabbing his hands.

'The idea that I would cheat on you and then hang out with that person in front of you . . .' Luca shook his head.

'No, of course you wouldn't do that,' Mo said. 'And I did trust you. Do trust you! You just looked so comfortable together.'

'We get along,' Luca said, like he was explaining something very simple to someone very slow to catch on, and it did seem simple now, Mo thought. They just got along. What was wrong with that? Nothing! She cringed inside, seeing the truth of it.

'Luca, I'm sorry. I've been stupid. I'm new to relationships, that's all. I don't know how they work.'

She anxiously studied Luca's face. He wasn't smiling. He seemed to be weighing her up with his eyes, but then he reached out one finger and gently pressed the tip of her nose.

'What?' she said.

'Apology accepted,' he said, and they walked back towards the house.

'You two all right?' Mo's mum asked as they passed the garage. 'I thought you were rowing maybe. Don't worry, I wasn't listening in.'

'We're OK, thanks,' Luca said.

'The course of true love never did run smooth,' she called out after them. 'Shakespeare, *A Midsummer Night's Dream.*'

Neither replied.

'You're welcome,' she said.

17

'*Are* we OK?' Mo asked nervously, once she and Luca
were up in her room.

'Yes, we're OK,' Luca said, looking steadily at Mo.
'Although I didn't expect you to be the jealous, suspicious
type. Doesn't seem very, what's the word . . . ?'

'Cool? Together? Trusting?'

'Yeah,' Luca said, smiling now, 'all that.'

'It wasn't just that I didn't trust *you* – it's Vanya really.
Something about her gets under my skin. I need to get
my head straight. She was actually really nice last night.
Sorry again.'

'You don't need to be jealous of her, Mo, and you
don't need to push me away.'

'OK,' Mo said quietly.

'Stop running from your feelings for me.'

'I'm not running anywhere,' Mo said.

'You're running from your feelings because they're so
powerful. I get that being with me is overwhelming – it
would be for any woman of course.'

'Luca . . .' Mo growled, realising she was being teased.

'Just remember – gratitude! Your boyfriend is amazing and all you need to do is embrace that, embrace him in fact.'

He held his arms out wide. Mo punched him, not very hard, in the stomach. He fell to the floor, curled up, pretending to moan with pain.

'Big boys don't cry.'

'That's sexist,' he said. 'Come on Mo. First you're jealous and now you're horribly sexist.'

Mo laughed. 'I'm doing OK at being Vampire Queen though,' she said.

'Well, that *doesn't* surprise me,' Luca said, still on the floor but sitting up now. 'Any more news from the Vampire King?'

'He sent a Christmas card but other than that, nothing.' Mo passed the card to Luca.

'Looking good, Stevie Baby,' Luca said. 'Did he forget to get fully dressed? He's not wearing anything on top.'

'I think maybe a bear ripped his shirt off,' Mo said.

'And he killed it with his bare hands and then drank its blood?'

'Almost definitely,' Mo said, and then smiled at Luca, who smiled back, and his smile seemed to zap all the tension from her body.

'Mo, it's your chauffeur here,' her mum called up the stairs a few hours later. 'Dinner's ready. Are you all right walking downstairs or do you need a lift?'

'Your mum is so funny,' Luca said as they went downstairs.

'Your mum is so funny,' Luca said again, when they were back in Mo's room later. 'She kept up the chauffeur jokes the whole way through dinner.'

'At least it meant she didn't quiz me on my mysterious new friend on a motorbike,' Mo said. 'Luckily Vanya doesn't look much like a vampire.'

'No lace or crushed velvet,' Luca said.

'Yeah, she didn't need a wardrobe makeover, did she? Already cool.' Mo sighed.

'What?' Luca said.

'I wish she hadn't come to my house. She saw way too much. What if she talks? Tells the other vamps what she saw?'

'She won't,' Luca said.

'How come you're so sure?'

'I know her better than you do,' Luca said.

Mo pulled a face then apologised. 'Sorry, I'm not jealous. I'm *not*. I trust you. We've been over this.'

'Maybe you should go and see her while I'm away,' Luca said. 'Get to know and trust her yourself.'

'Oh, I don't think so,' Mo said, frowning. 'I'm the queen! It's not a good idea for me to hang out with my subjects. I realise that now.'

'I think it's up to you, Mo. Your rule, your way, remember? Anyway, you guys have stuff in common. She likes science and reading. You like science and reading. And you both like me.'

Mo clocked his cheeky smile and sighed loudly, but inside she felt a pulse of joy at Luca making one of his 'aren't I excellent?' jokes. This was familiar, solid ground, the kind of ground she was grateful to be on. He would be flying home in the morning to spend Christmas with his family. She wanted their last hours together to be happy and for them to part with no doubts hanging over their relationship. And they did do that, on the doorstep, for some time, until Mo's dad told them to 'break it up' and Luca left, walking backwards across the gravel and smiling.

So, it turns out Vanya is gay.

Mo was lying in bed the next morning, messaging Lou.

No! So she wasn't trying to SEDUCE Luca. Relief!

I guess. I still feel weird about her.

Maybe you fancy her? Lou pinged back.

I don't.

Another message from Lou pinged in.

Think about it. You go along for fifteen years thinking you don't need any kind of relationship, you just want to study, do lots of maths and work for YouTube.

The UN, actually.

Whatever.

Then suddenly, wham! All your hormones wake up and you don't just want a boy – Luca – you want a girl too.

Lou! Shut up! Mo messaged back. Anyway, your hormones don't 'wake up', that's not a biological thing.

I think it's exciting, Lou replied. Go for it!

It's really NOT that. The weirdness I feel is something else. Don't know what. I actually think I need to keep Vanya out of my life. Put some boundaries up. Anyway, Christmas shopping?

They arranged to go on Monday, and in the meantime more letters from the vampires arrived. Jimmy sent a card from Jamaica, complaining about how sunny it was. Natasha wrote requesting some cream for her stiff joints and Sven asked for 'a modernistic blade to wield against vegetal matter.' That's a new axe for cutting down trees, Mo decided, but bought him a small penknife instead. Putting a sharp blade into the hands of a Viking vampire felt counter-intuitive.

Olga and Lenka asked if they could get a gel manicure if they promised not to eat the nail technician. I wish they'd take as much care over their intellectual development as their appearance, Mo thought, booking the treatment but ordering them a copy of Michelle Obama's autobiography, too. They also asked for some eyeliner and cleansing wipes. 'Single-use wipes are bad for the environment, girls,' Mo wrote back. 'They contain plastic and do not biodegrade, even when the packet says they do.' She made a note to send them a clip of fatbergs in the sewers once they were online.

'They'll have to learn to do all this stuff for themselves soon,' Mo muttered as she punched in her Dark Card details yet again. 'I said I wouldn't be their mum, and that's kind of what I'm being right now, but as soon as they're online, this stops.' Vanya must have visited all the vampires by now, Mo thought. She expected an email from her any day, but in fact she got a personal visit. It was four days before Christmas. Mo had been shopping in Middle Donny with Lou.

'Good luck getting your cast removed tomorrow,' Mo said, once they had got off the bus at the Lower Donny stop.

'Cannot wait!' Lou said. 'I'll be able to give proper hugs. I can't take my hands off my crutches without them falling over.'

'Off your *crotches*, as Danny would say.'

'Yeah, and when I do try and hug someone I hit them in the crotch with my crotches.'

Mo laughed and kissed her friend on the cheek.

'Love you,' she said, walking off.

'Love you more.'

Mo's shopping bags were bulky – a new cushion for her mum, a massive book about the history of carpet-making in Turkey for her dad. As she turned down the lane that led to her house she was wondering if she should have bought more sticky tape and something for Nipper when she spotted Vanya up ahead. It was too dark to make out details, but she recognised the silhouette and abundant hair and, of course, the motorbike.

'What is it with this lane?' Mo muttered to herself, hastily spraying on some I'm-not-a-human perfume and smoothing her hair. 'Bogdan always met me here, and now Vanya.'

She quickened her pace and straightened her back, walking assertively towards her.

'Good evening, Vanya,' she said, reaching for a regal tone.

'Hello, Queen Mo,' Vanya said, and then pointed at her bags. 'Been shopping?'

Mo felt her heart twitch. Did vampires go shopping? Oh well, this one does, she decided quickly, steadying herself. My rule, my way.

'Yes,' said Mo, determined not to blather.

'Buying more books about leadership? I read Michelle Obama's autobiography the other day. It's great. Have you read it?'

'Of course I have,' Mo shot back, then softened a little. 'Actually, I just sent it to Olga and Lenka. She's one of my heroes. Disciplined, fair, hard-working.'

'A good role model for anyone, human or vampire,' Vanya said.

Mo felt suddenly silly. It was like Vanya had seen inside her, spotting her fan-girl adoration of the former

First Lady, and quickly contrasted it with the here and now: Mo, the Vampire Queen, just back from the shops, walking home in jeans and a puffa jacket.

'Anyway, didn't mean to surprise you, but I was passing so I thought I'd let you know that everyone is online now.'

'Good.'

'They took a while to get it, but they should be able to email, and Francis the Mountaineer in particular was enjoying googling pictures of sunsets.'

'Good.'

'They were all wearing their new clothes. Big improvement. They look more like us now, and we're cool, right?'

Mo wasn't sure if Vanya was being serious. If she was, Mo thought, do I *want* to be in some kind of cool-girl mini gang with her?

'Natasha's discovered she loves bingo and plays it most evenings with her friends from the retirement village. Oh, and the Tartan Fangs have taken up tai chi.'

'What? They didn't tell me that.'

'It's very new development.'

Mo nodded and, unable to resist a little more positive feedback, said, 'So they seemed content?'

'Yeah. They love having you as queen. No one had bad word to say about you.'

Mo gave a small nod, and watched as Vanya reached for her helmet and squashed it down onto her head.

'Listen, before you go, sorry for rushing off the other night, when I was round at yours,' Mo said quickly.

'No problem,' Vanya said.

'I shouldn't have gone to your home and I'd prefer you to keep away from mine too, even though it's only my temporary address. Don't come here again – it's best that queen and subjects have clear boundaries.'

'Sure, OK. I understand.' Vanya nodded. She hopped onto her bike. 'Keep good work up. I'm proud of you. We all are.'

Then she revved the engine and sped away. Mo walked down the lane towards the lights of home, thinking not about how well she was doing as Vampire Queen but about Vanya being proud of her, and wondering why that felt so important.

18

To make the most of the vampires now being online, Mo decided to host a Christmas Zoom meeting the very next day and emailed them invitations with a link. Luca logged on from his family home earlier so he could chat with Mo.

'This is going to be perfect,' she said. 'No travel involved and zero chance they can guess I'm human if they can't smell me or touch me. Love it.'

'Change your background though,' Luca said. 'I can see your bed and Mr Bakewell.'

'Oh god, yes. Not very vampiric. Here we go. Mountains. Perfect.'

'I can't wait to see twenty vampires wrestling with modern technology. It's going to be hilarious.'

It was.

Natasha was the first to appear on the screen, her usually wild grey hair falling in a straight bob around her face. Clearly Olga and Lenka had used their straighteners on her.

'Natasha, you're on mute,' Mo said.

Natasha was talking – Mo could see her mouth working.

'It's the little microphone icon at the bottom, Natasha. You don't know what a microphone is? Down there, with the line through it.'

'. . . never get the hang of this. What's going on? Is it this? Or, wait a minute –'

'Natasha, I can hear you now. You're not on mute any more. That's great,' Mo said. 'Can you just move the camera a bit? I'm looking up your nose.'

New faces appeared. Derek popped up, waving. Sven arrived. He was wearing a headband like a 1970s tennis player, but at least it was less intimidating than his Viking helmet.

'Greetings, my liege, on this blessed eve,' he said.

'Hello, Sven,' Mo said. 'Hi, Pat. Hi, Richard – can you hear me OK?'

'You ruddy bet we can,' Pat said, hooting with girlish laughter. 'It's like you're in the same room. It's an actual and total miracle.'

Pat started stroking the screen. Even Richard seemed to be smiling, though he was sitting behind Pat and obscured by her big tangled up-do, so it was hard for Mo to tell.

'Nice mountains behind you, Your Majesty,' Pat said.

'Oh, they're not real,' Mo said.

'They are. Mountains are completely real. Ask Francis.'

Mo didn't bother explaining about backdrops, and anyway, the Tartan Fangs had just joined.

'Guys, you've got some sort of filter on,' Mo said, trying not to smile.

'What's that mean?' Malcolm asked.

'It means the computer has put a kitten face over each of your faces,' Mo said, biting the inside of her lip so she didn't grin. Luca was making no such effort. He had muted himself but was quite obviously howling with laughter.

Mo quickly messaged him privately, telling him to get a grip or turn his camera off.

'Look at the screen – can you see how your faces are covered up?' Mo said.

The three guys squinted in.

'Who's done this?' Malcolm roared. 'Nobody puts a kitten on my face, do you hear me?'

They patted each other's faces. Donald got up and Mo realised he'd gone to check behind the screen.

Olga and Lenka were using the chat box now. Kitten emojis began spooling up the side of the page, then crying-with-laughter faces, shocked faces, hearts, then actual vampire emojis.

'Is that a real kitten?' Pat muttered, her eyes wide, fascinated. 'Did a witch put a curse on them? Human witches can be so absolutely vindictive.'

'It's just a picture of a kitten,' Mo said. 'I'm going to put you three in a breakout room with Vanya; she can help take that off you.'

The Fangs and Vanya disappeared from the screen.

'What's happened to them?' Natasha shrieked.

'It's OK,' Mo said. 'They will be back in a second. Ah, here they are, with normal faces again. OK, let's start our meeting. I am pleased to see you wearing your new clothes. You all look very smart.'

The vampires grinned and spoke at once, creating a babble of voices.

'Maybe mute yourself unless you want to speak,' Mo said. More fiddling about, confusion. Mo decided to press on.

'I would like to start with a mindfulness exercise, to help you focus on the present,' she said. 'Not on the past, or the future. This is to help you get free of your worry about vampire hunters and the P-word that we don't speak of.'

'The purges,' said Derek.

'I thought we weren't supposed to say it.'

'Maybe we need to reclaim it, make it our own,' Derek said. 'That way, we can rob it of its power.'

'Lovely idea, Derek,' Mo said. 'OK, so, I want you to close your eyes and picture a lemon.'

'Are lemons the yellow ones or the green ones?' Natasha asked. 'So long since I ate fruit.'

'The yellow ones,' said Derek. 'The green ones are limes.'

'Oh yes, I remember now.'

'Really picture that lemon,' Mo encouraged them.

'We used to hate fruit,' said Olga.

'And vegetables,' Lenka added. 'What was that green stuff we had to eat?'

'Spinach.'

'No, the other one, looked like little trees.'

'Broccoli.'

'I don't really like lemons,' Derek piped up. 'They're very sour.'

'Well, you don't really like lemons because you don't really like any food, do you?' Pat said. 'You eat blood and you're a vampire. We've been through this before, Derek.'

Derek hissed.

'Picture something else then,' Mo said.

'A spleen?' said Natasha.

'If you like,' said Mo. She noticed Luca's camera was off, which probably meant he was laughing uncontrollably. Mo pressed on.

'Everybody OK with a spleen?'

They all nodded.

'Good. Excellent. Then let's begin.'

19

'Now,' said Mo, using a soft, slow voice, 'I want you to hold that spleen in your hands. How does it feel? Is it heavy?'

'Mine's quite heavy,' Pat said, her eyes closed and her hands cupped in front of her. 'It's a big spleen.'

'Try not to speak, please, just imagine this in your mind,' Mo said. 'Hold that spleen. Notice its weight. Now, think about its texture. Does it feel smooth? Bumpy? Wet? Is it soft and spongey, or dense and hard? Now I want you to sniff it. How does it smell?'

Luca popped up on-screen again, his eyes huge as traffic lights, unable to believe that he was hearing his girlfriend ask twenty vampires to imagine sniffing a spleen.

'I want you to squeeze that spleen a bit and catch the drips in a glass,' Mo said, and watched as the vampires made squeezing gestures with their hands. 'Now raise the glass to your lips and drink.'

They pretended to drink. Olga and Lenka smiled. Derek licked his lips. Sven grunted with satisfaction.

'Now, slowly and gently, open your eyes,' Mo said.

Blinking, the vampires refocused on her.

'How was that? I hope many of you could actually feel and taste that spleen. Could you?'

'Its pungent taste recalled to me a Nordic agriculturalist I once dined upon,' said Sven.

'I thought it was more like honey,' Olga said.

'We used to love honey,' Lenka added.

'But why are we drinking an imaginary spleen?' Pat asked.

'It shows that your thoughts can be mistaken for reality,' Mo explained. 'Your imagination is so powerful you can believe that what you're thinking is real. There was no spleen, and yet you felt it and tasted it.'

'So what?' Pat shot back.

'Well, every time you worry about vampire hunters out there waiting for you, remember your worries are just fantasies, they're not actually real. Then simply come back to the here and now. Be grateful for today. The future is unknowable; today is all we have.'

The vampires were quiet and thoughtful. Even Pat.

'You can practice the spleen exercise any time you feel tense or worried. Or work on your breathing.'

'I hardly think I need to do that,' Pat chuntered. 'I've been doing it for hundreds of years.'

'I'll email you a link to some guided breathing exercises,' Mo said. 'After all your years of anxiety, this could be very helpful.'

'Well, I certainly feel nice and relaxed,' Natasha said. Others nodded.

'I just feel hungry,' Pat said. 'I'm dying for a bit of real spleen.' And she did a squeezy thing with her hands while grimacing in a way Mo found slightly repulsive. Time to wrap it up.

'Very well,' Mo said. 'Let's adjourn this meeting of the British vampires. I will invite you to another online meeting soon.'

'But can we meet again face to face?' Derek asked. 'Some social events, maybe.'

'I rejoice in carousing heartily during the non-daytime hours,' Sven added.

'Aye, we'd welcome that too,' said Malcolm. 'Perhaps an all-you-can-eat human buffet? With dancing.'

'How about something that will really boost your health and well-being?' Mo said.

'That's an all-you-can-eat human buffet,' said Malcolm. 'No boost like it.'

'Maybe Your Majesty was thinking of a yoga retreat? Or a perfume-making workshop? Or some art therapy,' Derek offered. Someone's discovered TripAdvisor, Mo thought.

'Art?' Pat roared. 'What do we need with art?'

'We could do some life drawing,' Derek said.

'Only if I can eat the model afterwards,' Pat said. 'There's no way, no way at all on this tiny stupid planet, that I can stare at a human for hours and only draw him.

That's like staring at the menu and never ordering any food. Forget it.'

'It was just a suggestion, Pat,' Derek huffed. 'Have you got any better ideas?'

'Well, I do have an idea, not for a silly drawing lesson, but for something more ambitious,' Pat said.

'Murals? Street art?' Derek said.

'Shut up, Derek,' Pat snapped. 'You see, Queen Mo, I got a letter from my cousin Ludmilla who lives out east. It was all the usual news, you know – we visited the coast in the summer, Bob's back is still playing up, blah, blah – but then she mentioned that there's a rumour going around that the Vampire King will get married this summer. He's been doing up his castle. He's been sending out vampire emissaries to check out possible brides. Ludmilla was very totally excited about this. Vampire weddings are famously decadent, you know? But if this is true, this would make him even more powerful. It would consolidate his power in Europe, and whoever she is, she might get ideas about chucking you off the throne here quick sharp.'

'I see,' said Mo.

'You don't actually really sound like you *do* see, Majesty,' Pat snapped impatiently. 'The point is, now is the time to strike, Queen Mo. Just say the word. I will happily help you with this.'

'A coup d'etat?' Mo said.

'A what?'

'A rebellion? Is that what you mean?'

'Yes!' said Pat, the word becoming a long, excited hiss. 'Knock that useless, arrogant king off his fat throne and take charge. You could rule Great Britain and all of Europe. You'd do a much better job than that spoilt-brat medallion-wearing twerp.'

The vampires were licking their lips, nodding, leaning into their screens. Everyone except Vanya, who was calmly and silently observing.

'I told you when we first met, I'm not doing that,' Mo said, as firmly as she could. The vampires slumped back, disappointed. 'If I or you or any one of us kills him, we could bring hundreds of vampires from the East down on us, seeking revenge for their king.'

'Cowpat ploppings!' said Pat. 'They all hate him as much as we do. They would be ruddy grateful. Get rid of the useless ninny peacock.'

'It's still too risky,' Mo said. 'It could turn into a vampire civil war. We could all die, and then where would we be?'

'Dead?' said Derek.

'Yes, exactly. Do you want to be dead?'

'We already are,' he replied.

'More dead, then? Extra dead?'

'No, OK, we don't want that. That sounds bad.'

Pat threw up her hands. 'I still think it's the right path. Revenge on him for being a failed leader for so long, and an excellent promotion for you, Queen Mo.'

'No. I forbid it,' Mo said, staring sternly into the camera. 'Now is the time to enjoy some new vampire freedoms, not lose them all again by crossing the Vampire King. He's extremely violent and easily upset. He needs careful handling. Leave him to me, understand? No more talk of a coup.'

Some vampires shrugged, others nodded. Pat crossed her arms across her chest like a child refusing to apologise for smearing chocolate spread on the cushions.

'Let us end the meeting with a pledge of allegiance to me.'

'Again?' Derek said. 'We did that when we met at the hotel.'

'Someone's feeling needy,' Pat muttered.

'I can hear you, Pat,' Mo said.

Pat muted herself and blathered something to Richard over her shoulder.

'So, do you all still swear allegiance to me, your queen?'

'Of course we do,' said Derek. 'Why wouldn't we?'

'You've done more for us in a few days than the Vampire King did in decades,' said Natasha. 'Personally, I'm so grateful.'

'Yeah, you're the best, Queen Mo,' Olga and Lenka said, firing off a stream of emojis: balloons, stars, hearts. 'But could we also get mobile phones?'

'My fealty remains as massy as the fjords of Norseland,' said Sven.

'Thank you,' said Mo, trying to sound regal and not delighted (as she actually was). 'Massy is good. Our strength lies in our unity. Proud vampires of Great Britain standing as one.'

'There's no I in team,' Derek chipped in, grinning.

'I still think you should overthrow the Vampire King, but whatever, I'm behind you,' Pat said. 'We all are. No traitors here. I totally hate traitors. Death to any traitors – right, everybody?'

The other vampires nodded and hissed.

'Good. Let's end here then,' said Mo. 'Be well, my loyal vampire subjects. Goodbye.'

Mo watched as the vampires one by one worked out how to exit the meeting and disappeared from the screen, leaving just her and Luca behind.

'That was fantastic,' he said. 'Hilarious, but also fantastic.'

'Sven really enjoyed his spleen juice.'

'He totally got into that!'

'And Olga and Lenka were all over the emojis. These are vampires fit for the twenty-first century. Makes King Stevie's Chat Bat look like an antique.'

'Them all wanting to stage a coup and put you on the throne isn't quite so good though.'

'I know,' Mo agreed. 'I wish they would shut up about that. It's treason! They could get me in serious trouble. And I can't possibly do it – I've got GCSEs this summer.'

'They'll be spending hours on their laptops from now on anyway. They'll forget all about him.'

'That's the goal,' Mo said. 'Right, I'd better go. I'm sleeping over at Lou's tonight. She had her cast off today. Apparently, the skin underneath has gone really pale and got long dark hairs growing out of it, like a werewolf.'

Luca's eyes pinged open.

'You don't think she is one, do you?' he gasped, then he laughed. 'Joking!'

'I thought you were going to tell me werewolves exist too.'

'No chance!' Luca said. 'Vampires, yes, but werewolves? Forget it. Humans turning into oversized wolves on the full moon and running around eating other people? That's the stupidest thing I've ever heard.'

'Yeah, way more stupid than humans becoming undead creatures of the night that suck blood and can only be killed with a stake or sunlight,' said Mo.

'Exactly,' said Luca. 'Say hi to Lou from me. I wish I could be there to examine her extremely hairy and withered leg. Sounds great.'

'I'll tell her you said that.'

20

Mo spent a lot of the Christmas period eating. She watched films in Lou's bed with Lou and Nipper, munching on crisps and, for a seasonal change, mini mince pies. At home she tucked into the succession of big meals her dad prepared, starting on Christmas Eve with Mike's Massive Cracking Crimbo Creation, as he liked to call it. (Bit over the top – it was just a stew.) By the time the doorbell rang at 6 p.m. on the 29th, Mo felt she waddled to open it. Her hair was tousled from a post-lunch doze on the sofa and the top button of her jeans was undone.

'Luca!' she gasped.

'Hi,' he said, his trademark full-beam smile bathing her in delicious honeyed warmth, his perfect teeth gleaming like sunlight on freshly fallen snow.

'Who's that?' Mo's mum asked, on her way to the kitchen. 'No! Is it Luca?'

She elbowed past Mo and squashed Luca into a huge hug, then ushered him into the living room, where Mo's dad fired off a few quick questions – 'How long did it take you to get here? Did you come via Middle Donny or straight through the village? Many cars on the road? Foxes on the road? Badgers on the road?' – which Luca nodded and smiled through until both parents went to the kitchen to get more food.

'You weren't due back today,' Mo said, finally alone with him.

'Thought I'd come back early. I was missing you.' He beamed at her.

Why is it you only realise how much you've missed someone once they come back? Mo thought, beaming back. Then her parents returned with sandwiches and mince pies. The TV was showing a cheesy Christmas film, the lights on the tree were flashing – they weren't supposed to be, the wiring was faulty – and Mo sat quiet and close against Luca, feeling the warmth of his body soak into hers.

'It's good you're back – you can help me carpet the garden tomorrow, ready for Kate's party,' Mo's dad said.

'I didn't know you could carpet gardens,' Luca said.

'You can carpet anything.'

'Can you carpet a dog?'

'Don't be ridiculous, but anything that stands still long enough you can carpet.'

'A well-trained dog?'

Mo elbowed him.

Despite having heard numerous carpet-laying anecdotes, Luca still showed up again early next day to help.

'Your boyfriend's a natural at carpeting,' Mo's dad said to her later that morning. 'He's talented. He could go far.'

'In the world of carpeting? Or in the world?' Mo asked, hoping it was the latter.

'Is there a difference?' he replied. 'I'm going to speak to him about it. If you won't join the family business, maybe he will, once he's finished his technology widgets course.'

Mo had a lot of objections to this, but before she could voice them her dad had marched back over to Luca and was shouting, 'Use the knee kicker!' which sounded pretty aggressive to Mo, kind of like a martial-arts move, but Luca understood and reached for the right tool.

In the afternoon, Lou came over to help decorate the house and garden. She brought the bunting that just a few weeks before Mo had hung up in Lower Donny Village Hall, to greet the Vampire King. Today, though, they strung it over the front door and between the two apple trees that flanked the – now carpeted – lawn. Lights hung from the tree branches and the smell of sausage rolls and punch filled the house.

Neighbours flooded in from 6 p.m., including Mrs Spreadbury and the members of the Lower Donny crochet club. They burst into coos when they saw Luca again.

'They seem to like your boyfriend,' Dad said. 'A good carpet technician always commands respect.'

'What's he on about?' Lou asked, once Mo's dad had moved away.

'Don't ask. Ignore my dad. That's what I tend to do. Let's go get some punch. Mum's been brewing up her special recipe.'

'What's special about it?'

'You'll see,' Mo said, passing Lou a glass. They both took a sip and then winced.

'Oh my god that's bad,' Lou said, spluttering into the back of her hand. Her eyes were watering. 'Like squash mixed with onions? Is there booze in it?'

'Nope.'

'But there is sugar. So much sugar. It's so sweet it's making my mouth do weird things. I can't breathe. Quick, outside.'

They ducked into the garden.

'Do this, Lou,' Mo said. 'Poke your tongue out. Lick the air, it helps.'

Lou stuck her tongue out and the two of them licked the cold night air until their giggling got too much.

'Looks like you're enjoying my punch,' Mo's mum called from the kitchen window. 'How about a top-up? There are secret spices in that recipe that only I know about.'

'Any sugar?' Lou asked.

'Just a pinch,' said Mum.

They collapsed into giggles again.

'What's so funny?' Luca asked.

'We're having a massive sugar rush,' Lou explained. 'Come on, let's dance. No more cast and crutches. I want to move!'

She grabbed Luca's hand and led him to the dance floor. Mo followed, hovering awkwardly.

'Come on Mo, dance!'

They pulled her in and Lou and Luca began bouncing up and down, forcing Mo to bounce with them, which she did, laughing and soon shrieking and then breaking free and moving her own way.

'Yas Queen!' Lou shouted, applauding. 'Watch her go. You're actually really good, Mo. Who knew?'

Mo didn't reply; she was too caught up in the music. The air was cold but she felt warm, the blood pink in her cheeks and her eyes sparkling while Luca, who was carrying Lou on his back, did laps of the dancefloor.

'Check out the crochet-club members,' Lou shouted down to Mo. 'They have all the moves. Whoop! Whoop! Go crochet! Go crochet! Go crochet!'

They danced for ages, until Mo's dad grabbed the mic at the end of the evening and did a speech about his undying love for Kate, which Mo couldn't hear because she had stuffed her fingers in her ears. Then they began their slow dance.

'We are *not* watching this,' Mo said, and she grabbed Luca by the hand and led him quickly away.

'Will my parents never stop being embarrassing?!' she said once they had made it to the dark edges of the garden.

'They're sweet. Still so in love after all this time.' Luca pulled her towards him. 'Shall we slow-dance too?'

'Oh no, no, no, it's too cringey,' Mo protested, but he was gently swaying now.

'Remember when we danced in Middle Donny town square that time?'

'Seems ages ago,' Mo said. 'We weren't even together.'

'But you were crazy about me.'

She poked him in the ribs.

'Now, we are together, you're queen, the vampires are happy and there have been no more threats from the Vampire King. Just take it all in, Mo.'

'It is going pretty well.'

He tipped her and she shrieked.

'It's going brilliantly,' he said, bringing her upright again and kissing her.

'Ah, wonderful,' said a voice in the shadows.

Mo and Luca sprang apart and stood very still, scanning the darkness.

'Who's there?' Luca called out.

'You know me plenty well,' said the voice. It was familiar. The face too, when it appeared from the darkness. Piercing eyes, short grey hair, narrow lips.

'Bogdan!' said Luca, rushing up to him.

'Dear Luca,' he said, beaming. 'I'm so exciting to see you. And Queen Mo, here you are.'

Mo shook her head angrily and marched towards Bogdan.

'What the hell are you doing here? This is my Mum's birthday party. Do you want to get me in major trouble?'

'Surprising visit!' he said, his eyes sparkling. 'I mean no harms. I just arrived in Great Britain and am plenty wanting to see you both.'

'But why have you come? I thought you were in the Caribbean.'

'I told him he could,' Luca said.

'What?'

'He was sending postcards to me too, saying he was lonely. I told him to come over if he wanted to, for a visit.'

'And I did want to, and now I am here,' said Bogdan, grinning.

'Mo, it's OK, as long as he doesn't feed on anyone,' Luca said. Then he turned to Bogdan. 'You won't drain any of Mo's family or friends, will you, master?'

'Hang on, I'm the master around here now,' said Mo.

'I thought you didn't want me to call you that,' Luca said.

'I don't, but still – don't go mastering Bogdan, he's retired. Bogdan, it's nice to see you, of course it is, but please go away!'

'Can I meet you later, after guests have gone?' he asked. 'I am missing you.'

A voice called from the dance floor: 'Mo! Where are you? We're cutting the cake.'

'That's my dad,' Mo whispered. 'All right, in the shed at midnight. But for now, get away, far away.'

Bogdan bowed and retreated into the darkness.

'A vampire at my mum's party. Not good! He should have warned us he was coming over.'

'Nice to see him though?' Luca said.

Mo didn't answer. She glanced nervously over her shoulder, into the dark. Did she glimpse a shape, moving towards the bushes? There was only a sliver of moon, not enough to see clearly. She stared harder now. There, again! A flicker of movement. Someone walking away. Bogdan? But it was smaller, faster.

'What are you looking at?' Luca asked.

'I thought I saw something . . .'

'Probably just Bogdan, leaving like you said. Come on,' Luca said, tugging Mo forward. 'Cake time.'

21

Everyone was gathered in the kitchen where a huge cake sat on the table. Mo's dad sliced it up with a long, sharp knife – 'First the lasagne, now this,' Luca whispered – and Mo's mum handed out pieces.

'It's almost eleven,' Luca said. 'Will they definitely be gone by midnight?'

'Definitely,' Mo said. 'Lower Donny people party hard but they don't party long. They've been waiting for the cake, but they'll start leaving soon.'

She was right. By midnight everyone had gone. Only Mo's mum and dad were still around, clearing bottles and stacking the dishwasher. They didn't notice Mo and Luca slip out to the shed.

'I'm getting déjà vu,' Mo whispered to Luca. 'Walking across to the shed to meet Bogdan.'

She pictured the turning ceremony that had taken place here, Bogdan's blood pooled into a child's plastic beach bucket, Mo pretending to drink it, and then roaring, fake fangs in, transformed. The Vampire Queen!

She remembered Bogdan's face too, full of childish delight and wonder.

They pulled the shed door open. Inside, Bogdan was sat comfortably in the armchair, like he'd never left. He leaped up when he saw Mo and Luca and held his arms wide. Mo hugged him, thinking, Sure, why not, hugging vampires is totally normal for me now.

'Do I look plenty well? I tell you Mo, being retired is very nice and relaxed. No more worries, you know? No big stress.'

'You look great,' Mo said. 'Even got some colour in your cheeks, which is rare for a vampire.'

They laughed.

'Yes, yes, yes, retiring is good, but I was feeling a tiny bit boring, so I thought, come see my favourite non-vampire ruler and her familiar, yes? And after this, a little road trip back to the old country. I need to visit my tailor. The clothes on my Caribbean island are plenty nasty. Flowery shirts and loose shorts. Bleurrgh! Anyway, enough about me, how are you? Mo, you look radiant. Luca is caring for you properly?'

Mo blushed a little.

Bogdan patted Luca on the back in a paternal way and then sat down again. 'And how is reign as Vampire Queen?'

'It's good,' Mo said.

'The other vampires – they are happy?'

'I think so,' Mo said. She decided not to mention that Pat kept salivating about killing the Vampire King.

'She's being modest,' Luca butted in. 'She's a great leader. Really cares about the vampires.'

'Excellent. I knew this would be case,' said Bogdan. 'Sounds plenty impressive, Mo. That's the trick, is it not? Getting balance right. If the vampires don't respond to you, the Vampire King will think you're weak. But if they like you too much, he'll think you're a threat.'

'I'm not a threat,' Mo said.

'Not popular enough, he'll think you're a loser queen. Too popular, he'll think you're dangerous.'

'I'm not dangerous either,' Mo said, louder this time.

'Don't command respect, he'll think you're pathetic. Command too much, he'll think you're after his throne.'

'I'm not!' Mo shouted, her words sharp with anxiety. 'All I want is to do my job well and support my subjects. I don't want to offend the Vampire King, or his wife, if he ever gets married. There are rumours that he might. Did you hear?'

Bogdan shrugged.

'I don't ever want to see the Vampire King again! That's the truth,' Mo continued. 'He's already threatened to remove me if I don't make the British vampires loyal to me.'

'Ah yes, always ready with some threats. He carries them in his pocket like a child carries sweeties. Anyway, as I was saying, it's about balance. Not powerful enough, he'll think you are baby kitten. Too powerful, he'll think –'

'I get it,' Mo said, 'but how will he actually know how I'm doing? He's miles away. Have you heard something? Does he plan to come over again?'

Bogdan shrugged. 'Probably not. He really did not like it here, but even so, he will be getting the sense of how you're leading. He has many powers. Remember when he threw me across Lower Donny Village Hall? Psychokinesis. Rare power in a vampire, but not his only one.'

'So, what, is he telepathic too? Does he have laser vision? What?'

'Just take it from me, Mo, he will know,' Bogdan said firmly.

Goosebumps crept up Mo's arms.

'Anyway, my dear, no need to look worrying. We will hope all remains nice, but good to be cautious where Vampire King is concerned. He is pretty ruthless, as we know, sometimes dangerous and always, told be truth, a bit of pain up arse.'

Mo smiled.

'I can say that, now that I'm retired,' Bogdan added, winking. 'Well, my friends, it is time for me to go.'

He stood up and buttoned his heavy coat, stretching it over his belly which, Mo noticed, had grown a little since he'd retired.

'I have a dinner date. Nice man from car-hire company. He doesn't realise he's my dinner yet, but he will soon enough . . .'

He winked again. Luca pushed the shed door open and Bogdan stepped out onto the grass. Mo and Luca followed him.

'Well done, you two,' he said. 'I feel tiny bit like proud dad, standing here looking at you both. Gah! I must go before I am getting emotions. See you soon. Farewell.'

He reached out his hand to shake Luca's and then withdrew it at the last minute and cuffed him gently around the cheek.

'Hey,' Luca laughed. 'You're not my master any more. I could take you down.'

'I would like plenty much to see you try,' Bogdan teased back, raising his fists and hopping about.

Luca ducked and bobbed and landed a playful punch on Bogdan's side, then Bogdan popped him on the shoulder and Luca cried out, 'Ow!' in mock horror and rolled around on the grass like an injured footballer. Mo watched them, thinking how like two big kids they looked, play-fighting on the lawn on a freezing December night. As a result, she didn't notice the figure approaching from behind. A man, coming out of the darkness of the garden. A man walking quickly towards them, his broad shoulders hunched. Until he shouted out.

'Hey, what's going on?'

Mo looked over.

'Dad!' she gasped. He was running now, then suddenly there, right behind Bogdan. He slapped a hand down on his shoulder and spun him around. Bogdan, shocked and angry, hissed loudly. Mo saw a glint of fangs. She saw Luca scrabbling to his feet. She ran, calling out, 'Dad, get away!' hoping to warn him off this ancient but deadly vampire, hoping to alert Bogdan about who he was hissing at, but then she stopped, suddenly, frozen to the spot as her father reached into his coat, pulled out a wooden stake and, in one swift and powerful movement, plunged it deep into Bogdan's heart.

Mo's mouth gaped in a silent scream. She saw Bogdan stagger backwards. He looked confused. He glanced down at the stake, baffled to see it sticking out of his chest, dark blood spreading from around its buried tip. Then his gaze flickered unsteadily over to Mo, to Luca running towards him, before he collapsed face down onto the grass.

Mo didn't move. She couldn't move. Her dad was by her side now. 'Mo, are you safe? Are you OK?' he asked urgently. He cupped her face in his hands and looked deep into her eyes. 'Did he hurt you?'

Slowly, Mo shifted her gaze from Bogdan to her father's face.

'You killed him,' she whispered. 'Oh my god, Dad, you killed him.'

'It's OK,' he replied. 'That wasn't a real man. That was a creature of the night. A vampire. He's dead now. Properly dead. He won't be coming back. You're safe.'

Mo blinked and looked back to where Bogdan lay. Luca had turned him over and was studying his face. He took off his coat and laid it over Bogdan. The stake, still sticking out of his chest, poked up like a tent peg underneath.

'There's no need for that, Luca,' Mo's dad called over. 'Vampire scum don't deserve any respect.'

Mo could see Luca's jaw working. He was biting back words. She imagined him screaming in his head: 'He was my master and a human once too.' Instead, he asked, in a quiet, tense voice.

'What will you do with the body?'

'Bury it,' Mo's dad said. 'I'll call Jez and get him over to help.'

'Jez?' Mo shrieked. 'Why Jez?'

'He's a vampire hunter too. Well, he's in training. Still a rookie, but he's got the potential to be a really good slayer, and as I'm the last of the vampire hunters, I thought it was time to enlist some fresh blood, so to speak.'

Mo's mouth opened and closed like a netted fish, but no words came out.

'Sorry, love, there's a lot you don't know. I can explain everything. Come on, let's get you inside into the warm. You've had a big shock. Then we'll get rid of this disgusting bloodsucker.'

22

Mo's dad went over to Bogdan, yanked out the stake and then turned and walked purposefully back to the house. Mo and Luca followed. Something made Mo pause on the doorstep and look behind her. The moon was out now, illuminating the drive, and there, standing just beyond the gate, quite clearly, was Vanya. For a few seconds Mo stared at her and Vanya stared back, but then she was gone, suddenly disappeared. She had been the figure in the bushes earlier when Bogdan showed up, Mo realised. Why was she here?

'Kate, guess who just staked a vampire in the garden?' Her dad's triumphant voice reached her. Then her mum's terrified one:

'Here! There's a vampire here?'

Mo went inside.

'Was,' said her dad. 'He's an ex-vampire now.'

'You staked him in front of Mo?'

'He was attacking Luca. I had no choice.'

Mo glanced at Luca. His face was still but his eyes flashed with pain. The two of them sat down heavily. Mo squeezed Luca's hand under the table. He stared flatly ahead and didn't squeeze back.

'Whoa! Still got it,' said Mo's dad, holding both fists up in victory. 'I can tell you're shocked that there are still vampires around, Mo. You probably thought they didn't exist, right?'

Wrong.

'Thought they were just something from stories.'

Also wrong.

'And you couldn't know I was a vampire hunter.'

Right. That bit definitely came as a surprise.

'I had thought most of these bloodsuckers were gone,' he went on. 'We tried our best to eradicate them from Great Britain. A team of vampire hunters, around twenty years ago, went on a mission to stamp them out once and for all, but they're like cockroaches or boomerangs. They come back.'

The purges! Mo thought. Oh god. Oh, no, no, no. My dad was involved in the purges. My actual dad!

'Well done for fighting back,' he said, patting Luca on the shoulder, 'but punches are never enough when it comes to vampires. The only thing that can stop them is a stake. I can give you one to keep on you at all times. OK, good, let me call Jez, then it's time for a celebration.'

Mo glanced at Luca. His face was set as stone. Mo's mum put cups of tea in front of them and squeezed

152

her daughter's shoulders. They sat silent until her dad returned to the kitchen.

'Jez is on his way,' he said. 'Cheer up, everyone! Killing a vampire is something to feel good about. If we hadn't just had a party, I'd suggest we have a party.'

Mo looked at her hands, painfully aware of Luca motionless beside her.

'But why was it here, Mike?' Mo's mum asked. 'What did it want?'

'I don't know,' he said. 'I'm pretty sure it wasn't British. The clothes suggested Eastern Europe – the stitching, the buttons – and the accent too.'

'But he didn't speak,' Mo said.

'It hissed. You can tell where a vampire is from by its hiss,' he said. 'Black Sea region, I'd say, probably turned three to four hundred years ago.'

Six hundred actually, Mo was thinking, but wow, Dad knows his stuff. All this time, there was another vampire expert in the house, although admittedly coming at things from a very different angle.

'I reckon he was alone. They usually are. Nasty, solitary creatures with no friends.'

'Was he after you, Mike?' her mum asked. 'Is your cover blown?'

'No, he was genuinely surprised to see me. The look on his face when I staked him!'

He pulled a comically surprised expression and waved his arms around. Nobody laughed.

'Don't worry, guys. The main thing is, I got him. The Biter didn't let me down.'

'The Biter?' Mo asked, feeling dread rise in her throat.

Dad patted his pocket. 'My trusty stake. I've had The Biter for years. He's seen a *lot* of action.'

Mo swallowed, but her mouth was dry. There was a knock at the door.

'That will be Jez,' said her dad, getting up and putting his coat on. 'Luca, want to help us bury this filthy thing?'

Luca blinked a few times, the offer taking him by surprise.

'Coming,' he said.

Mo's dad dived outside.

Mo followed Luca to the door. 'You don't have to do this.'

'It's all right. I want to,' Luca said. 'I can make sure he's buried with care, not just tossed in a ditch.'

Mo blinked back tears. 'He would have wanted you there,' she said, hugging Luca hard. 'Oh god, I'm so sorry.'

'Hurry up, Luca,' Mo's dad called from the garden. 'Get out here if you're coming. We could use your muscle.'

Back in the kitchen, Mo's mum was spreading oven chips on a baking tray.

'Your dad always likes steak and chips after a staking,' she said, sounding apologetic. 'Terrible pun, but you know him, he loves terrible puns, almost as much as he loves killing vampires. Only, we haven't got any steak. He'll have to make do with chips.'

Mo slumped down into a chair.

'It's a lot to take in, isn't it?' her mum said.

'My Dad is a vampire hunter,' Mo replied. 'Yes, that definitely feels like news. Sure. Yup. Hadn't expected that. I thought carpets were his thing, but now it turns out it's murdering.'

'Well, eradicating a threat, really. Think of it like pest control.'

Mo shook her head.

'You mustn't worry, Mo,' her mum went on. 'Your dad is really good at vampire hunting. He's killed loads. Don't wince. They're vampires after all. It's best they're wiped out.'

'They were human once.'

'Well, technically, I suppose. Not any more though. They're dangerous. That vampire could have killed Luca, then you. Oh, Mo, I can't bear to think about that. Here, in our garden, at my birthday party.'

She started nervously wiping surfaces.

'Why didn't you tell me about Dad?' Mo asked.

'To protect you,' she said. 'We didn't want you to be scared, and anyway, he doesn't do much staking any more. There's been no vampire activity for years, until Clive Bunsworth and that teacher of yours.'

'Mr Chen,' Mo said. 'So you knew they were murdered by vampires? I mean, *were* they murdered by vampires?'

'We suspected, yes, but then it seemed to go quiet. Anyway, hopefully the one Dad just finished off was the same one that killed them, and now he's gone, so we're safe again.'

The front door opened and Dad, Jez and Luca came back into the kitchen.

'Sorted,' Dad said. He was wearing a huge, satisfied grin. He poured a measure of whisky into three glasses and handed one each to Jez and Luca.

'Cheers! Another one bites the dust.'

He tossed back his drink. Jez took a self-conscious sip and then coughed a little. Luca just stared at his glass.

'How are you, Mo?' Dad asked.

She shook her head.

'Probably a bit shocked. You'll be OK soon. I have to say, *I* feel great. Nothing beats staking a vampire. The adrenaline rush! Wow, it's huge! I haven't done that in a while. Last one was a skinny little vamp I came across on holiday in the Alps a few years back, but to exterminate one here, on home turf – that's a big deal. That feels momentous, you know?'

He grinned at Jez.

'You should have seen me, Jez. Not going to lie, I was smooth. Hand on his shoulder, pivot him round, see the fangs. Then it was all just one beautiful swift movement. I grabbed the stake from my pocket, whipped it out and BULLSEYE! Drove it in.'

Luca slammed his glass down on the kitchen worktop. Everyone looked round.

'Sorry,' he murmured.

'Anyway,' Mo's dad went on, 'loads to learn from this, Jez. Number one?'

'Always carry a stake with you,' Jez said.

'Correct. Day and night. And number two?'

'Always check for fangs?'

'Good,' said Dad. 'When you get a confirmed sighting, act fast. Speed is of the essence. Vampires can really move when they're threatened. You have to be incredibly quick, incredibly decisive. Aim for the heart and aim hard.' He beamed at everyone. 'That's how you get a kill. That's how you protect your precious girl.'

He went to stroke Mo's cheek but she flinched away.

'I'm going to bed,' she said.

'I'm leaving too,' said Luca.

'Don't you want steak and chips?'

'I'm a vegetarian, Dad, and there's no steak anyway,' Mo snapped. She walked quickly out of the kitchen, pushing past Jez without speaking to him, and paused at the bottom of the stairs. Luca joined her.

'Sorry,' she said. 'I didn't know, honest. I'm as shocked as you are.'

He nodded.

'See you tomorrow?' Mo said, tears prickling her eyes again.

Luca nodded, opened the front door and was gone.

23

What do I do now? What the absolute hell do I do now?

The question was motoring through Mo's brain before she'd fully woken up the next morning.

She sat up in bed, clutched Mr Bakewell to her chest and tried to wrap her head around this new situation.

My dad is a vampire hunter. This – surely – changes everything.

I represent vampires but my dad kills them. It's like being head of the vegan society when your parents run an abattoir. This doesn't work, does it?

How can I face my subjects as the daughter of a vampire hunter? Not just any old vampire hunter either, one of the guys responsible for the purges. The very same purges that have left British vampires cowering in their homes for the last twenty years.

Mo went over to the mirror and stared at her face. 'What do I do? What do I do? What do I do?' she muttered, hoping her reflection would chuck back a workable answer. Nothing came. The only thing she felt sure of was how the vampires would react. Answer? Terribly.

If they heard that Bogdan had been staked by a vampire hunter they would freak out. This was their worst nightmare coming true just weeks after they started to reclaim their lives, just weeks after Mo had urged them to put the past behind them, walk tall and be proud of who they are. They would be totally triggered – and totally furious. Could they trust her again? Did she have even a scrap of authority left? Would they stay loyal?

'Just when I thought everything was going well,' Mo groaned. 'Dad. You have ruined it all. Ruined it!'

She sat down at her desk, drumming her fingers as her panicked mind tried to find an answer to the question: What do you do when you're Vampire Queen and you've just found out your dad is a vampire hunter?

I could get turned, Mo thought. Become a real vampire. Divorce my family and my vampire-hunting dad. They might expect me to kill him though. Oh yuck. That wouldn't feel good. Or Dad might have to hunt and kill *me*. No, no, no, that's way too dysfunctional!

What else?

I could resign. Say it's for personal issues. Or a scandal. Abusing expenses, maybe? Unethical spending on my Dark Card.

Maybe I could just ask someone else to do the job. Elect a successor. Tracey Caldwell's feisty. Maybe she could rule? Then I could step down, go into hiding maybe . . .

Her thoughts fizzled out like a sparkler in the rain. She paced the room before finally stopping by the window, where she drew back the curtains. Over by the hedge, at the far side of the garden, was a mound of earth. It was person-sized. It was a grave. Bogdan's.

'Oh god,' she whispered, a new wave of horror crashing over her. Bogdan was murdered, after all those years undead. Six hundred of them.

She squeezed her eyes shut and only opened them when she heard footsteps on the gravel drive a few minutes later. Luca was striding towards the front door, a frown clouding his broad forehead and darkening his treacle-brown eyes. Then Mo heard the doorbell and Luca's voice downstairs. She felt her heart bounce at the sound of his footsteps on the stairs. Would he be angry with her? Was he grieving too?

A light tap on the door, then he stepped inside. He smiled. Not the full beam that used to liquidise her insides, but a weak hello that Mo could see, instantly, was dripping with sadness.

'I'm so sorry,' she said, rushing up to him. 'I know you cared about Bogdan. I did too.'

They hugged and then Luca took a strand of Mo's long hair and used it to wipe his tears away, which she found a bit weird but didn't say anything. It was the least she could offer him.

'I can't believe he's gone,' Luca said, sitting on the bed.

'And it was my dad that did it,' Mo said, her bottom lip quivering and tears spilling from her eyes. She swiped them clumsily away.

'God, my stupid, stupid dad. He's dumped me in this humongous mess. Why didn't he tell me about being a vampire hunter? Why did he lie about it?'

'Well, the success of his work probably depended on him keeping his identity secret,' Luca said in a weary voice, 'and he didn't want you to worry about him facing down vampires, even though that's exactly what you like to do too. You have more in common than you realise.'

'We have *nothing* in common,' Mo fumed. 'I've been tasked with improving their lives; he's busy trying to wipe them off the face of the earth.' She began pacing again.

'You know what,' she said, jabbing the air with her finger. 'I can *never* trust my dad again. Never. He's ruined *everything*. He's a liar, who keeps really big, fat secrets.'

Luca raised one eyebrow slowly, but said nothing.

'Oh, don't give me that,' Mo said. 'It's right that I haven't told my parents about me being Vampire Queen, especially knowing what I know about Dad now. It's *my* business.'

Luca shrugged.

'What? You're not seriously saying I should have told them?'

'I just think there's dishonesty and secrets on both sides of this family.'

Mo folded her arms across her chest and marched over to the window. Seeing Bogdan's grave again popped her anger, like a pin in a balloon. Her shoulders slumped and her tone became quiet.

'I'm sorry,' she said, turning back to Luca. 'I'm in shock. I'm stressed and I don't know what to do. I feel really terrible too. So terrible. It's my fault that Bogdan died – he came to see me.'

'He came to see *us*,' said Luca. 'Anyway, it's on me. We were play-fighting. Your dad thought he was attacking me.'

'Dad would have killed him anyhow, Luca,' Mo said, sitting next to him and squeezing his hand. 'He would have seen he was a vampire and done it. It's not your fault and it's not Bogdan's fault for coming. It's nobody's fault, except my dad's.'

Luca flopped backwards and stared at the ceiling.

'I thought he'd be around forever,' he said, his voice small. 'I should have protected him.'

'It happened too quickly. There was nothing you could have done.'

Mum called from the kitchen, 'Come and get some food, you two. I'm doing eggs.'

Luca sat up.

'Does this come between us?' Mo asked, her face pained and nervous. 'My dad killing your previous vampire master?'

He shook his head.

'When you first met Dad, I was worried he'd be embarrassing. Now I wish that was all I had to worry about.'

'He's definitely making it hard for me to bond with him,' Luca said, trying to smile and failing. 'I finally get introduced to him, he fires a thousand totally stupid questions at me about have I ever eaten soup with a teaspoon or something, he decides I'm acceptable and I think, OK, I can relax. Now, though, it turns out he's a vampire hunter. What if I don't find *him* acceptable?'

'I know. I feel the same. The big joke is he thinks he's just protected me, when in fact he's landed me up to my neck in trouble.'

She put her face in her hands and groaned.

'Are you coming?' her mum shouted again.

'We should eat,' Luca said. He took Mo's hand, pulled her to her feet and they limped towards the door.

'Wait, Luca, there's something else,' Mo said, pausing. 'I saw Vanya last night in the garden.'

'What?'

'Yeah, when we first met Bogdan, but then after the killing too. She was over by the gate.'

'Definitely her?'

Mo nodded.

Luca rubbed his forehead, creased now by a frown. 'Did she see the murder then?' he asked.

'Must have done. What if she talks?'

'She won't,' he said.

'How can you be so sure?' Mo said, her voice high and strained. 'I saw her before Christmas in the lane and she promised to stay away. Then there she is again, in my garden, on the night Dad goes staking crazy.'

She clasped her hands together and tapped them against her mouth. 'I need to speak to her. Oh god, more problems. I need to swear her to silence.'

'She won't say anything,' Luca said again. 'I know she won't.'

Mo shook her head, a panicked look in her eyes. 'Wish I could be that certain. With Vanya, I never am.'

'Come on,' Luca said, taking Mo's hand again. 'Don't think about her for now. Let's go get some food.'

Downstairs there was toast, grilled tomatoes, baked beans and fried eggs piled up on the table.

'Tuck in,' Mo's mum said. 'Always nice to have a big brunch the morning after a party.'

'The morning after you find out your dad is a vampire hunter,' Mo said.

'I thought you'd be impressed,' her dad said. 'I know I'm not on TikTok or whatever, but I'm a real-life vampire hunter, love. It's quite cool, isn't it?'

'It's violent, Dad, and weird and aggressive and gross.' Mo stared at him, fury in her eyes. He looked shocked and sat back in his seat.

'I wasn't expecting that reaction. Hopefully you'll come to see it as a good thing when you've calmed down.'

'Calmed down? You have kept this from me my whole life, lied to me basically, and now I have to let off the party poppers, do I? Well, sorry to disappoint, but this is a huge thing for me. Huge. You're a vampire hunter, Dad!'

'And proud of it. I saved Luca's life and your life last night.'

'All right, all right, stop shouting, both of you,' Mo's mum said.

'I thought Mo might be just a tiny bit grateful.'

'Why should I be? How do you even know if I was in danger? Or Luca?'

'Mo! It was a vampire. Don't be so naive. He was fighting Luca and he would have killed and drained all of us if I hadn't got him with my stake. I'm amazed you don't see that. I know you're a vegetarian, but still.' He snorted.

Mo glared at him.

'Look, you're obviously upset.'

'You think?' Mo shot back.

'But I'm not. Want to know how I feel today? Luca, do you? I'll tell you. I feel relieved that I killed him. A father protecting his daughter – that's powerful. On top of that, I've performed a public service. We can all sleep a little more soundly because of what I did.'

'You took a life, without asking any questions or giving any reasons, just because he was a vampire. What gives you the right to do that? Maybe that vampire had friends and family who are devastated now.'

Mo's dad laughed, then clocked Mo's expression.

'Oh my god, you're serious, aren't you?' he said. 'Look, love, you can't afford to feel sentimental about this. There's no point going all human-rights lawyer. You have to understand that vampires are outside of humanity. They are not humans. They *destroy* humans. They drink our blood. Their presence pollutes our lives; it infects our society and corrodes everything we are, all that we hold dear – life, love, family. They cannot be tolerated in this country, on this island, do you see? That's why I have devoted my life to expunging them.'

'Expunging?' Mo said. 'You're an *expunger* now.'

'Is that funny to you?'

'No, it's cool. Love having an *expunger* for a dad.'

'Mo, I don't understand why you're being so difficult about this?'

'She's upset, Mike,' Mo's mum said. 'She's just discovered vampires exist.'

Did that weeks back actually, Mo thought.

'That they live among us.'

Yup, knew that too.

'She also witnessed you killing one last night.'

Bogdan. His name was Bogdan.

'How many fifteen-year-old girls have experienced that?'

'I understand it's a bit shocking, but it was for the best, Mo, I promise you,' Dad said. 'We're all a lot safer now.'

All of us safer? Mo wanted to shout. Really? You've just taken out one of Europe's oldest vampires who, until recently, was working for Europe's nastiest, most powerful vampire – the Vampire King of the East. Vanya almost definitely witnessed it. If, or rather when, my – until now – loyal subjects find out, they are going to be triggered, panicked and super angry. They are going to want me to respond too, and by respond, I mean kill you. Or they may try to do it themselves. So now I can't decide who is in more danger. Me, the Vampire Queen, who has let a staking happen on her territory, or you, Dad, the vampire hunter who drove the stake in.

Mo shoved her chair back noisily and ran upstairs to her room. Luca excused himself and left too.

'She'll come around Mike,' Mo heard her mum say. 'Give her time, that's all.'

24

Time, though, was not what Mo needed. Time alone in her room was just time to feel anxious about this latest development, to replay Bogdan's murder in her mind, like a horror film, or stress about what would happen if – when – the news came out.

She flipped open her laptop and fired off an email to Vanya with the subject: 'URGENT – READ THIS THE SECOND YOU WAKE UP!' In it, she insisted that Vanya explain why she was in Mo's garden last night and ordered her to keep quiet about anything she saw.

Then Mo grabbed her coat and cycled over to Lou's.

'Oh no, what's happened? Did you have a fight with Luca?' Lou said, clocking Mo's broken expression.

'No, it's my dad. He's done something really bad.'

Lou's face lit up, sensing drama.

'He's not having an affair, is he? Maybe it's a midlife crisis. Or could be the male menopause. It's totally a thing. Have his boobs got bigger?'

'Lou! Please.'

'Keep an eye on that. He can probably get medication for it.'

Mo laughed now, a grateful burst from behind the hands pressed against her face.

'Look, it's complicated and super secret. Can we go for a walk?'

Lou tried to look serious and mature, but her eyes sparkled with anticipation as she quickly put Nipper on the lead and zipped up her jacket.

Mo strode ahead and was halfway across a field when she turned to Lou and dropped her news like a bomb.

'My dad is a vampire hunter.'

'What the . . . ?'

Mo held up her hand to silence her and continued. 'And last night, he . . . He . . .'

'What?' Lou asked, leaning in.

'Last night he killed Bogdan, the vampire who ran you over. Luca's master. Him.'

'No! Your dad? Mike Merrydrew? Sure it was him?'

'Yes,' said Mo, exasperation sharpening her voice.

'Did you see it happen? How did he do it?'

'With a wooden stake that he calls The Biter and keeps in his pocket.'

'Oh . . . My . . . God!' Lou said, her face appalled, delighted, amazed. 'Was there loads of blood? Was it super gory?'

'I don't really want to talk about the details,' Mo said.

'You probably should though. Don't bottle it up, you'll get PTSD.'

'It's not PTSD I'm worried about. I'm worried – actually that's a massive understatement – I'm totally freaking out about what to do next.'

'You probably need to bury him; you can't have a dead vampire lying around. Health and safety. Where did it happen, by the way?'

'In the garden, near the shed, but they've already buried him. Dad and Luca.' Mo edited out Jez. That was one detail she didn't feel she could tell.

'Oh, grim. That must have been hard for Luca. He liked Bogdan, didn't he?'

'I liked him too.'

'Really? He ran me over, Mo.'

'He wasn't perfect.'

'Terrible driver,' Lou muttered.

'Luca is really upset and I am upset and just *so* stressed. What if the other vampires find out?'

'Wow, not often you need advice from me,' Lou said. 'You really *are* crapping it. OK, well, just say he died of natural causes, peacefully in his sleep.'

Mo shook her head impatiently. 'Vampires don't die like that. They either live forever or they are terminated violently – stake or sunlight. There's nothing in between. He would never go out in the sun, so they would know he was staked.'

'Well just don't tell the vampires about the murder. It's simple. Zip it.'

'It's not going to be that easy,' Mo said. 'Vanya – she was there last night. She must have seen it. She could tell the others.'

'What the hell was Vanya doing there?' Lou asked. 'Man, this is complicated. I guess just tell her to keep quiet too. Command her to. You're the queen.'

'Yeah, you're right. I've emailed her already. I should probably speak to her as well. God, it's extra stress though. Extra, extra stress.'

Lou grabbed Mo's hand and stared hard into her eyes. 'It will be OK, Mo. Look, you get Vanya to shut her mouth and then you do the same. Hush it all up and move on. That's what leaders do when something goes wrong, isn't it?'

'Bad leaders do that. I'm trying to be a *good* leader. I don't know, Lou, it's not very honest. Would it work? I just say nothing and keep on ruling?'

'Yes.'

'Forget about my dad and his hyper violent and weird alter ego.'

'It's not that weird,' Lou said. 'My dad used to collect empty crisp packets. That *was* weird. Partly why Mum divorced him. Hunting vampires is actually kind of dramatic, you know?'

Mo shook her head.

'Cooler than carpets anyway.'

'He's still geeky about them. Odd combo really –
vampire slaying and carpet laying.'

'That sounds like a rap.'

'Or a really niche seller on Etsy.'

They began walking back across the field.

'Mini Battenbergs and hot chocolate back at mine?'
Lou said.

'You had me at Mini Battenbergs,' Mo replied.
'Thanks, Lou. I feel a bit calmer now.'

It didn't last. When Mo got home later that afternoon,
Jez was in the drive. He was helping her dad unload some
bags from the back of the car. They were putting them
into the garage freezer.

'Ah, Mo, now that you know about my life as a vampire
hunter, no need to hide what we're doing,' her dad said.

'What *are* you doing? Looks suspiciously like disposing
of the dismembered corpse of something you've just
murdered. Is that another vampire?'

'I wish,' her dad said cheerfully. Clearly butchering
vampires put him in a buoyant mood. 'It is meat though.
It's for training, isn't it, Jez? Staking training.'

Jez nodded and rubbed his hands together nervously.

'I don't understand,' Mo said, and I'm not sure I want
to, she thought.

'Simple, you string the meat up and then you stab it.
Gives you a feel for how it will be when you stake the real
thing. You need to get a sense of the meaty resistance.'

'Meaty resistance?'

'Yes, I mean, obviously a pork roasting joint isn't quite the same as a vampire's chest, but you'll get an idea.'

'Of the . . .'

'Of the meaty resistance, yes.'

Mo noticed her fists clenched by her side, her jaw tightening. She looked over at Jez. He didn't make eye contact and something about that made Mo press on.

'Have you actually met a vampire yet, Jez?'

'No, not as far as I know,' said Jez.

'Excited about it?' Mo asked. 'I suppose you won't have time to get to know him or her. There won't be any chit-chat, will there? You'll have to strike fast, just like my dad told you. How will that be? Your first kill. Driving that stake in, dodging the ribs and aiming for the heart. Sharpened wood against soft flesh. Oh wow, it's going to be great, isn't it?'

Jez shifted uneasily. 'We're doing a service,' he said. 'A public service.'

'A public service that involves killing,' Mo said.

'All right, Mo, that will do,' her dad said. 'We've been over this.'

'What else has my dad been telling you, Jez? That it's big and manly and brave to hunt vampires? It's what tough guys do in their spare time?'

Jez shook his head, frowning.

'You know what would have been a good public service that you could have done? You know what would have been brave?' Mo said, her words tumbling out in an angry stream. 'You could have asked Tracey Caldwell not to pick on me like she used to on the bus. All those names she called me, all those times she made me feel small and scared. That's the kind of public service I would have liked. Instead, you just sat there.'

'What's this?' Dad said, looking between the two of them. Jez didn't speak. 'Tracey who?'

Jez licked his lips nervously. Mo glared at him for one second more, then turned and marched into the house.

25

That evening, an email from Vanya plopped into Mo's inbox.

'I'm sorry I came to your house again. Maybe we should meet to talk about it?'

No explanation of why she was there, Mo noticed. She groaned quietly, feeling exhausted.

'Tonight, 8pm, in the lane,' she emailed back, and then texted Luca to ask him to come over too.

At 7.45 Mo reluctantly put on her long black dress and Vampire Queen robe and snuck outside with Luca.

'What the . . . ?!' Mo said, breaking into a run. Vanya was walking across the gravel drive towards the front door. Mo raced up to her and yanked her back towards the gate.

'What the hell do you think you're doing?' she hissed. 'Were you going to knock on the door?'

'What the hell do *you* think you're doing, grabbing me like that?' Vanya shot back, snapping her arm away. 'I was early, that's all. What's the harm?'

Mo glowered at her, clenching her jaw with fury.

'Anyway, you told me come, and I'm here,' Vanya said, glowering back.

Mo felt a few fat drops of rain land on her face, felt the wind shift and blow her hair around. It was cold. She suppressed a shiver.

'Let's go to the shed.'

It was warmer and dry inside. Mo flicked on the light and looked at Vanya. She was wearing her usual mix of biker jacket, silk blouse and tight black trousers, plus expensive-looking ankle boots decorated with studs. Mo took it all in instantly. She clocked the big hoop earrings, the heavy black eyeliner and a nose stud she hadn't noticed before.

Mo, by contrast, felt like she was dressed in a pair of curtains. She spread her palms against the velvety sides of her robe, hoping to wipe off some sweat.

'Your Majesty,' Vanya said, 'how can I help?'

Mo flinched – so patronising! – but she couldn't protest. She did need her, after all. She needed her to stay quiet.

'Bogdan was murdered yesterday night. I know you saw it, because you were here. I command you to stay silent on this. I cannot have the other vampires or the Vampire King finding out.'

'I won't tell anyone,' Vanya said. 'You can trust me.'

'I don't want the vampire hunter's identity revealed either.'

'Because it was your dad?'

Mo flinched.

'Correct.'

Vanya nodded calmly. 'It's kind of awkward, isn't it? Your dad's a vampire hunter. You're the Vampire Queen.'

Mo glanced at her and thought, She's enjoying this. Knowing everything, watching me squirm. Mo wanted to reach for something solid to hold onto to stop herself from swaying.

'Look, do you promise to stay loyal and keep your mouth shut?' she snapped impatiently.

'Of course.'

Mo nodded, felt her shoulders drop a little. Maybe she could contain this, just as Lou had said. Then . . .

'Shhh!' It was Luca. He was pointing at the door. They all froze, and then heard scratching. He tiptoed over, slowly opened it and peeped out.

'It's a Chat Bat,' he said, and then let it flutter in. It settled on the armchair. The three of them stared at it while it sat there, doing nothing, saying nothing until eventually it opened its mouth.

'*So, I'm sensing that Bogdan is dead.*'

Mo felt her legs go watery. It was the Vampire King's voice.

'*And I'm also feeling that he was staked by a vampire hunter.*

'*This is not very good – who likes a staking? Not me! But Bogdan was old, and I had no use for him any more. (Wasn't he in the Caribbean?) You must give Bogdan a good funeral though. Since it's vampire tradition – as you well know – to bury our departed exactly seventeen days after they were slain, that means the sixteenth of January. Get all the British vampires out to celebrate his life. Make it the send-off he deserves. No bunting. A proper vampire funeral.*

'Sadly, I can't be there. There's another uprising brewing. This time it's the Vampire Freedom Front. Fools. I must crush them. I'm sure you're disappointed not to see me, and you should be, but when you're the king, them's the breaks. Anyway, I will send my new emissary – the one who replaced Bogdan – to represent me instead. The new Bogdan saying farewell to the old. How fitting!

'Laters.'

The bat fell silent. Luca shooed it out of the shed door. Mo could feel herself beginning to shake. She was blinking rapidly, her mind whirring, her fists clenched, and then she turned to Vanya, a look of cold hatred in her eyes.

'You!' she said, in a deep and menacing voice. 'You told him. You told the Vampire King!'

'No, I didn't, I swear,' Vanya said.

Mo noticed that Vanya actually looked worried, a change from her usual ironic gaze.

'You're a snake! A spy working for the Vampire King. That's why you're here. That's why you have been stalking me!'

'That's not true,' Vanya said.

'Mo, remember what Bogdan said, about the Vampire King's weird powers? And the Chat Bat said he *sensed* Bogdan was dead, he didn't say someone had told him.'

Mo made a 'pffft' noise and waved Luca's words away.

'How could you?' she said, still glaring at Vanya. 'What have I ever done to you?'

'Mo, stop, please,' Vanya said. 'Take breath. Listen to me. It was wrong of me to come to your house last night, I'm sorry for that, but I'm not a spy for the Vampire King. Never have been. Never will be. That arrogant, preening narcissist? Forget it. I would never do that.'

Mo blinked rapidly.

'Do you believe me?' Vanya persisted.

'Why should I?'

'Because I'm telling the truth,' Vanya said, moving towards Mo.

'Don't come near me,' Mo shouted, her voice shaky. 'I need to think, *think*. What am I going to do? I have to punish you somehow, yes, you must be punished, and then I'll have to tell the other vampires.'

She chewed her lip, her gaze darting around the shed, settling nowhere.

'Look, why don't you sit down?' Vanya said.

'I don't want to sit down.'

'Please? I have something to tell you.'

'I'm fine here, thanks,' Mo said. 'And I don't want to hear anything you have to say, OK? Shut up. Just shut up right now.'

'Mo,' Luca said, putting a hand on her arm.

She shook it off fiercely. 'I know, how about I pay you to go and never come back? You want money, don't you? You'll do anything for it. That's why you agreed to spy for the Vampire King, isn't it? For the cash. Fine. I have money! I have a Dark Card. Go on, name your price, let's get this over with. How much to never see you again?'

'Mo, stop. I don't want your money.'

Mo blinked back tears. She had a strong urge to parrot back *I don't want your money* in a juvenile, sing-song voice and then blow a massive raspberry. Instead she turned away, painfully conscious of Vanya's greedy gaze.

'I need to show you something,' Vanya said, reaching into her jacket.

'I don't want to see it,' Mo screamed. 'This isn't show-and-tell. Whatever's in your pocket, you can stick it where the moon don't shine,' she added, feeling herself unravelling.

'Mo, if you would just listen, this might all feel better.'

'This?' Mo shrieked, waving her arms about. 'This! You mean the fact that you've been spying on me and observed a murder – ooh, result! – by my human dad.'

'I am not a spy, Mo, and I don't work for the Vampire King. I had my reasons for being here last night. Please let me explain.'

'Are you jealous of me? Or my role? What's behind all this, eh? You obviously want me dead. And I may be soon. The vampires will riot when they hear I let Bogdan get slayed. If they find out it was my dad who did it, or that I watched it happen and didn't stop it, they could mutiny, take me out, and who could blame them? I have let them down, but if you hadn't been poking and prying and watching, I might just have been able to contain this complete and utter horror show.'

She made her hands into claws and shook them in the air, her eyes wild.

'Mo, calm down,' Luca said. 'You can trust Vanya.'

'Stop defending her,' Mo cried out, spinning round to face him. 'Are you still sticking up for her? She was spying on us.'

'That's not true. How many times?' Vanya said, sounding impatient now. 'Look, I get that you're stressed –'

'I'm not stressed, I'm angry, that's what I am. And sick of you.'

Vanya shook her head and moved towards the shed door.

'I should have stayed away,' she said, irritated. 'I was about to explain, but you're not ready to hear it. I don't know why I bothered.'

'You bothered to come because I'm your queen. The Vampire Queen,' Mo thundered back. 'While you're here, on this territory, in my shed, you serve me, OK? I'm your leader, and you're here because you obey me. *You* obey *me.*' She jabbed Vanya's shoulder.

Vanya took a step back, looked down at the floor, pursed her lips.

'Or maybe not. Maybe you came to rub it in. To show off how you've been laughing at me all this time. Spying on my home, my family, me. Silly little Mo, who thinks she can rule. You wanted to bring me down before you even met me. I get it. I understand everything now. So just get out. I command you to get out. Get out of my shed. Now!'

Vanya stepped towards the door, but Mo hadn't finished.

'I can't believe you. We're almost the same age, but you seem to hate me. I feel sorry for you. You're unfeeling. You're unfeminist! What happened to sisters sticking up for each other?'

Vanya's mouth dropped open.

'Female vampires should be feminist vampires; they should be sisters. They should look out for one another.'

Mo was panting now, struggling with her feelings, fighting to work out who she was – vampire? Human? Queen? Feminist? Little girl being laughed at by the big kids?

'Mo, I'm sorry,' Vanya said.

'Stop calling me Mo. It's *Queen* Mo to you. You're just a lowly vampire, you're nothing, remember? You're just a stupid cow.'

'Don't say that.'

'I'm the boss, I'm the queen, I'm in charge,' Mo yelled. 'I could stab you right now, with this, with this . . .' She looked around the shed and grabbed a wooden tool shaped like a carrot. Her dad used it to make holes in the ground for planting, but now Mo held it up in her right hand like a dagger – or a stake.

Vanya laughed.

'Really?'

'It's a dibber!' Mo shouted, hearing how stupid that sounded and feeling even more furious and out of control.

Vanya stepped towards her. 'Please, Your Majesty, put that down now.'

She held out her hand. Mo slapped it away. Vanya, reflexively, slapped her back. Mo shoved Vanya on the shoulder, Vanya snarled at Mo and pushed her hard.

'Stop!' Luca shouted. 'What are you doing? Are you actually fighting?'

They were – suddenly slapping and squealing and tussling in a tight angry knot. Mo squashed Vanya against the shed wall while Vanya muttered, 'Get off me!' and tried to squirm free. Vanya ducked and swerved, but Mo grabbed her in a headlock. With her free hand, Vanya reached up, trying to squeeze Mo's nose but scratching her face instead. Mo staggered backwards, feeling the sting of it.

'You absolute . . . Get out!' she yelled, hurling herself once more at Vanya and this time bundling her towards the door, like a security guard ejecting a drunk from a nightclub. Vanya's heels caught on the shed door frame and, rather than stepping backwards, she fell. Mo, caught off balance, fell on top of her and then she felt the dibber thump into Vanya's chest beneath her, right where her blouse was open to reveal her milk-pale skin.

Mo heaved herself up, panting. She stared down at Vanya. She was lying motionless on the grass, deep, dark blood staining her pale shirt. Mo glanced at the dibber. There was blood on its tip.

'Oh my god, oh my god,' Mo muttered. 'Have I . . . ?'

'I think she's OK,' Luca said, kneeling next to her and searching for a pulse. Mo didn't move. She could not stop staring at Vanya, her arms flung out to her sides. Have I just killed a vampire? Killed Vanya? What just happened? Then she saw Vanya stir, open her eyes and groan.

'You're alive,' Mo said.

Luca helped her sit up. Vanya shook her head and touched the wound on her chest, examining the blood on her fingertips.

'Well, not technically, but I get what you mean. You didn't manage to stake me through the heart with that thing.'

'It's a dibber. I dibbered you,' Mo said, her voice small and anxious.

'Were you trying to kill me?'

'No. I don't think so. I don't really know what happened.'

'Nope, me neither,' Vanya said, standing up. 'A lot of slapping.'

'Hair-pulling too. Do you want a plaster for that?' Mo pointed at Vanya's chest, where thick red blood still glowed.

'Nah,' she said. 'I've had worse. I've definitely *done* worse.'

Mo nodded and watched as Vanya walked away.

'Sorry,' Mo called out, and Vanya turned and looked calmly back at her.

'It's all right,' she said. 'I understand, and for the last time, I'm not a spy. I promise. OK?'

Mo nodded and then Vanya disappeared into the darkness of the garden.

26

When Mo woke the next morning, the sun was out, making the frost on the grass sparkle. Friday the 1st of January. The annual Lower Donny New Year's Day walk was due to start in a few hours, and Mo always went.

All the villagers came, wearing their Christmas jumpers to traipse through the fields, around the duck pond and past the church. The vicar had put a sign up, hoping to pull in new congregation members.

'GOD GOOD, SIN EVIL, DETAILS INSIDE.'

The walk ended in the vicarage garden. Mo and Lou were the last to arrive. They grabbed a couple of mince pies and retreated to a remote corner to eat them.

'How did you get that scratch on your face?' Lou asked Mo.

'I told my parents I did it with tweezers when I was plucking my eyebrows,' Mo said.

'You never pluck your eyebrows.'

'Yes, but they don't know that.'

'So how did you get it?' Lou asked again.

'I had a fight with Vanya.'

Lou grabbed Mo's arm. 'Did she get you with her fangs? Was she trying to bite you?'

'No, it was an actual fight.'

'Punching?'

'Slapping and wrestling.'

'Old skool. Love that.'

'I started it. In my dad's shed. Yesterday.'

'Like when you pushed Danny Harrington up against the hot-dog van at Halloween?' Lou asked.

'Kind of, but also different,' Mo said. 'With Danny, I felt this pure rage – quite exciting really – but with Vanya I was a mess. It was a big fat emotional hissy fit. I really lost it. I'm pretty sure I called her a cow.'

'A what? Who calls anyone a cow? Mo, that's hilarious.'

'It's not. I wanted to cry and shout and pull her hair. Actually, I did pull her hair. Then she scratched my face while I had her in a headlock.'

'Oh my god,' Lou said, eyes sparkling. 'This sounds amazing. I wish I'd seen that.'

'Luca saw it.'

'Shut up! He didn't!' Lou put her hand over her mouth 'Sorry. I kind of want to laugh now.'

'It's not funny. It's really, really bad. The Vampire King knows about Bogdan.'

'Vanya told him?'

'I *thought* so. I totally assumed it was her. It seemed to make sense. That's why we fought. But now I think I believe her.'

'Right . . . OK,' Lou said, frowning. She bit into her mince pie.

'I did stab her though.'

Lou sprayed crumbs and currants across the churchyard.

'You did what?'

'Yeah, with a dibber. It's a wooden tool for making holes in the ground for seeds. I fell on her and it went in her chest. I didn't mean to. She tripped. Or did I push her? It's a blur. I was shoving her out of the shed. She fell backwards and I landed on her and . . .'

'Was she all right?'

'Yes. She bled a bit. Messed up her posh shirt, but she got up and walked away. She was surprisingly nice about it too. She could have killed me. She's a vampire, way stronger than me. She could have drained me dry and chucked me aside like an old teabag, but she didn't.'

'So she is loyal then. Luca was right. You can trust her.'

'I think so,' Mo said. 'I just kind of, I don't know, feel it.'

She brushed sugar off her fingertips. 'Anyway, kind of doesn't matter, because I've got even bigger problems to deal with now. The Vampire King wants me to organise a funeral for Bogdan, which won't be easy as he's already buried in my garden. He insists that all the British vampires attend, which means I have to tell them what happened.'

She tried to smile at Lou, but felt tears pool in her eyes.

'My only plan was to keep Vanya quiet – obviously too late for that! – and hush up Bogdan's death. I've got nothing now, Lou. No clue what to do. Oh god, when the vampires hear that Bogdan was staked by a vampire hunter . . .' She shook her head rapidly, panicking.

'They will fall apart. They will riot. They may come after me. I'm toast. Dad too. We're both vampire toast!'

'Not if the vampire hunter is dead,' Lou said.

'Lou!' Mo screeched. 'I can't kill my dad.'

'I mean fake it. Photograph a body on the ground. Use Luca maybe. Stage it, take a pic, done. Tell them you ripped his head off or stabbed him.'

Mo shook her head again, even more frantically. 'They would never be convinced by that. It's not enough. Anyway, Dad's still a vampire hunter. He's still a threat. He could strike again. Or I could end up accidentally leading him to the vampires, or the vampires to him, with very nasty results.'

She bounced her fist against her forehead then smoothed her hair with trembling fingers.

'I think all I can do is distance myself from the whole thing. I'll tell them Bogdan was staked but say I wasn't there and don't know who did it, so there's nothing I can do.'

'That could work,' Lou said.

'I need to tell them soon too. Get it over with.'

Lou nodded.

'It's not great though, is it, as plans go . . . ?' Mo said, chewing her lip.

'But they won't turn on you,' Lou said. 'They love you.'

'Correction – *loved* me, past tense, before all this . . .'

'They *will* stay loyal, Mo. You're a great leader and the only one they've got. They won't throw that away.'

Mo stared at Lou, her eyes a little wild. 'Yes, well . . . I have to hope you're right.'

27

At seven o'clock that evening, Mo opened her laptop and
began letting the vampires into the Zoom meeting she
had called. Subject heading: SOME NEWS. She had put
the mountains backdrop up again, which hid Luca, who
was sitting behind her on the bed.

Mo watched the vampires appear on-screen and
then, with shaking fingers, she unmuted her mic
and spoke.

'Thank you all for logging on. I won't keep you long.
It's dinnertime after all.'

She cleared her throat.

'I have some news. Bogdan, a great and ancient
vampire who many of you knew, is no more.'

'No more? What does that mean?' Derek asked.

'Ended. Terminated. Not alive, not undead. Just dead.
Regular dead.'

Sven let out an animal roar of grief and thumped
his chest with his fist. 'My coronary organ is painfully
fractured.'

'How did he die?' Pat asked, her eyes narrow with suspicion.

'Yes, how did it happen, Majesty?' Olga and Lenka said in unison.

'Was a pointed wooden instrument inserted crudely into his thorax?' Sven asked.

All three Tartan Fangs were glowering. 'Your Majesty, was he staked?' said Malcolm.

They had zeroed in on the truth of Bogdan's death like sniffer dogs – quickly, accurately. What did I expect? Mo wondered, as she found herself nodding and then watched as the vampires dissolved into chaos. Sven was roaring something in tumbling, angry Danish. Derek had shot out of his chair and was nervously pacing his room. The girls were firing off emojis in the chat box – faces screaming, hearts with daggers in them – and Pat was screeching that she couldn't ruddy believe it.

Each little tile on the screen contained an outraged and terrified vampire, tearing their hair, screaming and hissing, banging their heads on their desks. Thank God I'm not actually with them, Mo thought. This is frightening enough on-screen.

'Please, can you all be quiet?' Mo shouted into her mic. 'Mute yourselves so I can speak.'

But Derek got in there first. 'Now that we know there's a vampire hunter out there,' he said, covering his mouth briefly and blinking back tears, 'what are you going to do about it, Majesty?'

Mo was ready with her line.

'Nobody saw it happen,' she said, not daring to look at Vanya. 'No one knows who the vampire hunter is, so there is nothing I can do, unfortunately.'

A riot of voices burst out of Mo's laptop again as the vampires unmuted themselves and shouted all at once.

'We're not safe, are we, Queen Mo?' Olga said.

'*Wuthering Heights* opens in a few weeks. How can I go on stage knowing there could be a vampire hunter out there?' Derek asked.

'Aye, and what about our tai-chi lessons?' Malcolm threw in. 'It used to be relaxing; it won't be now.'

'Can we move back in with you, Natasha?' Olga asked. Lenka nodded anxiously.

'This doesn't change anything,' Mo shouted, trying to regain control. 'It was a rogue attack. A one-off. I suggest you carry on as normal.'

Pat leaned towards her camera looking horrified. 'Carry on as normal? Pardon? Did my ears lose their minds? Carry on as normal, Queen Mo? What the damn cheeses are you on about? Have you chucked out your brain and replaced it with a lentil?'

'I think it's important to stay positive.'

The vampires were hissing now.

'Just refuse to be upset by this.'

The hissing rose to a shriek.

'Don't dwell on it.'

'It will be all we think about, Queen Mo,' Olga said. Lenka nodded and whimpered, 'I'm scared.'

'Me too,' said Derek. 'This is very triggering.'

'Maybe try some mindfulness exercises,' Mo said, smiling a tight, anxious smile.

Pat's eyebrows shot up. 'Is that the best you can offer? You, our brave leader. It's go picture a spleen and then just carry on, is it? While there's a vampire hunter out there picking us off. I don't think that's good enough. What about the rest of you? How do you feel about our queen doing a big fat zero of nothing to remove this vampire-hunter threat?'

Nobody spoke, but their faces had gone from scared to angry. This is it, Mo thought. The rebellion. The mutiny. It's coming.

'Listen, I know you're upset. I am too, but there is nothing we can do. Nobody knows who the vampire hunter is. I definitely don't know. How could I?'

'Really?' Pat said, peering at Mo.

'I wasn't there!' Mo protested.

'Where? Where did it happen?'

'Somewhere. A field somewhere.'

'Was it near my castle? Near Derek's house, Natasha's retirement village? We need to know where this hunter scum is operating.'

'I really don't know,' Mo said. 'Quite far from any of you, I think.'

'Wasn't Bogdan retired, anyway?'

Mo's heart was hammering in her chest. So many questions! She could sense Luca behind her, listening intently, tense.

'He was visiting.'

'Coming to see you?'

'Yes, maybe. I'm not sure. I didn't see him.'

The lies were tumbling out now, one after another.

'If he was coming to see you when he was murdered, why would he have been miles away from any of us including you? That doesn't make sense. Was he taking the bloody scenic route?' Pat asked.

'Maybe! Perhaps he was sightseeing, wanted to check out Durham Cathedral or something,' Mo said.

'So it happened near Durham?' Pat asked.

'No. Or at least I don't know. It might have been near Durham! But Durham was just an example. What I'm saying is, Bogdan was a very cultured vampire. It's totally possible he was enjoying some of Britain's finest tourist attractions before coming to see me. If he was coming to see me. Which I don't know for sure. We don't know. Nobody does.'

The vampires were silent now. They looked confused and nervous. Is that it? Mo wondered. Are we done?

'How did you find out about Bogdan's murder? Who told you?' Pat asked.

Oh great, we're not done.

'No one, I just heard. I'm the queen. I hear things,' Mo said.

'Did somebody witness it? Another vampire? A human informer? Who?'

'News just made its way to me. Word gets around in the vampire world.'

Mo felt horribly hot now. She tugged anxiously at the neck of her dress, feeling she couldn't breathe. Sweat was breaking out on her palms and she realised she was grinning a wide, tight grin like a hysterical shark.

'OK. Let's move on, shall we?' she said, her voice brittle. 'Let's discuss the funeral plans.'

But Pat wouldn't give up. 'So, someone found the body? Who was it?'

'Nobody did. Well, somebody did, I suppose, but I don't know exactly who . . .'

'You're scaring us even more now, Queen Mo,' Olga said.

'I'm confused *and* frightened!' Lenka added.

'Was it another vampire who found the body? It wasn't one of us, so who?'

Mo's eyes skittered across the vampires faces across her screen, all leaning in.

'Just give me a moment to think,' Mo said. 'I'm upset too and this is a lot of questions. Let me just . . .' She picked up a pencil and then put it down.

Luca reached forward and touched her arm, but Mo hardly felt it.

'Sorry, what was the question again?' She cocked her head as if straining to hear.

'We would like to know who found the body,' Derek said.

'Yes, of course!' said Mo, grinning at them. 'I don't have that information right now, but let me make a note here . . .' She grabbed the pencil again in her shaky fingers.

'Queen Mo, are you OK? You're being quite weird,' Olga asked.

'I am absolutely fine, thank you, Olga. How are you? Hair's looking lovely and straight.'

'Who found the body?' Derek repeated.

'Erm . . .'

'It's a totally simple question,' Pat said, and then began speaking very slowly. 'Who . . . found . . . the . . .'

'Me,' said a voice, clear and calm. 'I did. I was there for all of it. I saw the staking happen.'

It was Vanya.

The vampires looked shocked and suspicious. Mo glanced anxiously between them and Vanya, looking cool and composed.

'You were *there*? So who killed him? Who was it?' Derek asked.

Don't say Dad, don't say Dad, you promised you wouldn't say Dad . . .

'I don't know. It was impossible to tell. It was dark, the hunter had his hood up, it was over quickly. I didn't get a good look at his face.'

Mo breathed again.

'The queen is right,' Vanya continued. 'We can't know who did it. We need to move on.'

Mo felt a rush of gratitude, followed by a rush of confusion. What was Vanya doing?

'You seem pretty relaxed about this, Vanya,' Pat said. 'A vampire was staked and you witnessed it, but you just shrug your shoulders.'

'I guess I'm not wired up like you, Pat,' Vanya said coolly.

'Meaning?'

'Meaning I'm not angry and fearful. You guys can't seem to get over the purges, can you? Still jittery. Still refusing to let go. Still living in the past.'

'Don't talk to me about the purges, my girl,' Pat replied hotly. 'How would you understand – you weren't there. You've been a vampire for about five pathetic minutes.'

'I think you need to chill out, Pat, that's all. You'll give yourself an ulcer.'

Pat's face twisted with fury. 'How *absolutely* dare you?' she screeched, but Vanya held up her hand and leaned in to the camera.

'Sorry, that was my doorbell. I have to run. My delivery has arrived. The pizza's going in the bin obviously, but the delivery boy . . . I suggest you all do exactly what Queen Mo has advised. Stop cowering and get on with your undead lives. Stuff happens. Get over it.'

Then she was gone.

28

A loaded silence fell over the Zoom meeting and Mo realised she was holding her breath. She glanced at the remaining vampires on-screen in turn. Nobody spoke.

'Well, if that's everything, I'll end this meeting now,' Mo said. 'We can discuss the funeral another time.'

'Wait, Queen Mo,' Derek said.

'What is it?' Mo said, feeling her throat tighten.

'I feel deep down that something's not right. Someone is lying.'

'Well, it's not me,' Mo lied.

'Of course not, Your Majesty, so it must be Vanya.'

Mo felt a chill creep up her spine. Where was this heading?

'But I believe her. I believe she saw the staking.'

'Do you believe she didn't see who did it? How would she witness an attack but not get a look at the vampire hunter?' Derek asked.

'Aye, killing a vampire isn't done in two seconds flat,' Malcolm said. 'It's hard physical work. Bogdan may have struggled, so surely Vanya would have had time to see the killer.'

Mo felt slightly sick, remembering her dad plunging the stake in and Bogdan's horrified expression.

'Why didn't she help Bogdan?' Donald asked.

'Why didn't the hunter kill her too?' Duncan added.

'That snake!' Pat hissed, banging her fist on her desk. Mo jumped. 'You're all correct. You can't be at a staking and not see who did it, and what kind of a lame, cowardly vampire doesn't defend their fellow creature of the night when they see them get struck down by a hunter?'

The vampires all nodded and murmured in agreement.

'Also, what kind of vampire hunter doesn't kill both the vampires he comes across?'

Mo shook her head, struggling to keep up. 'Perhaps he didn't see her? Perhaps he was too busy, you know, killing Bogdan? Perhaps –'

Pat shouted over her. 'It's obvious, Queen Mo. Vanya is working with the vampire hunter.'

The vampires all hissed.

'What? No vampire would do that,' Mo said over the noise.

'Unfortunately, Your Majesty, many did, during the purges, to guarantee their own safety,' Derek said. 'They would reveal the addresses of other vampires, for the promise that they would not be staked.'

Mo's heart was rattling in her chest now. She had the terrifying sense that she was riding a runaway train.

'She has only been a vampire for about a year, so perhaps her loyalties were confused,' Natasha said.

'She turned up here out of nowhere,' Malcolm added.

'We know nothing about her,' Derek said.

Mo sensed the vampires goading each other on to a disastrous conclusion, but what could she say? The mystery of who Vanya was, why she had arrived suddenly at their first meeting, had troubled her too.

'I have never been sure about Vanya,' Pat said. 'I don't trust her. Do you?'

'Yes,' said Mo. 'I do actually.'

'Actually?' Pat seized on the word. 'But you didn't always?'

Mo felt herself blush. 'I, er . . .'

Olga leaned towards the camera, her face anxious. 'If Vanya is working for this vampire hunter, she can tell them where we live. She visited our homes to get us online.'

The vampires shrieked now, ignited by a real sense of panic. Olga and Lenka dropped a few more screaming emojis in the chat box.

'Forsooth, she heartily castigated our cherished vampire colleague Pat but moments ago,' Sven said.

'That's right!' Derek said. 'She disrespected Pat. We all have our disagreements, sure, but it's not right to speak to a fellow vampire like that.'

'Well, that's settled then,' Pat said.

'What is?' Mo asked, dreading the answer.

'Back during the time of the purges, we had a rule about how to deal with vampire snitches in the pay of filthy vampire hunters.'

'What rule? I don't know anything about this.'

'It's simple, Queen Mo,' Pat said. 'You must destroy her.'

'Destroy her?

'That is the way.'

'What way? Whose way?'

'The only way. These rules pre-date your time, Queen Mo. I know you want to modernise us, make us wear Lycra and go to wine bars or whatever, but you must respect vampire tradition.'

'Pat speaks well and truly,' Sven piped up. 'It is beholden upon you to commit fatal harm to Vanya for her great deficit of fealty.'

'Fatal what?' Mo said, her voice trembling.

'Aye, aye, you must exterminate her,' Malcolm said.

'End her, good and proper,' said Donald.

'If we can't find the vampire hunter, we can at least kill his source. That way, we are protected. We are safe,' Duncan said.

'But we don't have any evidence that she was working for the vampire hunter.'

'It's obvious,' said Pat. 'She's in on this. I knew I was right not to like her.'

'Let me talk to her,' Mo said.

'No talking. It's time to act. Actions speak louder than words, Queen Mo. We will never feel safe while she continues to exist around us.'

'I don't agree with murdering.' Mo's voice sounded small and weak.

'But you believe in us, in our right to live without fear of violence at the hands of murderous vampire hunters?' Pat said.

'Of course,' Mo said, feeling the last of any control she had evaporate.

'Then you must kill her,' Pat said. 'We demand it. We *need* it!'

'We trust you, Queen Mo,' Derek said.

'You're a powerful female leader,' said Olga.

'A role model to us,' said Lenka.

'It's the right path, Majesty,' Malcolm said sternly. Donald and Duncan nodded.

'It's unfortunately what she deserves,' said Natasha.

'Refuse to extend one trifling jot of clemency towards her,' Sven shouted.

'Restore confidence and safety to your vampire realm,' said Derek.

'Wipe out that traitorous, sneaky double-crosser,' said Pat, making an energetic crushing gesture with her fist. 'Working for a vampire hunter – that's the dirtiest low-life thing a vampire can do. That little worm. That infected cockroach. That stinking, mucky cheat. She needs to be shown who's boss.'

The other vampires roared now, like a crowd at a boxing match, drowning out Mo's stuttering 'But . . . but . . .' Only the girls were silent, watching Mo with wide, frightened eyes.

'Very good, Your Majesty,' Derek said, when finally everyone fell quiet. 'We trust you to exterminate Vanya – so thrilling, I wish I could watch! – to restore safety and security to our vampire existence. We are grateful, and pledge our allegiance to you once again.'

He laid his hand across his heart. The other vampires did the same. Mo felt her mouth go dry, felt her eyelids flicker nervously. She stared blankly at their pale faces, each one of them gazing out at her, calm now, trusting, you could even say loving.

No words came. No ideas. Mo's brain felt empty of all useful thoughts, like someone had broken in silently and stolen its contents. She swayed a little, and then felt her head bob in a curt little nod. She hit the Leave button. The screen went blank.

29

Mo stood up slowly and, without making eye contact with Luca, sat next to him on the bed.

'You OK? They were furious,' he said, rubbing her back. 'I guess when you email them tomorrow to clear it all up they'll be calmer.'

'Clear what up?'

'That you're going to kill Vanya, because you're not, obviously.'

'Obviously? Why obviously? You heard them. They were really, really clear about it. I've got to kill Vanya.'

'Mo, hang on, you didn't even agree to it. You didn't say anything. They got carried away, that's all.'

'That's what they do,' Mo said, her voice tense. 'They're vampires. They're easily triggered and always up for violence. God, I actually thought I was getting somewhere with them. I stupidly thought I was a good leader, reckoned I could do things my way. Considerate, committed leadership. But look what happened tonight! At the first mention of vampire hunters they panicked, the fangs came out and it was kill, kill, kill, because that's the traditional bloodthirsty ultra-violent vampire way!'

'You can stand up to them though. Stay true to who you are. *My rule, my way*, remember.'

Mo shook her head. 'Maybe this *is* the way, Luca. Killing Vanya is what I need to do. The vampires insisted. Perhaps I should. Maybe it's what all leaders do – they listen to their people and they're flexible when they have to be.'

'Mo, what's going on?' Luca leaned away from her, his face appalled.

'Besides, I've already dibbered her. I almost killed her then and I wasn't even trying. How hard can it be?'

'This is freaking me out, Mo. You really don't sound like you now.'

'Look, Luca, maybe killing Vanya is for the best. After all, even if she's not actually a spy for the Vampire King, she *was* spying on me, on us. She must know I'm human and that we're together. If that gets out, I'm in even deeper trouble.'

'But she didn't reveal who the vampire hunter was, Mo, just now.'

'She still could!'

'I thought you were beginning to trust her.'

'Well, it's not down to me any more.'

'Mo, you're the queen, remember. It's always down to you!' He stood up and moved away.

'Look, obviously I'm not happy about this,' Mo said, 'but it's a decisive move that will ensure the smooth running of my reign and, as a bonus, it keeps my big secret – that I'm not actually a vampire – under wraps. I'm safe. My subjects are loyal and happy. The Vampire King stays away. Dad's safe, you, Lou . . . It's good.'

'Good?' Luca exploded, spinning round. 'There's nothing good about it.'

'There is, it's just that you can't see it. You really like her and it clouds your judgement.'

Luca looked shocked. 'Mo, this isn't about me liking Vanya, this is about me not being OK with *you* planning a murder.' He stared at her, his mouth open with disbelief.

'Fine. Whatever,' Mo said, flapping her hand dismissively. 'The fact is, I have to do *something*.'

'Yes, but you don't have to do this. You don't have to kill Vanya.'

Luca went back to Mo and knelt down in front of her. He seized her hands and stared intently into her eyes. She pulled back a little, unable to hold his gaze.

'Email the vampires and say you are not murdering Vanya. Say you'll banish her or excommunicate her or something, but you don't have to kill her.'

'I can't do that, it would look weak.'

'You're the queen. You can do what you want.'

She shook her head. 'I need to go through with it.'

'No, you don't. Pull out. Change your mind. Tell them.'

'Luca!' Mo said, snatching her hands away. 'I am their leader. I have to be strong. I can't flip-flop around.'

'You're not being strong though, you're being completely irrational. Mo, come on, this isn't the way. Why not talk to Vanya? Find out why she just stood up for you. She was trying to tell you something last night, but you wouldn't listen.'

Mo laughed, slightly hysterically.

'Luca, that all sounds very lovely, but I have promised to kill her, remember?'

'You did not promise!' Luca shouted now, eyes blazing with frustration.

'I have to listen to my subjects. I'm supposed to represent them.'

'Represent them, yes, but not be bullied by them.'

'Backtracking now would look silly and pathetic. It would make the vampires panic even more. They want me to kill Vanya and I'm going to. It will be like when we had our dog Ronnie put down. I didn't like it, but it was for the best.'

'Did you kill him with a stake?'

'No! The vet gave him an injection.'

'Then that's nothing like what you plan to do to Vanya,' Luca shot back.

'Well, possibly, blah, blah,' Mo said. 'You know, it's actually really tiring being understanding all the time. Listening to all the arguments and weighing it all up.

There are times when, as the Vampire King told me, you have to be ruthless.'

'So you're aiming to be like him?' Luca said, his cheeks colouring. 'The guy who nearly killed me and your best friend. He's your role model now, is he? Seriously?'

'I have tried to rule well, Luca,' Mo said, rubbing her forehead like she was auditioning for a paracetamol advert, 'but it's so hard to stay true to what you believe with all these angry vampires and violence and fangs and hissing and problems, problems, problems. Every solution in the vampire world is about destruction. It's never, why don't you have a chat, talk it through, agree to differ. It's kill, exterminate, murder. It's like cancel culture with fangs.'

Luca didn't reply.

'It's too much for me. Surely you can see that. All my fancy ideas about how to rule. I was an idiot. A total idiot. They were way too ambitious. I can't stand up to the vampires on my own.'

Luca shook his head. 'What's happened to you?' he said, his voice quiet. 'I don't know who you are any more.'

'I'm the Vampire Queen, Luca, and it's a *really* tough job.'

'That doesn't mean you have to go ahead with a dangerous, horrible plan like there's no other choice.'

'There *is* no other choice,' Mo said, looking at him suddenly, her eyes full of tears. 'I might be the queen and the Chosen One, but I'm also a human in a vampires' world. I'm vulnerable. Maybe actually, Luca, I'm scared. Have you thought of that?'

Mo waited for Luca to reach out to her, soothe her, tell her it would be OK. He didn't. He stood up slowly. 'There are always choices, Mo,' he said. 'You just have to look for them.'

'Oh, well, brilliant, thanks for the support,' Mo snapped, throwing her hands up. 'You're my familiar, remember? You're meant to be on my side.'

'I am on your side, but you don't seem to realise that.'

'You're not! You're not helping at all.' She was panting now. 'Maybe I can't trust you. Maybe you do prefer Vanya. Maybe you're in love with her. Maybe . . .'

'You're talking total rubbish, Mo!' Luca snapped. 'We've been through all this. Vanya is like a sister to me. Of course *you* can't understand that. You, the precious only child.'

Mo felt like she'd been slapped.

'I miss home, you know?' Luca went on. 'I miss my family, my brothers. Did you ever think of that? Did you ever even ask about them or about how it is for me, living hundreds of miles from home? No! Never. Being with Vanya, someone from my own culture who I am completely comfortable with, feels good, but that's all.'

Mo blinked back tears. The truth of it hit her and she felt ashamed, and her shame made her lash out.

'Well, go and be with her then!' she stormed, her cheeks burning.

'What?'

'Go and work for her, be with her, hang out with her, whatever it is you want. You obviously care for her more than me, and you really don't understand how hard it is being Vampire Queen. You, the chilled-out nice guy, always there with a smile, never having to actually do the work, the hard, relentless work of leading. You're just the familiar, not the ruler. It's barely a job at all. You have no schoolwork either, no parents in the background who you have to keep happy. Your life is so incredibly easy, Luca, and you don't even realise.'

Mo had shouted the last few sentences. Her eyes were blazing and she was breathing hard.

'I have always tried to support you, Mo,' Luca said, hurt but also furious. 'I understand the difficulty of your role, but you chose to be Vampire Queen without becoming a vampire, remember. It was your choice.'

'I was trying to keep everyone happy!' Mo shouted again. 'I'm always trying to keep everyone happy. Now I'm just trying to keep the vampires happy so we can all stay alive, but you don't get it. You want to talk about morals and principles and your beautiful, wholesome relationship with Vanya. God, Luca, why don't you just go to her then? Go on, do it. Let's call it a day. That's what you want, right? So let's end it, here, today.'

'Are you serious?' Luca looked stunned. 'Do you mean that?'

'Yes,' said Mo, folding her arms.

'I can't believe you're saying this.'

'Well, believe it. We're done for now. Over. Let me get on with my job. You're free to go. Do what you want.'

Luca looked at her for a few seconds, then stood up and walked out of her bedroom, slamming the door behind him. Mo stayed where she was, sitting on the edge of her bed, staring at the carpet.

30

'Dad, I was wondering if you could train me to be a vampire hunter,' Mo said. She carried on tipping cereal into her bowl and didn't see her father's face crash through emotions like toppled dominos – shock then suspicion then curiosity then glee.

'Mo, I don't think that's a good idea,' said her mum, but Mo didn't reply. She began spooning cornflakes into her mouth, staring blankly in front of her. Considering she'd just agreed to murder Vanya and had broken up with Luca, she had slept well and woke feeling calm and unemotional. She had a plan, after all. An admittedly poorly fleshed out and rather violent plan, but still . . . It went like this:

1. Learn how to stake vampires from Dad
2. Stake vampire (Vanya)
3. Persuade Dad to retire as vampire hunter

'Well . . .' her dad said.

'It's incredibly dangerous,' Mo's mum interrupted, gripping her coffee cup.

'Why do you let Dad do it then?' Mo asked, without looking up.

'That's different, Mo. He's a grown man.'

'Not very feminist, Mum,' Mo replied. 'Men can go out and fight vampires, but us little ladies need to stay home and do embroidery.'

'That's not what I said, and what's got into you this morning? You seem really . . .'

'Really what, Mum?' Mo said.

'There's a mean energy coming off you. It's not like you at all.'

A mean energy. Fair enough, Mo thought with a shrug, I'll take mean, though really I just feel . . . what? Nothing. Flat, heavy, numb. Thoughts usually cascaded through Mo's mind, one after another, second by second, like a waterfall in the rainy season. Now, though, there was nothing but a thin trickle heading weakly towards one inevitable end: killing Vanya. There was no debating the killing any more. Mo wasn't chewing her lip or wondering, 'Can I?' or 'Should I?' Instead, it felt like a boring job she had to get done, like hanging up the washing or writing a thank-you note to your aunt for the book token she sent, before she could do something more fun. Would that be getting back with Luca? Mo couldn't go there. One thing at a time. She couldn't even picture him any more. In place of his image – the deep brown eyes and honeyed smile – there was a grey blank.

'Look, of course women can do anything men can.' Mum was talking again. 'But that doesn't mean I'm OK with you going out and taking on vampires.'

Too late, Mo thought. She carried on chewing, staring ahead of her.

'You're too precious, Mo. My only child. And you *are* still a child.'

'I'm nearly sixteen.'

'I know, and you're very mature, but even so . . .' Her words trailed off.

'See it as self-defence,' Mo said, finally looking up at her mum. 'A sensible precaution. I can't always rely on my dad racing in to save me.'

'But if you're out with Luca, he can protect you,' her dad said. 'I can supply him with stakes. He's strong.'

Mo dropped her spoon and shoved her bowl away. 'I don't need a man to protect me. I can do it myself. If you'll train me. But if you prefer to stay stuck in the 1950s and imagine I need to be chaperoned by a member of the male sex every time I leave the house, be my guest, Dad.'

That little burst of anger, like a firework stuck into the damp November earth, blazed up brightly but soon sputtered out.

'Sorry,' Mo murmured. 'We broke up, actually.'

'You and Luca? Why?' Mum said.

Mo shrugged. 'It's complicated.'

'Oh, love, how sad.'

Mo shrugged again, or was it more of an irritated twitch? 'It's fine,' she said, eager to move off the topic. 'So will you train me, Dad? You're training Jez. Train me too. I can take over the family business and then you can retire. Haven't you staked enough vampires for one lifetime?'

'Oh, I don't know. I see it more as a vocation than a job,' her dad said.

'You're exposing yourself to risk. Maybe you should hang up your crucifix and pass on your stakes, you know?'

'Let me think about it. Obviously it's great to see you taking an interest.'

'Maybe I'd have taken an interest before, if you hadn't kept it all a secret.' Mo couldn't resist the jab.

'Look, I understand the value of you being able to protect yourself, but being a vampire hunter is a whole other ball game. It's nasty work killing nasty creatures. It's incredibly risky. People think you just whack a stake in their heart. Everyone knows that's how you finish off a vampire, right? But in fact it takes knowledge, training, strength and loads of stuff to do it, and to do it right. Vampires are dangerous. *Really* dangerous. Not just the fangs, but their strength. There must be something in a blood-only diet, because they are all incredibly powerful, even the puny-looking ones.'

'Strong enough to rip someone's head off?' Mo asked.

'You bet,' said her dad. 'Wait, why do you ask?'

'Oh, no reason.'

Her dad squinted at her for a second then carried on talking. 'There was this one vampire I killed twenty-odd years ago, up near the Scottish borders. Skinny, malnourished-looking guy who lived out in an old derelict farmhouse. Local people tipped us off about him. Claimed he'd been draining their sheep. I mean, that's low. Vampires will sometimes feed on livestock, but it's a sign that they're struggling.'

'Or maybe they just don't want to kill humans any more?' Mo threw in.

Her dad looked annoyed. At being interrupted? Or at the suggestion that a vampire might have a moral compass? He pressed on with his story.

'I got the gig to go and stake him and I arrived at the farm close to nightfall. It was raining and cold. Horrible night. From outside I watched him light a few candles. He seemed to be talking to himself. Pacing up and down. I got the sense that he wasn't, you know, all there.'

Wow, Mo thought, it's not enough to look down on this guy for being a vampire, now you want to slam him for possible mental health problems too. Way to go, Dad. Working that empathy muscle. Then she remembered Malcolm talking about Uncle Stewie. The last vampire killed in Great Britain (if you ignore Bogdan, and

Bogdan's grave, a messy heap of earth in the corner of the garden), back in 2002. He was a poet. Was this the same vampire? Had he been reciting verse? Is that what her dad saw and failed to understand? Mo felt the heat drain from her cheeks.

'Anyway, I thought, this one's going to be an easy kill. A doddle. I knocked on his door, thinking to stake him the second he opened it, but that's the thing. He didn't open the door.'

'What did you do?' Mo asked, drawn into the story now.

'I kicked it open and went inside.'

'And?'

'He was nowhere.'

'Had he materialised?'

'How do you know that word?'

Her dad's eyes drilled into her suddenly. Quick, say something, Mo!

'What word?'

'Materialise.'

'Did I say that?'

'Yes.'

'Oh, sorry, I've got my period,' Mo said, shaking her head with ditzy energy.

Her dad looked baffled for a split second then pressed on. 'Anyway, I was picking my way through his rooms, holding my stakes out like this –' he gripped two teaspoons and raised them like daggers either side of his head – 'but I couldn't see him anywhere. I was about to leave, thinking he'd legged it, when all of a sudden he swung down from the rafters, screaming – and I mean, screaming – and kicked me right in the centre of my chest.'

Mo gasped.

'I flew backwards and hit the floorboards, banged my head pretty hard. Then he was on me. Literally on me. Crouched on my chest, pinning my arms to the ground.'

'Oh god,' Mo mumbled, picturing it all, appalled.

'He was strong. *So* strong. Physically slight, but the weight of him – it was like being sat on by a rhino, you know?'

'What happened?'

'I nutted him, right between the eyes,' he said, smiling at the memory. 'He fell backwards, I leaped up and then *BOOM!* – I gave him the double.'

'The double?'

'One stake, then the other. Bish, bosh.' He enacted it with his teaspoons.

'The moral of this story is, vampires are stronger than they look, and they're sneaky too.'

'Mike, that's enough reliving your glory days as a vampire hunter now, don't you think?' Mo's mum said, looking anxious.

'The glory days clearly aren't over though, are they?' he said. 'There will always be more vampires out there to vanquish.'

'Good reason to train me up then,' Mo said, getting up from the table. 'And anyway, I thought you expunged them, not vanquished them.'

'Same difference,' said her dad.

31

Mo spent the rest of the day on the sofa.

'You must be ill,' Mum said around lunchtime, feeling her forehead. 'You never normally watch daytime TV. Or any TV really.'

Mo didn't respond.

'Is it heartbreak? Over Luca?'

Mo shook her head, irritated. Heartbroken over a boy? Mo thought. How pathetic. As if! I'm about to commit a murder in order to cement my rule over twenty violent vampires and, admittedly, that is affecting my mood a bit, but all Mum sees is a little girl crying for her boyfriend. Very. Annoying.

Mo gripped the remote firmly and focused on the TV, letting the flickering images gradually numb her. Just before dinner, her dad called her into the kitchen.

'What's going on?' she asked, sensing tension. 'Has something happened?'

'Sit down, please,' he said. 'No need to worry. I just wanted to give you this.'

He reached behind him, and when he turned back he was holding a box, about thirty centimetres long and covered in what looked like green leather.

'This is for you. It was mine originally. My first one. Now I'd like you to have it.'

Mo flipped the lid open. Inside was a stake, resting on a bed of red velvet. It was made of dark brown wood with a carved handle.

'It's beautiful,' Mo said, feeling uncomfortable about calling a murder weapon attractive. It was like complimenting a serial killer on their hair.

She examined the intricate carving on the handle. Art and death, united again, like on all those ornate swords she'd seen in museums, their stinging blades offset by beautifully sculpted handles and hilts, as if their bloody purpose had to be prettied-up to make it acceptable.

She took the stake out of the box and laid it across one hand.

'Not like that,' said her dad, grabbing a nearby spoon firmly in his fist to demonstrate. 'This is how you do it.'

Mo folded her fingers around the handle and gripped it. If my vampire subjects could see me now, she thought, with a queasy little flip of her belly. She could understand why vampires favoured ripping off the heads of other vampires. Using a stake, the exact weapon vampire hunters used against them, was too much like going over to the enemy.

'You won't use that in training, mind you,' Dad said. 'You can use the basic stakes that Jez and I whittled. Keep this one for special occasions.'

Mo tried to picture what special occasion might involve staking a vampire. Or maybe killing a vampire *was* the definition of a special occasion, in her dad's world.

Mo looked up at him. A broad grin split his face.

'Welcome to the family,' he said, throwing open his arms like a mafia don.

Mo hugged him reluctantly. 'I already am family, Dad.'

'I know, I know, I mean the vampire-hunting family. Now, when shall we begin?'

Mo's phone rang in her pocket.

'Sorry, it's Luca,' she said, feeling blood rush to her cheeks. She sprinted upstairs and said hello.

'Just checking in, as your familiar,' he said, his voice cold and business-like. 'Wondered if you need me to do anything, oh great Queen?'

'You don't have to sound so bitter.'

'I'm not bitter,' Luca shot back. 'I'm being professional. I'm still your familiar. Unless you want me to take a break from that too?'

Mo sighed. 'No, it's OK. And I, er, don't need anything from you right now.'

'Cool.'

Silence for a bit, then Luca spoke. 'What are you doing then?'

'I was watching TV, but now I have to do something with my dad. Some cooking,' she spluttered. 'We're making a quiche together.'

A quiche of lies, her brain unhelpfully added.

Another painful pause.

'Right, well, see you around,' Luca said.

'Yup,' Mo replied, and the line went dead. Mo stared at the phone for a second, like it had insulted her. Luca had hung up. He *never* hung up like that, without a proper goodbye. She tossed the phone onto her bed. Men! Who needs them? I must focus on my job, she told herself. Secure my queenly authority. I can patch up my relationship with Luca after that. If I want to. I might not want to.

The kitchen was empty when Mo got back downstairs, but she noticed the garage lights on and spotted her dad inside. She went to join him.

'What are you doing?' she asked, her face crimping with disgust. He was hanging an old string shopping bag on the garage wall, and on closer inspection Mo saw that it contained a huge piece of meat.

'Don't worry – I'm sure we'll still be able to roast it after we're done,' he said, smiling.

'After we're done doing what?' Mo asked, and was about to mention again that she was a vegetarian when her father handed her an undecorated stake.

'Now,' he said, standing back and folding his arms. 'Hit it.'

'Hit what?'

'Hit the pork,' he said. 'With the stake. Imagine it's a vampire.'

'Is this about the meaty resistance?' Mo asked, remembering her dad unloading the car the other day with Jez.

'That's right,' he said. 'You're not staking custard, you're staking a body. Go ahead. See how it feels.'

If you'd shoved a microphone under Mo's mouth and asked her to comment on what was happening, she wouldn't have been able to say a thing. A tiny voice in her brain was murmuring, 'excuse me, Mo, are you sure this is entirely appropriate? The Vampire Queen taking lessons from her vampire-hunter dad so she can kill one of her vampire subjects?' But the chain-gang chant of necessity – got to do this, got to do this, just kill Vanya, just kill Vanya . . . – drowned it out.

Mo picked up the stake and gripped it in her fist.

'Hold it up,' said her dad, 'and drive it in powerfully. Put some body weight behind it.'

Mo approached the hanging pork. Hate meat, hate meat, hate meat, she thought. She pulled her hand back. Stabbing, stabbing, stabbing, she thought. Stabbing meat, stabbing meat, got to do some stabbing meat. Then, screwing up her face, she darted her hand forward. A squelchy thud was followed by the glockenspiel plink of the stake falling to the floor and then her dad laughing.

'You barely scratched it,' he hooted. Why was he enjoying this so much?

He handed Mo the stake and she tried again. This time she managed to keep her eyes open, but felt her arm tense and pull away slightly at the moment of impact. Not a convincing staking.

Her dad took the stake from her and perched on the edge of their old picnic table, like a football manager giving a half-time team talk.

'Let's take a step back,' he said.

Mo gratefully stepped away from the bag of pork.

'Not literally!' He was laughing again. 'What I mean is, let's think about why you're doing this. Why do you want to kill vampires?'

No immediate answer sprang to mind. Because I agreed to? Because I said I would? It all sounded a bit limp, and Mo couldn't afford to admit to herself – or her dad – the corner she'd backed herself into.

'To keep myself safe?' she eventually said.

'OK, sure,' said her dad. He shifted his position and stared meaningfully at Mo.

'I kill them because they make me angry. Furious. They have weird rituals and strange powers. Materialising, for instance. They drink blood, for god's sake. That's not real food. What's wrong with fish and chips?'

'I don't eat fish and chips either,' Mo muttered.

'They come over here, kill our humans, ruin the peace and safety of our neighbourhoods,' he thundered on. 'They don't belong in this country.'

Mo could feel herself getting tense now, getting drawn into an argument. You can take the girl out of the debating society . . .

'But Mrs Kumari at mum's nursing home wasn't born here. Neither was Mr Kowalski down the road or the Afzal family or –'

'Mo, come on, that's different. Mr Kowalski doesn't feast on human blood. I've queued up behind him in the village shop. A lot of crisps in his basket. A lot.'

'Every culture has its own rituals though, doesn't it?' Mo went on. 'Its own way of making meaning, governing, setting boundaries.'

'Mo, Mo, I know you want to work for the UN and everything, but that's really not the point when it comes to vampires. They are a dangerous menace and they have no business in this country.'

'That's why you kill them?'

'Absolutely, and I kill them effectively by connecting with my sense of right about how wrong they are. Understand?'

Mo sighed. 'What if they'd like to live alongside us,' she said, remembering how the vampires had told her just that.

'They should stop bloody well killing us then, shouldn't they? Right, come on, Mo. Try this again. Connect with your anger. Connect with your belief in justice. Let it pour through your arm and power your stake and –'

'Arrggghh!' Mo yelled, hurling herself at the hanging bag of pork. She drove the stake in forcefully with one furious blow, her teeth clamped hard together, her mouth a twisted grimace. Then, panting, she stepped back.

'Nice,' her dad said, clapping. 'Now *that's* the way to kill a vampire.'

Mo wasn't listening. She sprang back to the stake and furiously yanked it out of the meat. Then she thrust it in again, and again, and again. With each blow tiny grunts of effort that morphed into squeals of tantruming confusion burst out of her, until her dad came and placed his hands on her arm and gently pulled her backwards.

Mo was panting and sweating.

'OK, Mo?'

Mo windscreen-wipered her hands quickly over her eyes, flicking tears away.

'I'm fine.' She handed her dad the stake and marched out of the garage.

'You did brilliantly,' he called after her. 'I knew you would. You're my daughter after all.'

32

Mo took a long shower when she got back into the house, and after she'd dried her hair and drunk a hot chocolate she began to feel calmer. She flipped open her laptop and found a batch of vampire emails in her inbox. She didn't bother opening them. There was no need. The subject header on all of them was: HAVE YOU KILLED HER YET?

Where was Vanya now? Still in her quiet country home with its comfy sofa and tasteful rugs. Still ignorant of Mo's plan to end her life. Mo flicked open her diary. When should she do it? It must be soon. Her vampire subjects were impatient for blood.

Her pencil hovered over the page. She could train all day tomorrow, Sunday, and do it on Monday evening. Maybe Dad would let her stake some beef for practice? Plenty of meaty resistance there. Or a whole chicken? Then Mo squinted at the dates again and realised with a heart thud – school went back on Monday.

'How could I forget that?' she gasped. Her uniform was in a filthy pile at the bottom of the washing basket and she had not even unpacked her bag, let alone done any of the holiday homework she'd been set.

Mo knew why. She understood that she was already light years away from that studious girl she used to be. She was Vampire Queen now – and man was it demanding – with only hours to go before she had to fulfil a commitment to exterminate one of her subjects.

To stave off the terrifying images of plunging the stake into Vanya's milky-white chest that were massing at the sides of her mind like hungry predators, Mo began tidying her room. Memories of staking the bag of meat flooded back as she grabbed pencils not in her fingers but, without thinking, in her clenched fists. She gathered up her uniform in a messy bundle and flung it hastily into the washing machine. The sound of water rushing into the drum seemed to unleash a waterfall of anxious thoughts.

'Come on, Mo,' she scolded herself aloud as she grabbed her textbooks and stuffed them into her backpack. 'You have a plan. You *love* a plan. Stick with it. The vampires are insisting you do it, and you don't go back on your word. They can rely on you. They can trust you. That's what makes you a great leader.'

A great leader who commits murder.

'No!' Mo gasped aloud, desperate to stay on message. Quick, do something, anything, her brain seemed to shout. I know! Demonise your opponent. Yes! The perfect swerve away from trickier moral issues of killing and ethics and . . .

Vanya started this, Mo thought. She's slippery and untrustworthy. She appeared in our community out of the blue, wormed her way into our lives, spied on me and Luca. She can't be trusted.

This was better, Mo decided. A bit of righteous indignation to keep her on the right path. The only path. Kill Vanya.

She tossed her water bottle into her backpack.

'Stick with the plan.'

She stuffed some pens in the front pocket.

'Stick with the plan.'

She zipped the bag up smartly.

'Stick. With. The. Plan.'

Then she sat down on her bed. She became aware of the sound of her shallow breathing and then of the wind outside. It had been blowing softly in the afternoon, but now it was gusting, rattling the windows and churning the leafless branches of the trees into a frantic dance. The gathering storm outside seemed to match the swirling turbulence of Mo's internal world.

'Pathetic fallacy,' she muttered.

The ping of a text message roused her. Maybe it was Luca, Mo thought, back on my side, ready to support me when I kill Vanya.

In fact, it was Jez.

Hey great news about you training as a vampire hunter. Your dad told me. Maybe we could train together some time?

Then there was another message.

Also have been thinking about what you said, about how I didn't do anything when Tracey was having a go at you. I'm sorry. I'd like to talk to you about that maybe some time?

OK, Mo pinged back, not knowing what else to say. She was taking lessons from her dad so she could kill Vanya. It didn't feel like a 'yay' moment. As for revisiting the Tracey Caldwell years and Jez's role in them . . . Mo felt far too preoccupied with the here-and-now, the heavy burden of being Vampire Queen, to give much thought to that.

She realised how far she'd travelled since October when Bogdan first appeared. The naive certainties of her old life with The Plan for great exam results and a glittering career had been trampled on by vampires and violence, love and Luca and loss, joy and chaos and one thing after another after another.

Mo saw everything clearly now, saw herself in pin-sharp detail. Her plan to rule with human values in a vampire world, without blood being spilled and heads being ripped off, had been idealistic and unrealistic.

It was time to grow up, and I have, Mo thought. This isn't the debating society any more. This isn't the All-Donnys Spelling Bee Challenge (of which I was the youngest ever winner, in 2014), this is ruling over vampires. It's dog eat dog, vampire eat vampire. Survival of the fittest in a dangerous world. The only way to keep these bloodsuckers satisfied is with violence. Not too much, but definitely some. The time for words is over.

She punched a clenched fist against the palm of her hand and pursed her lips. Yes. Time to get real. This meant forgetting Luca's despair at her new plan. It meant forgetting Luca altogether, at least for now. It meant never telling Lou about it either. It meant dispatching Vanya without a thought for her motivations and feelings. Hey, at least her dad was proud of her. He was family after all. Blood is thicker than water. And vampire blood is even thicker. I've seen it. Very sticky!

'Think of Macbeth,' she said, grabbing her copy off the bookshelf and flicking through its well-thumbed pages. 'That part about being so deep in blood that he might as well keep going to the other side, because it would be just as much trouble to go back.'

There you go, she thought, finding the quotation with ease. There was Macbeth, all crushed and fatalistic about the loads and loads of murdering he would have to do to keep his throne. That's how I feel, Mo thought. I'm in too deep now. I've got to get the job done. Maybe I won't have to kill as many people as Macbeth did. So far I'm only planning to do one, and she's not even a real person; she's undead. But I need to get on with it. Turning back is not an option.

Again she heard the wind outside. The garage doors banged angrily, rattling the bolt and eventually blasting open. Her dad ran across the gravel to secure them. Would the pork joint, peppered with staked holes, be blown from its nail and fall to the floor among the puddles of oil and dirt. Who cares? Mo thought. I'm a vegetarian. Maybe Macbeth was a vegetarian too.

33

The storm continued to rage, and when Mo went to her window at first light after a disturbed night's sleep she could see the damage. Tree branches down, tiles whipped off the roof and smashed into mosaics on the gravel drive, flowerpots rolled into random corners of the garden and a bench lying on its back.

Her phone rang.

'Have you heard?' Lou gasped. 'A tree fell on the sports hall, broke the roof and knocked out the power. School won't be opening on Monday.'

'Sorry, how old are you again?' Mo asked.

'Oh, come on. School being closed is seriously exciting. Apparently it might not reopen for a whole week. Do you want to go and see it?'

'I should probably catch up on some homework this morning,' Mo said.

'You? Not done your homework? Did I wake up in a parallel universe? Did I slip through a portal to an alternative realm? Did I –'

'But why don't we go and have a look later?'

Something about seeing the sports-hall roof smashed to smithereens appealed to Mo, who was just hours away from committing her first vampire killing. Violence, destruction . . . Bring it on. There would be lots of time to train with her dad now, and with school closed there was no reason why she couldn't head over to Vanya's tomorrow, ready for when she woke up in the evening and . . .

'Yes! Can we? Let's!' said Lou, excited.

The homework Mo actually got on with was staking rather than statistics. This time, a gammon joint.

'Still the meat of the pig,' her father announced, dropping a fat pink slab into an old pillowcase, 'but great practice all the same.'

He hung it from a tree in the garden and invited Mo to take aim. She felt less squeamish this time, more impatient. She staked the joint with ruthless efficiency, her eyes narrowed, fist clenched, arm muscles tense, no hesitating.

'Nice work,' Dad said approvingly.

'Very good,' said her mum through the kitchen window.

'I think I've got this,' said Mo, a nasty taste of metal prickling her mouth. 'Can we stop now?'

'Sure, although I've got lots more to teach you. There's vampire tracking, vampire history, classic vampire attack styles and how to defend against them.'

Mo walked into the kitchen and sat at the table. Her dad followed.

'Here, I've made you a hot chocolate,' her mum said. Mo wrapped her hands around the warm mug. 'If you give me some of your tops – your blue coat maybe and favourite hoodie – I can stitch pockets inside for your stakes, so they're always handy.'

A handy stake pocket, Mo thought. A quaint way of describing what was the equivalent of a gun holster.

'Are you OK with this now, Mum?' Mo asked.

'I've thought about it,' she said, 'and realised that unfortunately there are a lot of bad people out there, Mo. You training with Dad means you will be able to protect yourself against anyone, human or vampire. You mentioned self-defence, and you're right. It's a sensible precaution.'

'Except I can't really use a stake on a man, or can I? Is it legal to murder people with stakes in the street? I'm pretty sure I'd still get in trouble for that.'

'Don't be smart, Mo,' her dad said. 'Your mum's just pointing out that the training will help you defend yourself, make you a bit streetwise.'

Mo nearly choked on her hot chocolate. 'Sorry,' she said, wiping her mouth on the back of her hand. 'I've just never heard you say streetwise before. It was a shock.'

Her parents exchanged frowns.

'Look, love,' her mum said, trying to sound soothing but with an edge of exasperation in her voice, 'there are lots of things we need to think about now you're almost sixteen and beginning to go out there.' She pointed at the window. 'There are lots of conversations we need to have, now you're almost an adult.'

Mo pushed her empty mug away from her. 'Can they wait?' she asked. 'I've learned a lot, thanks, but for today I think I'm all talked out.'

'Sure,' said her mum.

'Of course,' said her dad. 'You did some brilliant staking today, Mo. I'm proud of you.'

He stood up and hugged her. 'That's my girl,' he said.

As Mo padded upstairs, she realised that for all her academic achievements and spectacular grades, it was her staking some gammon in the garden that her dad was most delighted by. She didn't know whether to scream or feel proud.

34

After lunch, Mo took a deep breath and called Luca. The hard edge to his voice when he picked up was unmissable.

'Will you drive me to Vanya's house tomorrow?' Mo asked.

Silence.

'Are you going to say anything?'

He didn't.

'You're still my familiar. You said so yourself yesterday.'

More silence. Then he said: 'I'm not going to do that.'

Mo felt like she'd been punched.

'What?'

'I'm not going to drive you to Vanya's.'

'That's not very helpful,' she said (sounding hurt). 'You have to obey me,' she said (sounding spoilt).

'I don't agree with what you're planning, Mo, so sorry, I won't be able to help with this one.'

Mo blinked hard, struggling to process Luca's words.

'Fine, then I'll go on my own,' she said, and quickly ended the call.

Feeling angry and shaken, Mo leaped on her bike and cycled over to Lou's house. She pedalled fast, cycling out her complicated feelings. By the time she arrived she was out of breath but calmer. They caught the bus to Middle Donny to look at the school. They weren't the only spectators. It was as if the tree, by falling so squarely on the sports hall, was expressing every student's occasionally felt desire to smash the school up. It seemed to call to them as a symbol of rebellion.

'It is so totally mashed,' Lou gasped, her eyes wide, taking in all the damage. The caved-in roof, broken windows and men in high-vis jackets swarming around it, with Mr Pascal the headteacher looking on grimly.

They watched as a lorry with a crane drove slowly up to the hall, parked up and anchored itself to the ground with stabilisers. More men in high-vis and helmets now busied about and soon the crane rose up over the fallen tree, the man inside wielding a chainsaw like it was Excalibur.

Mo spotted Jez over to one side and smiled at him.

'He's coming over,' Lou whispered. 'All right, Jez?' she called out. He nodded at her, then quickly turned to Mo. 'Could I have a word with you?'

They walked off towards the tennis courts.

'I'll wait for you here,' Lou called out behind them.

'Did you get my texts?' Jez asked. 'Of course you did. You replied.'

A dash of red coloured his cheeks. Oh my god, Mo thought, he's nervous.

'Yeah, well, I am really sorry I didn't do more when Tracey was being mean to you.'

'That's OK,' said Mo. 'I shouldn't have mentioned it. I don't need a man to defend me.'

'No, I know, but you don't need a man to spectate when you're being unfairly treated.'

Wow, Mo thought, he's articulate too. This isn't the frowning, monosyllabic Alpha Jez I thought I knew.

'Apology accepted,' Mo said, smiling quickly at him then going back to studying the ground in front of her.

'I also thought about what you said about vampire hunting. It being macho. You're right, I hadn't really considered what it would be like to kill a vampire. Honestly, don't tell your dad, but I'm still not sure what I think. I mean, they used to be human once.'

Mo almost winced. That was what she always used to say, but hearing it today, the day before she was due to kill Vanya, stung like vinegar in her eyes.

'It's like, a rabid dog is still a dog, right?' Jez went on.

Mo didn't reply, although she made a mental note to recruit Jez for the debating society once things settled down.

'Have you started your training yet?' he asked.

'Yesterday,' said Mo. 'Dad had me staking pork. This morning was gammon.'

'Classy,' said Jez. 'I started out on venison, and by venison I mean a deer that got hit on the road.'

Mo made a puking sound and then began laughing.

Jez's eyes squeezed up to become two small, happy twinkles as he grinned at her. 'Is Luca training too?' he asked. 'I know your dad would love it if he did.'

'No. Luca doesn't agree with it. Definitely doesn't agree with *me* doing it.'

'Because you're a woman?' Jez asked. 'That's sexist.'

Jez the feminist. Equal opportunities for all, including vampire hunters. What next?

They had looped back around and were near the group of students again. Mo felt conscious of Lou's eyes on her.

'So, well, let me know how you get on and if you need any help or, I dunno, you won't need any help from me, will you? But anyway . . .' Jez stuttered to a finish and smiled softly and quickly at Mo.

Lou came up to them now, glancing between their two faces. 'Oh, sorry, did I interrupt something?'

Really? Mo thought wearily. Did Lou have to suspect a romantic subtext behind every interaction Mo had. Luca, Vanya, Jez – Lou had paired them all up together at one point or another. Her imagination had all the subtlety of a string of emojis – hearts with bows around them, round yellow faces with kissing lips and winking eyes.

As soon as Jez was out of range, Lou grabbed Mo's arm.

'What the actual?' she said, her eyes lasering into Mo's. 'Are you best mates with Jez Pocock now? Or more? I can't keep up. Just a few months ago nobody knew your name. You were just the sad-girl neek. Now you've got a boyfriend who's really good-looking *and* the school's most popular boy wants to hang out with you. Who are you and what have you done with my best friend?'

Lou was joking, but Mo couldn't laugh. If you knew what I'm going to do tomorrow, then you really wouldn't recognise me.

'Is this revenge on Luca for hanging out with Vanya?' Lou asked.

'It's not anything,' Mo snapped.

'Sorry,' said Lou, looking not sorry. 'Where is Luca anyway?'

'Lou, I love you, OK,' Mo said, her smile not matching the desperate look in her eyes, 'but I really don't want to talk about Jez or Luca or anything right now.'

'Oh, OK,' said Lou, looking confused and hurt.

'I just want to go home.'

35

Monday morning. Mo's parents were back at work and school was closed. Mo had told Lou she still had homework to do so couldn't see her and was now lying in bed, her headphones pouring the most complicated science podcast she could find into her ears in an attempt to distract her from the day's scheduled events. It wasn't working. She kept thinking about Luca. She was about to go and kill Vanya and he wouldn't be there to support her, as boyfriend or familiar. She realised how much his presence always reassured her. Him just being there, smelling like a cinnamon bun, making rubbish jokes and being kind and calm and . . .

Mo ripped off her headphones and reached for her phone. She swiped through the hundreds of photos of him, pausing over the ones that showed his treacly eyes twinkling or the sun picking out the golden strands in his dark hair. Then she jumped to her contacts, quickly tapped on a number and listened. It rang and rang. He wasn't answering.

'Come on, come on . . .' Mo muttered, chewing her lip, suddenly desperate for him to pick up. 'Please answer, please . . .' and then . . .

'Hello?'

The voice sounded surprised, wary even.

'It's me, Mo.'

'Hi, Mo.'

'Did you mean it when you said you'd help me, if I needed it? I've got something important to do today.'

'Er, sure.'

'Great. Meet me at the bus stop in Middle Donny in an hour. Bring your stakes. Thanks. Bye.'

Mo tossed the phone aside. Her jaw was set, her face as hard as granite. If you won't help me, Luca, she thought, I'll take the next best thing. Jez. He's available, he's up for it, he's supportive. There.

She began filling her backpack, throwing in the fancy stake her dad had given her and stuffing in her robes. It's important to look the part when you're killing off one of your subjects, Mo decided. Then she walked quickly to the bus stop. Usually when she stood here she was on her way to school. Today . . . She resisted finishing the thought.

The bus pulled in and Mo instinctively made for the seat halfway up on the left that she and Lou always took. Someone was already in it though. Mo blinked and focused.

'Lou! What the hell are you doing here?'

'No, what the hell are *you* doing here?' Lou shot back. 'You're supposed to be doing homework. You're obviously not.'

Mo shifted, her face pained.

'Vampire business?' Lou guessed.

Mo sighed and sat down. 'Yes. I've got to, erm . . .'

'What?'

'Do a thing.'

'What thing?'

Mo shook her head and stared straight ahead.

'You're not going to tell me?'

'It's for your own good.'

'Oh, thanks, Mum,' Lou said, then she softened. 'Wouldn't it be good to share it?'

Mo didn't answer. She carried on staring straight ahead, arms folded, and the second they arrived at Middle Donny bus station she leaped up.

'We're here,' she said. 'See you around.'

Mo saw Jez as soon as she got off, leaning on a wall and staring so hard into space that a tiny frown line had appeared between his eyes. His face brightened when he saw Mo.

'Isn't that Lou?' he asked, pointing over at her.

'Don't think so,' Mo said, grabbing Jez's arm and leading him forcefully towards the Nether Slaughter bus parked on the far side. They climbed on board and Mo slumped down into the first seat she could find. Jez sat next to her.

'Are you going to tell me what we're doing?' he asked.

'Later,' Mo said, closing her eyes. She felt the engine rumble to life and heard the door closing. Then heard it opening again. Someone climbed on board, sat down behind them. The doors closed once more and the bus pulled away.

Mo felt lulled by the motion as it began to pick up speed, and then somebody spoke.

'Well, this is a nice little outing for the three of us, isn't it?'

Mo's eyes flew open and she spun around. 'Lou! What are you doing?'

Lou was peeping through the gap in the two seats and beaming at Jez and Mo.

'I'm coming with you, wherever you're going. It's bound to be dangerous or you would have told me, and you might need help.'

'I don't,' Mo said.

'Except Jez is here. What's that about?'

'I'm here to help,' he said.

'See!' said Lou.

'Only I don't know what we're doing yet,' he added.

'Lou, get off the bus,' Mo said.

'Can't, we're already moving. Too late.'

'You can't come. You need to get off.'

'Not going to, so forget about it.'

Mo glared at her.

'So, what *are* we doing?' Lou asked. 'Might as well tell us now. Jez, you want to know, right?'

'Erm . . .'

'Jez wants to know. I want to know. Tell us.'

'Just something.'

'What?'

'Just, you know . . .'

'No.'

'Just killing Vanya,' Mo suddenly blurted.

'Who's Tanya?' Jez asked.

'Vanya. She's a vampire,' Lou explained. 'Vampires exist.'

'I know, actually,' said Jez.

'Do you? Well, I got run over by one and almost eaten by another,' Lou shot back.

'All right, all right, this isn't a competition,' Mo said, sounding like a stressed-out mum with bickering kids. 'Jez, Lou did almost get eaten by one. The one that attacked you in the lane by my house, in fact. Remember when you mysteriously banged your head?'

Jez went a little pale.

'And Lou, Jez is training to be a vampire hunter with my dad. That's why he's here. To back me up when I kill Vanya.'

'You're actually going to kill her?' Lou spluttered. 'Mo, killing Vanya doesn't sound very you.'

'Don't!' Mo said, holding up one finger as a warning. Her eyes were burning into Lou's and her voice was sharp. 'Don't start. I have to do it. I'm going to do it. You wouldn't understand. OK?'

'OK,' Lou said, leaning back into her seat a little. 'Whatever the unhinged lady wants. And you're right, I don't understand.'

'Not sure I do either,' said Jez, frowning apologetically. 'You haven't completed your staking training yet. Neither have I. Should we call your dad for backup?'

Mo let out an exasperated gasp. 'I can see now it was a mistake bringing you, Jez. And Lou, you should never have got on this bus. Both of you should go. Now.'

'No way,' said Lou. 'I've paid for my ticket. I'm coming. No arguments. Anyway, why are you killing Vanya?'

'Can we talk about this in private?' Mo said. She squeezed past Jez and went to sit at the back.

Lou followed.

'I am going to kill Vanya,' Mo explained, 'because the other vampires want me to.'

'That's it?' Lou looked shocked. 'That's the only reason? You're meant to lead them, you know, not the other way round.'

Mo shook her head impatiently. 'I have to do it. Vampires only understand violence. Kill or be killed. It's like Macbeth. Keep on being tough to hold onto your throne.'

'Macbeth died in the end.'

'I didn't know you'd read it.'

'Only the revision notes, but I'm almost a hundred-per-cent sure he died.'

Mo said nothing.

'I thought Michelle Obama was your leadership role model, anyway, not Macbeth,' Lou went on.

'That was before I became Vampire Queen. Now I see how hardcore it is. I've got to be tough. Really tough. Tougher than Michelle.'

'What if she fights back?'

'Michelle Obama?'

'No, Vanya.'

'I won't give her the chance.'

'Are you kidding?' Lou said. 'It's a basic survival instinct, and anyway, you already had a fight with her and you told me how she could have messed you up but didn't. If you come at her with a stake, she won't be so polite this time.'

Mo shook her head again, trying to shake off the truth of Lou's words.

'I've done some training with Dad now. I'll stake her through her heart. Jez can give me a hand, if I hit a rib or something. Then it's over.'

Lou shuddered. 'Mo, you're freaking me out. This is dangerous. You're choosing to do something really super risky and grim and . . . What's happened to you? Did someone swap you with a fembot in the night? Can I have the real Mo Merrydrew back, please?'

Mo didn't respond. Her phone was ringing. Luca. Now? Really?

'Hello?' Mo said. She could hear rushing traffic in the background.

'Mo?' His voice sounded urgent. 'I'm with Vanya, in the car.'

'With Vanya?'

'Yes. She needs to speak to you. She asked me to bring her to you.'

Mo let out a groan.

'Luca, I . . . You know what I have to do. I am going to do it today. No more chatting and –'

'She has to speak to me,' came a muffled voice.

'Who said that? Was that her?'

'Yeah, she's inside her travel coffin. Must have woken up. I'm surprised you could hear that. Anyway, where are you?'

'On a bus,' Mo said.

'Where exactly?'

'I don't know. A big road. I can see some trees, a field . . .'

'Mo, find out where you are.'

Mo felt herself beginning to shake but did as Luca asked. She walked to the front of the bus with Lou following her and sat down behind the driver. He wore a name badge that said:

'HI, I'M KEN – DRIVEN BY EXCELLENCE!'

'Ken, where are we, please?' Mo asked.

'On the M5,' he replied.

'Put me on speaker, Mo,' Luca demanded. And then, 'Where on the M5?'

'Coming up to the Pethering Services, Junction 24,' Ken shouted helpfully so Luca could hear.

'Get off there,' Luca said. 'I'll be with you in about half an hour.'

What the . . . This wasn't in the plan. The taking-the-bus-to-kill-Vanya plan. The plan Luca had totally opted out of, as boyfriend and familiar. What was going on?

'I can't just drop you off,' Ken said, staring sternly ahead at the road. 'This is the no-stopping service to Nether Slaughter. No. Stopping.'

'We urgently need to get off,' Mo said.

'Which part of "no" and "stopping" do you not understand?' Ken asked.

'Please? We'll jump off really quickly. The services are only a mile away. There's the sign.'

Ken shook his head grimly. Mo felt sick with stress.

'Oh, this is shredding my nerves,' Mo moaned, but Lou didn't answer. She had gone back to her original seat and was reaching into her lunch box. She pulled out a sandwich and peeled back the top slice of bread. Then, after a few quick movements, she limped back to the front.

'This is actually an emergency, Ken. My leg has got pus coming out of it, look.'

Ken glanced nervously over his shoulder at Lou's leg and grimaced.

'Must be where I recently broke it. It's got infected. Mo didn't want to panic you, but we really need to get off this bus so our friend, who is a specialist doctor in wounds and infections and scurvy, can take a look.'

'I can't do it. If my manager found out I stopped a no-stopping service . . .'

'Oh my god, it hurts *so* badly,' Lou wailed.

'It's against company policy.'

'Mo, pass me something to bite down on for the pain!'

'I could be fired for this. I've got a wife and three kids and a tortoise.'

'I think it may even have maggots coming out of it!'

'All right,' Ken suddenly snapped, gripping the wheel with white knuckles. 'I've got you. Hold on tight now, people, we're diverting via Pethering Services.'

He hit the hazard lights and slammed his hand down on the indicator. Then he threw the wheel hard to the left. As the bus swung across the outside lane, car horns blared, but Ken didn't waver. He leaned on the wheel, face like stone, and swerved onto the slip road that led to the service station with a screech of tyre rubber on tarmac.

'Awesome, Ken,' Mo shouted. 'You really are driven by excellence.'

Braking hard like a jumbo on a runway, Ken managed to slow the coach down and bring it to a stop.

'Thank you, Ken,' said Lou, limping off.

'Jez, we're out of here,' Mo shouted, beckoning him to follow.

Ken nodded at them. 'Hope your friend can help. If not, call 999. You might need an ambulance for that,' he said. Then he popped the doors shut and pulled away.

Mo looked down at Lou's leg. 'What is that stuff?'

'Mayonnaise,' Lou said. 'Little bit of ham too.'

'Right. Thanks. Shall we go and wait by the picnic tables?'

36

They waited quietly. Jez stared his stare, Mo was preoccupied with what Vanya might want now – and where that left her plan to kill her – and Lou was preoccupied with the spaniel that was licking the mayonnaise off her leg.

'Is this OK with you?' its owner asked, smiling apologetically. 'He does love his condiments. Once ate an entire bottle of hoisin sauce.'

Finally a car sped into the car park and pulled up next to them.

'What the hell is he doing here?' Luca said, spotting Jez.

'Well, *you* didn't want to help me,' Mo said, opening the back door. There wasn't much space. Wedged in at a roughly upright angle behind the driving seat was a coffin.

'Bagsie the front,' Lou said as soon as she saw it.

Mo squashed herself up against the coffin and Jez dropped in next to her.

'People are pointing at us,' Lou said as they drove out through the car park.

'It's because of my pimped-up hubcaps,' Luca said.

'Is it?' Lou said.

'No, of course it's not,' said Luca. 'It's because we've got a coffin on the back seat.'

'I knew it,' Lou said.

Luca pulled onto the motorway and urged the car forward. Mo tried not to make eye contact with him in the rear-view mirror. She stared at her knees, the knees that were clamped tightly together to avoiding touching Vanya's travel coffin on her right and Jez on her left.

'Where are we going?' she asked, feeling oddly self-conscious. Talking to Luca used to feel easy. Now, not so much.

'Back to Vanya's,' he said. 'If it gets dark before we make it there, she asked me to stop the car.'

'Is she asleep?' Lou whispered, looking over her shoulder and pointing at the coffin.

'I guess so,' Mo whispered back.

They drove on in silence for several minutes, but when the sign for the next services appeared, Lou pointed at it.

'Can we stop and get some food? Most of my sandwich is now in that spaniel.'

Luca nodded.

'There, drive-through fried chicken,' Lou said, as they pulled in. 'We won't even have to get out of the car.'

Luca pulled up at the Cheeky Chick 'N' Pollo Shack. A young woman with heavy eyeliner and a bored expression appeared in the window. Her orange cap carried the Cheeky Chick 'N' Pollo logo – a rooster doing a thumbs up with one feathery wing and holding a chip in the other.

'Welcome to Cheeky Chick 'N' Pollo Shack,' she said, like she was reading the phone book. 'My name is Hayley. How may I help you?'

'One bumper bucket of wings,' Lou said.

'I'll take some fries,' Luca said.

'Me too,' Jez said.

'Mo, do you want fries?' Lou asked.

I'm on a mission to murder Vanya and now we're deliberating over takeout, Mo thought.

'OK, yeah,' she said. 'With extra ketchup, please.'

Hayley punched in the order and then leaned forward to peer further into the car.

'Anything else for you guys . . . ? Whoa!' Her eyes sparkled to life. 'Is that a coffin?'

'Yes,' said Lou.

'Cool. Empty?'

'Er, no actually,' Lou said.

Hayley's eyes grew wide. 'There's a dead body in there?'

'You could say that,' said Lou.

She grinned in amazement. 'This is wild! Where are you taking it?'

'Just out for a spin,' Lou said. Mo could feel herself starting to smile, but fought it. Luca was openly grinning now. 'It's what she wanted. She put it in her will. She was keen to stay active, get out and about, see a bit of the world, you know?'

'Yeah, that's really excellent,' said Hayley. 'Don't let death hold you back, isn't it?'

'Exactly,' said Lou.

'What was her name?'

'Va—'

'Valerie,' Luca interrupted, leaning across to look out of the passenger window at Hayley. 'Is our order ready?'

'Oh yeah, let me check,' Hayley said, eyes lingering on the coffin before she disappeared.

'Valerie?' said Lou, laughing at Luca.

'Here you go,' said Hayley, thrusting the bucket and bags of chips out through the hatch. 'Have an awesome day now. Travel safe, in this life and the next.'

She watched, smiling, as Luca drove away.

'Enjoying yourself, Jez?' Lou asked, twisting round to grin at him. 'You don't get this many LOLs hanging out with Tracey Caldwell, I bet.'

Jez had a mouthful of chips and only raised his eyebrows in a 'good point' sort of way. Lou gnawed at her wings greedily, breaking off to post chips into Luca's open mouth as he gripped the steering wheel and drove.

Mo's appetite soon failed though. She gazed gloomily out of the windscreen. They had left the motorway now and were trundling through an open landscape of blank fields and bald hedges. The task ahead – killing Vanya – was getting nearer with every mile and minute. Maybe I should think of her as Valerie, Mo wondered. It might help create some distance.

A tapping sound seized her attention. It was coming from the coffin.

'Hello, anyone there? I cannot open lid properly. Luca?'

'He's driving,' said Mo.

'Who said that?' Vanya said, shoving her coffin lid just wide enough to peep out. 'Oh, hi, Mo.' She waggled a finger through the gap at her. 'Are we nearly there yet?'

'Not far now,' said Luca. 'Go back to sleep. We'll wake you when we arrive.'

The fingers slid back inside and the lid clunked shut. They drove along in silence for a few more miles until Lou piped up:

'Sorry, but I actually feel a bit sick. Could we stop?'

Luca sighed. 'Can't you hold on?'

'People can't hold on to sick, Luca, it's biologically impossible,' she shot back, breathing now like a woman in labour.

'Open the window, get some fresh air,' Luca huffed, then muttered something about, 'We'll never get there at this rate.'

'Please Luca, I think I'm going to chun,' Lou mumbled, her hand over her mouth.

'All right, all right,' he said, 'just don't do it in the car. I vacuumed in here yesterday.'

Luca pulled off the road down a muddy farm track. Lou stumbled out and threw up into a hedge. Mo patted her back and handed her some water, then wandered down the lane a little, breathing in the sharp January air. Over on the horizon, the yellow winter sun was slipping below rags of grey cloud. Rooks were cawing noisily overhead, black flecks against the darkening sky. Mo watched the sun disappear completely and then felt Luca by her side.

'All right?' he asked stiffly.

'Yup,' said Mo.

'I really think you should hear what she has to say before you go ahead with your plan.'

'There's nothing she can say that will stop me,' Mo said.

Luca sighed heavily. He was about to speak but then looked over his shoulder. Something had caught his eye. Mo sensed what it was, felt goosebumps creep across her scalp. She turned. Vanya was standing in the lane, staring at her.

37

'I'll leave you to talk,' Luca mumbled, returning to the car.

Mo stared coolly at Vanya.

'You're up nice and early,' she said, her hand instinctively drifting up to the coat pocket that contained her stake.

'We need to talk,' Vanya said. She seemed different. She had dyed her hair black, just like Mo's, but that wasn't it. Her voice was unusually calm and quiet. Mo felt her heart race with fury. 'I haven't been completely straight with you, about who I am.'

'Bit late for that now. No one trusts you.'

'You know nothing about me though.'

'Doesn't matter.'

'It matters to me.'

'Yeah, I can't take that on right now.'

'You have to,' Vanya replied firmly.

Mo stepped angrily towards Vanya, one finger raised accusingly.

'I have enough to sort out already, thanks,' she said through pursed lips. 'Do you understand what you've done by saying you witnessed Bogdan being killed?'

'I was trying to help –'

'The other vampires believe you were working with the vampire hunter, that you're in his pay, thanks to what you said. They are angry and panicked and baying for blood and revenge and killings. And the thing is, you did witness the murder, didn't you? You were there all evening, watching me, sneaking around, peering out of the bushes like some weird stalker. What the hell was that about? Where do you get off spying on me in my private time? God! I'm so angry with you.'

'Then let me explain.'

But Mo had begun pacing in circles in the lane, mud squelching under her shoes, and then started in on Vanya again.

'As Vampire Queen I have to fix all this mess. Put it right. Sort it all out. More problems, more stuff to deal with, endless emails and letters and demands. Retaliate, Mo. Fight back, Mo. Be ruthless, Mo. Remember the vampire rules, Mo. This is how it's done, this is what we want, have you done it yet? Have you? Have you murdered Vanya yet?'

Silence for a second as that last line landed. Mo looked at Vanya. She didn't look shocked. She looked sad.

'Mo, I can explain. I told the vampires I witnessed Bogdan's murder to draw their attention off you. They were harassing you. I had to step in.'

Mo felt herself shaking. 'Had to? Really? Well, it didn't work. It failed in fact. Totally.'

'I could have told them it was your dad who staked Bogdan, but I didn't.'

'Good for you! Aren't you the moral example to us all?'

'Think about it, Mo,' Vanya said. 'I was trying to protect you.'

'Protect me!' Mo roared. 'And yet you are the one who was spying on me that evening. Poking around when I was at home. I feel sick when I think of it. Why were you even there? Why were you watching me? You have no interest in protecting me. You want to find out personal stuff about me and bring me down, don't you?'

Vanya was silent. Mo piled on.

'Why would you do such a low-life thing? What on earth persuaded you to do that? Why do you care about me so much?'

'I grew up in poverty, Mo,' Vanya said. 'We had nothing.'

'Did I ask for your family history?' Mo snapped, but Vanya continued.

'We were poor, not like you. My parents' lives were defined by having never enough, by sadness and shame and loss. A baby who died when I was five. They never recovered. Their grief contaminated our life, blighted my childhood. They died young. My father when I was thirteen, my mother two years later. I had to leave school, work two jobs, survive alone with no family. That's why I became a vampire.'

'Fine, OK, nice sob story, but I'm not interested. I feel *nothing* for you.'

Vanya winced. 'Don't. Don't say that.'

'It's true, and I'm glad because I have to kill you.'

'Stop saying that.'

'No, I won't. It's a fact. I've got to actually kill you now.'

'Yeah? Like when you threatened me with a dipstick in your shed?' Vanya taunted, suddenly sounding harsh.

'A dibber,' Mo growled through gritted teeth.

'Are you going to stake me?' she asked. 'Why don't you just rip my head off?'

'You're lucky I don't,' Mo said.

'I'd like to see you try,' Vanya snorted.

'Yeah?'

'Yeah!'

'Would you?' said Mo.

'I really would,' said Vanya.

'Don't tempt me.'

The two of them glared at each other for several seconds, until Vanya looked away, which Mo took as a victory. She wasn't sure if she could actually kill her, but she could sure as hell beat her in a staring competition.

'Look, Mo, hear me out. There's more,' Vanya said, calm again. 'I knew Bogdan too.'

Mo felt a chill creep up her back. 'What's Bogdan got to do with this?'

'He came to see me soon after I was turned, said he was looking for my sister. She died, I told him. No, he said, she didn't die, she was adopted. She was special, a child of promise, much desired by vampires.'

Mo's mouth had gone dry.

'Humans from another land took her to protect her, but Bogdan was now wanting to find her. He said her time had come. He said she had important calling.'

'What are you saying?' Mo was blinking rapidly. 'I don't, I don't . . .'

'You do, Mo,' Vanya almost whispered.

Mo shook her head quickly.

'I was angry at first,' Vanya went on. 'This child who had ruined my childhood, who was supposed to be dead, was actually living and thriving. She was special and destined for greatness. I had to see her, to look into her eyes and be sure she really was my kin. I wanted her to know that she had ruined Mother and Father's lives, make her sad like we had been sad.'

Vanya walked through the gloom towards Mo.

'But then I met her.'

Mo squelched backwards.

'And I asked about her. I watched her – call it spying, if you want – and I got to know her.'

'Stop,' Mo shouted. 'Stop. I don't want to hear any more.'

'So sweet, so good, so generous . . . My sister.'

Mo stuffed her fingers in her ears. 'La la la, I can't hear you.'

Vanya waited silently until Mo finally dropped her hands.

'I am Mo Merrydrew,' she said hurriedly. 'I was born in Middle Donny hospital to Mike and Kate Merrydrew, fifteen . . . nearly sixteen years ago and you are not my . . .'

Her words ran out. Vanya's pale face was glowing in the twilight, framed by her long black hair. Mo blinked rapidly. It was like looking in a mirror.

'You are not my sister,' said Mo quietly. 'You are not . . . my . . .'

She reached quickly into her pocket and pulled out the stake. With a shaking hand, she raised it.

'You're a traitor and I'm the queen and I'm here to punish you. That's what I have to do. It's what I *have* to do.'

Mo sounded desperate. There was a cornered animal look in her eyes. She gripped the stake with two hands, trying to stop it shaking, and walked towards Vanya.

'Get your fangs out,' she shouted at her, moving closer. 'Fight back. Lou said you would fight back.'

Vanya stood still as stone.

'Come on!' Mo screamed, getting closer still. 'Stand up to me. Get your revenge. If what you say is true, I ruined your life, didn't I?'

Still Vanya didn't react. The stake wobbled in Mo's hands. She took the last few steps towards Vanya and touched the wooden point against Vanya's chest, her eyes wild and terrified.

'Attack me!' she yelled. 'Why aren't you attacking me? Why . . . ? Attack me!'

Vanya looked calmly into Mo's eyes, holding her gaze. Mo felt the point of the stake against Vanya's chest, felt the tension in her arms, saw Vanya's cool, gentle gaze. With a tiny gasp she pulled the stake away, stepped back a few paces and doubled over, clutching her sides. Vanya moved towards her and laid a hand gently on her back.

'No!' said Mo, upright once more and wielding the stake, her hands still juddering like an ancient washing machine. 'I'm going to do it this time.'

'Look, I know this is lot to take in,' Vanya said, holding up her hands.

'They want you dead,' Mo screamed, her face contorted in misery. 'All the other vampires want you dead. I WANT YOU DEAD! You've ruined everything. You don't get to call me your sister. You don't get to tell me my parents aren't my parents. Who I was, what I was . . . all ripped to pieces. You can't do that. I won't let you do that!'

The tears were plummeting down her cheeks now. She pulled the stake back with both hands, high over her shoulder, then closed her eyes and thrust it powerfully forward.

'Mo! Stop!' Luca and Lou screamed. Mo felt no meaty resistance, only a tight pain around her wrists. Vanya's hands.

She was holding Mo frozen on the spot, the stake millimetres away from her heart. Mo stared into Vanya's eyes frantically, let out an angry, choking scream of despair and defeat and then went limp. Vanya loosened her grip and Mo let the stake fall. She staggered past her up the lane.

'Take me home, Luca,' she said, yanking the car door open. She clambered in and slammed it shut, then bent over, her face on her lap.

Luca looked towards where Vanya was standing.

'Go,' Vanya said.

'Sure?' Luca asked.

Vanya nodded. She didn't move, a black shadow against the twilight sky as Luca and Lou bundled into the car. Luca flicked on the headlights and as he reversed back up the lane Vanya was illuminated, her eyes glistening, her face still as a painting.

38

Mo stared at her lap for the whole drive home.

'Say something, Mo,' Luca urged, glancing at her nervously before looking back at the dark road ahead.

No response.

'Look, we heard what Vanya said, Mo. It must be a shock but, you know, it's nice having a brother or sister,' Lou offered from the back. 'It can be fun. Maybe you and Vanya could go shopping together.'

Silence.

'She is really cool too, like you said,' Lou added. 'A cool older sister. That's brilliant.'

More silence. Mo's pale cheeks were blotchy from crying, her eyelids red and swollen. She didn't move. Only Luca slowing down and pulling up outside her house seemed to rouse her from her torpor. Without saying anything, she got out of the car and walked slowly towards the front door.

Luca caught up with her. 'What are you going to do?'

'I need to talk to my . . .' she said in a quiet voice. Kate and Mike were clearly visible in the kitchen, eating dinner. She jabbed an accusing finger at the window. 'I need to talk to *them*.'

Mo opened the front door quietly and then stood in the kitchen doorway.

'Mo, there you are. You gave me a shock,' her mum said, spotting her finally. 'Where have you been? Dinner's ready. We would have waited, but I couldn't get hold of you. Oh, and Luca and Lou, and Jez too. Come in, all of you, I'll get some more cutlery.'

'Why didn't you tell me I'm adopted?' Mo said.

Mo's mum spun around to face her, gripping two plates.

Her dad stood up sharply. 'How did you . . . ?' he blurted.

'Come and sit down and we can talk about it,' Mo's mum said softly.

'I don't want to sit down,' said Mo. Her voice was razor sharp with anger. 'I thought the biggest secret in this family was that Dad is a vampire hunter. But no. There's more. Way more. Why didn't you tell me?'

'We were going to,' her mum said.

'When?'

'When you were sixteen.'

'On my actual birthday?' Mo put on a sickly American accent. 'Mo, honey, come right on over here, we've got a little something for ya . . .' Then she roared back into her own voice: 'It's the gift of finding out that your whole life is a *lie!*'

Her parents rocked back as if hit by the blast from a furnace.

'Oh, you guys,' said Mo, the American twang back. 'For me? Really? Oh, but you shouldn't have.'

She took a few quick breaths, then began again.

'First you don't tell me Dad is a vampire hunter. Then you don't tell me that you're *not* actually my parents. Anything else you'd like to get off your chest while we're at it? Any other big fat stinking family secrets? Mum, you're actually a lesbian lizard from the future? Dad, you're a hologram?'

Mo's mum came towards her, laid one hand on her arm. Mo snatched it away.

'I'm so sorry you found out this way.'

'How *did* you find out?' her dad asked again, opting to obsess over details rather than respond to emotions.

'Someone tipped me off,' Mo said.

'Who?'

'What does it matter?' Mo wailed. 'Does it change *anything*?'

'It doesn't change how much we love you,' her mum said urgently, pleadingly. 'Or that we are and always will be your mum and dad.'

Here Dad's head bobbed with tiny shaky nods as he gripped the back of the chair. For the first time ever, Mo spotted panic in his eyes.

Too bad. Panic all you want, she thought. She shook her head dismissively then ran upstairs. Luca looked at the floor. Lou hugged her sides. Jez checked his phone. They stood in awkward silence, listening to the sound of Mo thumping around in her room, snatching drawers open and slamming the wardrobe doors. She appeared moments later, carrying a bag.

'I'm going back with Lou to hers,' she said. 'She's my family now.'

'I really think we should talk about this,' Mo's mum said.

'What's the point?' Mo said. 'You had almost sixteen years to tell me. We could have talked at any time, but no. Nothing. Silence. And now you want a nice friendly chat about how I'm not who I thought I was. How you're not who I thought you were. How you were too cowardly or stupid or I don't know what to tell me that I'm not actually biologically yours.'

'Please don't leave,' her mum cried out, but Mo had pivoted round so fast her black hair flew out from her face and then she was running across the drive.

39

Back at Lou's house, Mrs Townsend welcomed Mo in, sensing her heartbreak like a cow senses rain. She settled her in bed and brought her hot chocolate and Mini Battenbergs, but Mo didn't eat or drink. By eight o'clock she was fast asleep.

The next morning, Tuesday, Mo woke feeling exhausted. Her blazing anger had collapsed in on itself like a dying star. It was replaced by a slow-motion nothingness that flattened her like a waterlogged blanket.

Lou appeared, hovering over her.

'There you are, Sleeping Beauty,' she said. 'Want something to eat? You didn't have anything last night, not even the Mini Battenbergs. You must be starving.'

Lou's mum appeared seconds later with a tray overflowing with food and brought more with each hour. The food wasn't the only thing that kept coming throughout the day. So did the anxious text messages from Mo's mum, asking when she'd be coming home and could they please talk.

Mo didn't reply. She stared gloomily at the ceiling and barely spoke. She was buried in cold, damp misery. She was adopted. Her parents were not her biological parents. Her real parents were dead. These were the facts, but Mo still had no idea what they really meant.

The following afternoon, Lou squidged under the duvet with Mo and lay alongside her.

'Thanks, Lou,' Mo managed to say, her first words for almost two days. Her voice sounded small and defeated. 'I don't know what I'd do without you.'

'You'd be finished. I keep telling you this.'

Mo tried to smile and failed.

'How are you feeling?' Lou asked.

'I don't know,' Mo said. 'I always knew I was different to Mum and Dad. It was more than just not quite fitting in. It was bigger than that, deeper.'

'You look nothing like them,' Lou added.

'I know.'

'At least this means you won't inherit your mum's varicose veins though,' Lou said gently.

'Or Dad's short-sightedness,' Mo added. 'Maybe there are some pluses. I am freed from their biology.'

'A strong independent woman,' Lou said. 'Especially the independent bit.'

Mo's face crumpled now, as a huge sensation of otherness, of feeling terribly alone, swept through her.

Lou spotted it and gripped her hand. 'What are you going to do? You can stay here as long as you want, but you'll probably have to go back home some time.'

'To speak to "my parents"?'

'Well, that, and you're going to need some clean knickers. Oh, and your uniform. School's open on Monday.'

Lou's mum popped her head round the door and beamed when she saw the two of them snuggled up in bed.

'This reminds me of when you used to have sleepovers, squashed up together in the same bed. I would come in and tuck you in, just like this.'

She began tucking the duvet under Lou and Mo – 'all nice and cosy' – making them giggle like little kids.

'You're so nice to me, Mrs Townsend,' Mo said.

'It's only what you deserve. You're like a daughter to me, love,' she said, stroking Mo's hair and cupping her face with her big warm hand. 'You and Lou have been friends so long. You're part of the family.'

Family, family, family. What did it mean? Biology, genes, nature more than nurture? Or something else? Love, care, unbreakable bonds. Did those bonds rely on conception and birth, or were they something that grew strong over years, like a sapling becoming an unshakeable tree?

'Anyway, I'm sure your mum would do the same if Lou was upset,' she added, smiling and then heading back downstairs.

Yes, she would, Mo thought. My mum is really kind. She's also funny and caring. She brings me hot chocolate and loves Lou and welcomed Luca into our home with open arms, like the best kind of mother does. Dad is great too. He wants good things for me. OK, yes, I wish he'd told me he spent his spare time staking vampires, but then again, I've hardly been upfront about my double life as Vampire Queen. Seems we've both been keeping secrets. Big ones. Whoppers.

Mo sighed loudly.

'I wish Mum and Dad had told me about my birth. I wish I had found it out from them – I *should* have – so I could understand who I am.'

'You're Mo Merrydrew, always have been, always will be. You're my best friend,' said Lou.

'Oh, don't make me cry, Lou,' Mo said, pressing her fingers against her eyelids.

'Sorry. It's true though. It doesn't change.'

Mo spent the rest of the week at Lou's, still quiet and withdrawn, sleeping a lot. Her mum continued to text and showed up at the house on Saturday afternoon and again on Sunday, but Mo refused to see her.

'I can't face her yet,' she told Lou. 'Or Luca or Vanya. Only you.'

Mo agreed to go to school on Monday though. The familiarity, the routine, the chance to put on a uniform and merge into a huge mass of other students felt manageable, reassuring even. At eight o'clock she rode the bus in with Lou, as they had so many times before. There was Jez on the back seat, there were Tracey Caldwell and Danny Harrington. All three nodded a short hello.

Once the bus had pulled into the school, Mo hung back and walked with Jez.

'All right?' he said.

'Yeah, no, don't know,' Mo said. 'Look, Jez, sorry. I shouldn't have asked you to come along with me, to meet Vanya. It was wrong. I was scared and Luca and I had broken up and you are training to be a hunter and so I –'

'I get it,' Jez said. 'I'm not surprised you were scared. I would have been. She seemed quite nice though, that Vanya. Could have attacked you, and didn't. Your dad said they're always ready to bite.'

'My dad doesn't know everything about vampires. Or about me,' Mo said. 'And it turns out I know nothing about him. He's not even my real dad.'

'Yeah, guess that was a shock too.'

Mo raised her eyebrows in a *you think?* way.

'But Mo, your dad he's, like, devoted to you. Seriously. I mean, I'd kill to have a dad like that.'

Mo sighed.

'Sorry, probably shouldn't talk about killing . . .'

'It's all right, and thanks, Jez,' Mo said, stopping and looking up at him. 'Please don't tell anyone about all this. Promise?'

'Of course. You can trust me. Not that you really need me, honestly. I mean, Luca and Lou, they're cool, right? They've got your back. You're lucky to have them.'

'I'm going this way,' she said, pointing to her left. 'Double maths.'

'See you,' he said and watched Mo disappear down the corridor.

Double maths was double numb. The words drifted past Mo, bounced off and were gone. She couldn't concentrate. When the bell rang for lunch, she made her way to the end of the playing field where she and Lou always ate their sandwiches.

'How's it going?' Lou asked.

'Not good,' Mo said, sitting down next to her and immediately starting to cry.

Lou hugged her until the sobs subsided, then passed Mo a tissue.

'I can't think straight,' Mo said. 'I feel so mixed up. It's sinking in still. I've felt angry and lonely and numb and confused. So confused. It's like you think you're on *Family Fortunes*, and you're this nice cosy team – me, Mum and Dad – but actually it turns out you're on *Mastermind*, alone in that chair, with the spotlight on you.'

'I didn't know you watched *Family Fortunes*,' Lou said.

'Suddenly it's all –' here Mo put on a serious TV-presenter voice – 'Mo Merrydrew, your specialist subject is how not to belong. You have two minutes starting from now. How long did you believe Kate and Mike Merrydrew were your biological mother and father? Fifteen years, ten months and seven days. Correct. When you dibbered Vanya in the shed, did you suspect that she was in fact your sister? Yes. I mean, no! I mean, maybe. Oh god, it's complicated. It's really, really complicated and messed up and confusing.'

Mo chewed her lip, then continued.

'I knew there was something about Vanya. We fought like sisters do, or how I imagine sisters do. I've never spoken to anyone like I speak to her, not even you, Lou. She even looks like me. You saw her, right?'

Lou nodded.

'She protected me too, and Dad. We could all be dead by now if she'd reported back everything she'd seen to the vampires. She saw Dad kill Bogdan and she kept it quiet. She knows about me and Luca *and* she knows I'm human, I'm certain she does. The biggest lie of all, which she could have passed on, but she didn't.'

'Of course she didn't. She's your sister. Sisters stick together. The good ones do anyway.'

Mo took a bite of sandwich and chewed it slowly. 'I wish I had known her when she was human,' she said. 'I wish I'd had the chance to meet my real parents too. Now it's too late.'

Her lip quivered as a wave of grief passed through her. Her birth parents, who loved her enough to give her up, were gone.

Lou held Mo's hand and they sat quietly for a while.

'Wow, my family is messed up,' Mo said, wiping her nose on the back of her hand. 'My dad isn't my real dad and my sister's a vampire.'

'You can't pick your family,' Lou said. 'You just have to try to get on with the one you've got.'

Mo nodded sadly.

'Your mum and dad are still your mum and dad, and you've also gained a sister. You always wanted a sister. Now you've got one. It's kind of a miracle.'

Mo smiled faintly at Lou. 'Maybe you're right. It's just a lot, you know?'

'Do you mind that she's a vampire?' Lou asked.

Mo shrugged. 'Vampires were humans once too. That's what I always say.'

'Good job you didn't kill her.'

A frown scudded across Mo's face. 'Why did I agree to that?'

'People do stupid things when under pressure from vampires,' Lou replied. 'You know that better than anyone.'

'Yeah, but I should never have agreed to kill her. Oh god, I nearly killed my own sister.' Mo's face contracted with horror.

'Nah,' Lou said. 'You were never going to do it.'

'You don't know,' Mo said, sounding offended. 'Dad had me stabbing gammon as training. I was good at it.'

'Gammon's gammon.'

'What do you mean, gammon's gammon?'

'I mean, you still wouldn't have killed Vanya.'

'I was going to do it!' Mo was annoyed now.

Lou shrugged, unconvinced. 'Doubt it.'

'Luca believed I was going to do it. He was really angry about it. That's why we broke up.'

'You broke up? How did I miss this? Is that why you were with Jez?'

'I wasn't with Jez, and yes, me and Luca had a fight about all this and I said we should take a break. I should probably talk to him about it, but my head is barely coping right now with all the family stuff. He'll understand. Anyway, can we get back to Vanya and how you think I'd never have killed her? I would have. I really believed I'd do it.'

'But deep down you knew you wouldn't, and probably even deeper down, right in the darkest, murkiest depths of Mo world, I reckon you knew she was your sister too.'

Mo stared into the distance, thinking.

'Yeah, you're probably right, Lou,' she said eventually. 'By killing Vanya I would have killed myself. Vanya is part of me. We're proper blood relations.'

She squeezed her hands into fists and brought them both up to her lips.

'And then there's my parents,' she said. 'They're, well, they're my parents. They've always been there for me. Always loved me. Raised me as their own, completely. To love a child you didn't even give birth to like they have loved me . . .'

'Yeah, because they could have sent you back, right?' Lou said. 'Like a parcel from ASOS. Wait, where are you going? I was joking, Mo. It's nearly time for geography. Come back!'

Mo had got up and was walking fast across the playing field.

'I've got stuff to sort out,' she shouted over her shoulder.

'But what shall I tell Mrs O'Toole?'

'Tell her I love her very much, but I've got something more important to do than plate tectonics.'

'Do you want a satsuma?' Lou called out, but Mo was too far away to hear, moving through the school gates and out of sight.

40

Mo ran down the lane to her house, her long hair streaming out behind her, and paused at the gate. She could see her mum and dad in the kitchen. Something about the way they were hunched over their mugs, backs curved and heads low, made her heart twitch. She vaulted the gate and ran into the house.

'OK, I'm ready to talk.'

Her mum shot up, beaming. Her dad pulled out a chair for her.

'Would you like some tea first?' he asked, sounding more nervous than she'd ever heard before.

'No tea, just the truth. Tell me everything. Why? How? When?'

Her dad took a deep breath and began, but despite seizing on each word hungrily, Mo couldn't stop her mind from chattering its commentary too.

'We were told about a baby in Eastern Europe, around five months old, who might be in particular danger from vampires,' he said. 'They wanted her, for some reason.'

I know that reason, Mo thought.

'Perhaps they wanted to kill her . . .'

Nope. Try again.

'Or use her to influence the human world somehow . . .'

Not that either.

'Perhaps they knew you would grow up to be good at debating,' he suggested.

I *am* good at debating, Mo thought, unable to resist the compliment. Still wrong though.

'Anyway, that baby was you.'

Well, duh.

'Naturally we didn't hesitate to take you. I then made it my life's work to protect you. Any father wants to do that for his child, but knowing that you were of interest to the vampire community made me extra vigilant.'

Not quite vigilant enough, Mo found herself thinking.

Then her mum spoke. 'We had wanted a baby for so long, Mo. I had three miscarriages, each one completely heartbreaking. It all seemed hopeless. I had basically given up on ever having a child. I had an inhospitable womb, apparently.'

How can a womb be inhospitable? Mo wondered. It didn't leave out any guest towels?

'But then you came along,' she said, her face melting with affection.

'I had no idea, Mum, about the miscarriages,' Mo said. 'All you ever said was that I was a much-longed-for baby.'

'You were! So wanted and so loved.'

No smart or ironic comment popped into Mo's mind now. Her mother's gaze had blazed through all her defences. She felt her bottom lip begin to tremble.

'And then you grew up.'

'Sorry to ruin it,' Mo said. There! Found it! That note of sarcasm which might just, *just* fortify the dam that was holding back a lake's worth of emotions.

'Then you grew up . . .' her mum repeated steadily, 'into a young woman so much more beautiful and clever and original and inspiring than I could ever have dreamed of. I still can't believe my luck that you're here, and that I get to be your mum. Every day you amaze me, Mo. Every day you make me proud. You have made my life so wonderful.'

And that was the dam gone. It didn't just leak, it gave way entirely. Mo threw herself into her mother's arms and blubbed uncontrollably. She felt shielded from the world by the intensity of their hugging and sobbing and affectionate protestations, which were mumbled into each other's neck and onto their shoulders in a snotty, tear-soaked mess.

Eventually Mo surfaced and took a huge, wobbly breath, only to repeat the cuddle with her dad. He squeezed her into his broad chest in a strong, reassuring, 'I've got you' kind of hug that also felt decidedly uncomfortable.

'Ouch, there's a pain in my chest,' Mo mumbled into his shoulder.

'I feel it too, Mo, I feel it too,' he whispered urgently. 'Maybe our hearts are breaking with love.'

'No, an *actual* pain.' She pulled herself free and flicked her dad's jacket open.

'Your stakes were digging in,' she said, pointing at them.

Mo's dad tossed them onto the kitchen worktop, mumbling, 'Sorry, sorry . . .' and looking so charmingly flustered that Mo was flooded with a great wave of liberating, hilarious love. She began to laugh, and soon they all did, catching the wave and surfing it until they were giggling together, in a teary, blotchy group hug.

Finally, Mo and her parents sat back down at the kitchen table. The atmosphere had the fresh, invigorated feel you get after a thunderstorm.

Mo felt able to ask a little more.

'Did you ever meet my biological parents?'

'No, you were passed to us through a third party,' her mum said.

'What did you know about them?'

'Very little. Everything was kept deliberately vague, in case any information might have interfered with our ability to bond with you. That was never going to happen. I fell head over heels the second I saw you.' She gripped Mo's hand quickly.

'They didn't tell us if you had brothers or sisters either,' she continued, 'but we've always assumed you didn't.'

Ooh, wrong assumption, Mo thought, but I'll get onto that.

'Of course, if you want to trace your biological parents we would support you,' Mum said.

'I don't.'

They nodded.

'I love you guys,' Mo said. 'Sorry I ran away to Lou's. I needed time to think.'

They nodded some more.

'We love you so much,' Mo's mum said.

'You should have told me about this though.'

'Yes, you're right, we should have been braver, spoken about it sooner. But it would have meant talking about vampires too, and Dad's hunting, and it all felt so complicated. But we should have done it. We were cowards. I'm so sorry.'

'How *did* you find out?' her dad tried again.

Mo held up a silencing finger. 'Yes, you were cowards, but I get it, I suppose.'

She moved towards the door and then paused. 'Look, I can't be sure I'll be fine about this all the time. Is that OK? I've got so much to think about. *So* much.'

'Of course, we understand,' her mum said, smiling anxiously up at her.

'But at least the truth is out.'

Well, most of it anyway.

'Are you going again?' her dad asked.

'There's something really important I have to do. I'll be back soon. I want you to meet someone.'

Mo dashed back and hugged her parents quickly and then ran outside.

41

It was already dark when Mo arrived at the gate to Vanya's house. There were no lights on, but Mo heard the sound of a motorbike engine rattling to life. She walked up the path and around the house. Vanya was in the garage, bent over her motorbike.

'Finally working?' Mo asked.

Vanya spun around, looking like she might hiss. Oh yes, Mo remembered, not good to walk up behind a vampire when they're not expecting it. But then Vanya's expression softened and became curious.

'Are you going to attack me again?' she said, wiping her oily fingers on a rag.

'No.' Mo pulled her jacket open. 'Look, no stakes. Promise.'

'Odd choice of weapon, anyway,' Vanya said, tossing the rag to one side. 'Wouldn't a Vampire Queen just rip another vampire's head off?'

Mo sighed. She sensed Vanya was teasing her.

'Look, can we talk? Please? Could we go inside?'

Vanya nodded and led the way.

'Did Luca really not fix your bike?' Mo asked, as they walked.

'No, but I just have. Luca means well, but he's a rubbish mechanic.'

They were in the living room now.

'Take seat,' Vanya said.

Mo sank down on the squishy sofa, exactly where she had sat before, and Vanya curled her legs up under her on the armchair.

Then Mo took a deep breath and spoke. 'I'm sorry I tried to stake you yesterday.'

Vanya nodded. 'I'm sorry I snuck around, watching you,' she replied. 'I should have told you who I was from the start.'

'Call it quits?' Mo said.

'Sure.'

'Great, that was easy.'

There was more to say, she knew there was, but how to get it all out?

Luckily Vanya spoke. 'I've made a decision actually. I'm going away, into exile. If I banish myself, you won't have to stake me to satisfy the other vampires. I promise I will totally disappear, so you can tell them you did it.'

'OK,' said Mo. She was being handed a neat solution, so why did it feel wrong?

'Not that you could ever stake me really,' Vanya added, with a sly smile. 'I don't think it's in you.'

'That's what Lou said!' Mo sounded outraged. 'I might have. I'm capable of all kinds of stuff when pushed hard enough. I pinned Danny Harrington to a hot-dog van once.'

'Ooh, scary. Anyway, I was prepared to take that risk. I trusted that some kind of sisterly instinct might kick in.'

'You trusted me?'

'Completely,' Vanya nodded. Tears prickled in Mo's eyes. She blinked quickly. 'Anyway, I knew you wouldn't do it, just like I knew as soon as I saw you that I couldn't attack you or ruin you.'

'We're as useless as each other,' Mo said.

'Totally hopeless. Runs in family.'

They both smiled.

'Once I'm safely hidden away somewhere remote, I'll let you know. Maybe we could write to one another.'

'Yes, I suppose so.'

'You might even visit, when things have settled down.'

Mo nodded weakly.

'We can chat online of course.'

'Yes,' said Mo, then she shook her head. 'What am I saying? I mean no. No actually.'

'Oh, that's OK, I understand if you don't want a relationship with me.'

'No. I mean, no to that plan. Don't banish yourself. I'm not even sure you can banish yourself. Don't you have to *be* banished by someone else? Anyway, don't go.

I've only just found out that I have a sister, that *you're* my sister. Please don't go.'

'This is good solution though. You can go back to ruling quietly, the vampires will be happy, the Vampire King too . . .'

'No.'

'We can pose some photos if you like. Me murdered by you –'

'No, that's not what I want.' Mo sounded forceful now. 'I want to get to know you. Here. I can't lose you right after I've found you.'

Vanya watched Mo, her eyes softening.

'You're family. My family. Sisters stick together. Or they can do, once they realise they're sisters, after a very long time not even knowing that the other one exists.'

Vanya smiled slowly. 'Sure about this? The vampires won't be impressed when they discover you didn't stake me.'

'They can suck it up!' Mo said. 'I'll explain that you're my sister and I'm not killing you. And neither are they. I'm back in charge. I'm queen. That's that. OK?'

'OK.'

'Come to Bogdan's funeral with me. I can tell them there, face to face. Get everything sorted. First though, I want you to meet some people.'

'What people?'

'Well, now that we're family, you'd better meet my parents.'

'Oh no, no, no!' Vanya said, cringing back in her chair. 'I don't think that's a good idea.'

'It's what I want and need. All of us together. A big messy brilliant family. No more secrets. Please?'

Vanya's cool, ironic gaze had become anxious, something Mo had never seen before.

'I still live with them, by the way, though I guess you figured that out.'

Vanya nodded.

'And I'm not . . .'

'Not what?' said Vanya, suddenly looking concerned.

'Well, I'm not actually . . .'

'Mo? What are you about to tell me?' Vanya said, looking really worried now.

'I'm not actually a vampire,' Mo said. 'Please don't hate me – I thought you'd guessed. Oh god, you look really shocked. I assumed you had worked it out. Does this change everything?'

Vanya had her hand to her chest. She was blinking fast, looking off into the distance, but then she turned to Mo and grinned. 'Got you!' she roared, chucking a cushion at Mo. 'Of course I know you're a human.'

'Oh thank god,' Mo said, grabbing the cushion and squeezing it to her chest. 'That's such a relief. Bit annoying obviously. I mean, I thought I was doing a pretty good vampire impression.'

'Well, I saw your house, your mum, your jeans.'

Mo winced.

'Relax! I'm happy for you. Being a vampire isn't the easiest gig going, and the fact that you're ruling *and* human is seriously impressive. I don't know how you convinced Bogdan and the Vampire King though.'

'Bogdan knew I was human in the end. I told him. The Vampire King did nearly kill and eat Luca and Lou, so it wasn't totally straightforward, but I am the Chosen One, so –'

'Are you certain about that? Sure Bogdan didn't make mistake? Get muddled up between two sisters?'

'You've either got it or you haven't, sis, sorry,' Mo fired back.

'Ouch,' Vanya said, but she wasn't hurt, she was laughing. 'Listen, this is what I wanted to show you, in the shed, before you dipsticked me.'

'Dibbered you.'

Vanya passed Mo a faded colour photo. A man and a woman, middle-aged, standing with a girl who was maybe eight or nine. She had two plaits and a serious expression. The man had his hand on her shoulder. The woman's face was pale and expressionless.

'That's you and . . .' Mo placed a curled forefinger against her lips.

'And our parents,' Vanya said softly.

Mo nodded but couldn't speak. She stared at the image for a long time, until Vanya stood up.

'Come on, we should go.'

Mo shook herself. 'Ready to meet my other parents?'

'Not really,' Vanya said. 'Ready to ride my motorbike?'

'Not really,' Mo said. 'I'm more of a bicycle kind of girl.'

'You'll love it. Just hold on tight.'

42

Mo was shaking when she finally got off Vanya's motorbike by the gate to her house.

'Hated that,' she huffed, once she'd yanked off her helmet. 'You drive really fast, and what was all that weaving in between cars? We could have been killed.'

'Correction, *you* could have been,' Vanya said.

'Being undead makes you reckless.'

'Nah, I was like this before I got turned. Anyway, I knew what I was doing. You're alive, aren't you? Which makes you a rubbish vampire but makes me a really good driver.'

They began walking towards the house.

'Your dad won't stake me, will he?' Vanya asked, when they got to the front door.

'I'll make sure he doesn't. Trust me.'

'I actually do.'

Mo nodded, and then rang the bell.

'Oh, Mo, it's you. Why didn't you let yourself in?' her dad said when he answered it.

'Dad, this is Vanya.'

Mo's mum appeared now.

'Oh, it's your friend from before, out in the lane. I remember, when you called me your chauffeur. Come on in then, both of you. Tea?'

'You'll have to invite her in,' Mo said.

Her parents looked confused for a few seconds and then her dad's face clouded over. 'What?'

'Invite her in,' Mo said. She reached for Vanya's hand and gripped it.

'She's a vampire? She doesn't look like one.' Dad's hand moved up towards the pocket that contained his stakes.

'Don't,' Mo said firmly.

He froze.

'She is a vampire, yes, but she's also my sister.'

'What?' her dad said again.

'Vanya is my sister. My blood relative. My biological parents did have another child. You're looking at her. She is not a threat. She's the one who told me I'm adopted. That's how I found out.'

Mo's mum put a hand to her mouth and looked as if she might cry. Mo's dad glowered, his eyebrows hunkering low over his eyes and the muscles in one cheek twitching.

'Now she's part of the family. Our family. You accepted me into your life and loved me, you can do the same for Vanya.'

'But . . .' Dad said.

'No buts!' Mo said sternly. 'We're going to stick together and support each other. You won't stake her. In fact, Dad, you're not going to stake any vampires ever again.'

'What?' he said again. It was becoming a habit.

'I know you see it as a public service, but I see it differently. I'm on the other side of the tracks.'

'Which tracks? What tracks?' he spluttered.

'Look, you might want to be sitting down for this. Can we go inside, please?'

They moved towards the kitchen.

'Erm, hello?' Vanya called from the front step. 'Are you going to invite me in or are we not doing that any more?'

'Sorry, sorry,' Mo said, rushing back to her. 'Vanya, will you come in please?'

Vanya did a little ironic curtsy and then stepped over the threshold. Mo led her to the kitchen and pulled out a chair for her at the table. Vanya sat down. Mo's mum smiled a strained, bewildered smile, but her dad shunted his chair back and folded his arms over his chest.

Mo glanced at the three faces – Vanya relaxed, Mum rigid with stress, Dad sullen and suspicious – and then spoke.

'So there's no easy way to put this, but I'm the Vampire Queen of Great Britain.'

Her mum blinked rapidly. Her dad leaned forward. 'The what of what?'

'You've heard of Great Britain, right, Dad?' Mo said, unable to suppress the sarcasm. 'Well, I rule over all the vampires that live in it, as their queen.'

He shook his head and put both hands up as if to push Mo's words back.

'Please let me explain. I know it's a lot to take in,' Mo said. 'I was approached by Bogdan, the vampire you staked, back in October. He told me I was chosen to lead the vampires here and basically urged me to do it.'

'Oh my god, you're not a vampire, are you, Mo?' her mum blurted.

'No. I faked the turning. I made Bogdan believe I'm a vampire and just kind of went from there.'

'Went from there?'

'Yes, I'm queen now, even though I'm still a human, and I've made it my mission to ensure the vampires are heard and respected and can start to lead more functional lives, alongside people.'

Mo's dad stood up now, both hands pressed against his head.

'Are you OK?' Mo asked.

'He looks like his head is going to explode,' Vanya whispered to her.

'But, but . . .' he stuttered as he paced up and down.

'Mo, I can't believe you've done this,' her mum said. 'You've been in so much danger. You've been meeting with vampires? Spending time with vampires?'

'Yes.'

'How can you even do that? How have they not killed you already?'

Mo shrugged.

'They like her. They respect her. She's the Chosen One,' Vanya said, matter-of-factly. 'She's doing good job.'

Mo's dad had bent over now, still clutching his head.

'When have you been doing this?' Mo's mum asked.

'After dark, obviously. Weekends. Remember that Christmas market? There was no Christmas market. It was a meeting with vampires.'

Mum shook her head and was about to say more when Dad suddenly shot upright, his hands now clenching the air dramatically.

'I have *totally* failed to protect you!' he said, his face desperate, the colour gone from his cheeks. 'I have completely failed as a father *and* a vampire hunter. The reason we adopted you was to protect you from vampires, and now this! I am a failure.'

'Dad, stop saying "failed" and "failure".'

'I should have sensed that the vampires had come for you at last, that that creature – what was his name?'

'Bogdan.'

'That Bogdan was here for you, that they had tracked you down. I got complacent. I knew I couldn't eradicate vampires, but I thought the purges had sent a clear message.'

'Maybe your vampire-hunting skills aren't as sharp as they used to be,' Mo suggested. 'You're getting old.'

'I'm fifty!' Mo's dad exploded.

'Not as old as some vampires,' Vanya chipped in helpfully.

'Exactly,' Mo's dad said, then realised who he was thanking and frowned.

'God, Mo, if only I had sensed he was sniffing around, pressuring you . . . I would have killed him sooner and you would never have had to take all this on.'

'Wouldn't have worked,' Vanya said. 'Mo would still be Chosen One.'

'But I could have hidden her better, got her away to somewhere really remote.'

'Lower Donny is remote enough, thanks,' Mo said. 'Anyway, Dad, being Vampire Queen is my destiny. I can't run from that. It was this destiny that sent me to you in the first place. This is why you took me away from my birth parents and from Vanya, to be raised in safety here.'

Mo's dad sat down. He stared blankly at the table. Mo thought she'd never seen him look so crushed.

'It didn't work though,' he said in a small, sad voice. 'They found you and I haven't protected you at all.'

'But I'm OK, Dad.'

'She's more than OK,' Vanya said. 'I don't think you two understand the daughter you have, sitting right in front of you. She could have given in to threats and become vampire, or she could have got herself killed, but she did neither. She followed a path that is uniquely her own – a human vampire leader – it's amazing! Not only has she survived, she is brilliant queen.'

'Well, I don't know,' Mo said, blushing. 'I've been making a mess of things lately. Stress got to me a bit. I even agreed to kill you.'

'We've been over this, sis,' Vanya said. 'Don't worry about it. You were never going to do it, remember?'

Vanya winked at Mo, who smiled back before they both became aware of Mo's parents watching them.

'You should be really proud of her,' Vanya said.

'You didn't fail at anything, Dad. Vampires have only been in my life for a few months, but you have been in my life always. You brought me up and cared for me. You and Mum were always there.'

Mo's dad shook his head sadly and rubbed one eyebrow.

Mo's mum stood up suddenly, both hands clasped in front of her. 'Tea?' she said. 'Maybe it's time for some tea.'

43

Mo's mum filled the kettle and then turned anxiously to Vanya.

'Is it OK for us to drink tea in front of you? It's not rude, is it? I've never had a vampire visit before, for obvious reasons, I suppose. Mike would not have been keen.' She let out a nervous laugh.

'Of course,' Vanya said. 'Tea reminds me of my human life. I was only turned a year ago. I still miss it.'

Mo's dad glanced up at Vanya, his face pained. Mo felt she could read his thoughts, could spot him finally letting in the facts – vampires were human once too.

'Can I get you anything else? Glass of water perhaps? I might have some mince in the fridge. You could suck on that, maybe? Would that work? Like a vampire lolly?'

'I'm good, thanks,' said Vanya, laughing.

Mo's mum switched on the kettle and dropped teabags into three mugs with shaky hands. She rubbed Mo's shoulders, her eyes darting everywhere. There was Vanya, still calm and cool, leaning back in her chair. Mo was next to her, studying her dad, who was staring at the table in front of him, his shoulders hunched.

'Well, this is nice, isn't it?' she said.

'Come on, Mum, it's weird, sure, but it doesn't have to be. Can't we figure it out? Be together as a family?' Mo said.

'Wait, whoa, hang on,' her dad said, shaking his head like he'd been woken from a dream. 'I've been a vampire hunter for thirty years – you can't expect me to welcome a vampire into my life just like that. How can I trust her?'

'How can I trust you?' Vanya shot back.

They looked at each other steadily.

'Fair point,' he said.

'We need to agree some rules,' Mo said.

'Some boundaries,' her mum added, nodding at Mo.

'We will set out terms so everyone feels safe. Vanya won't eat or turn anyone in the family or community, and Dad won't stake her. We can draw up a contract to make it formal. I love a contract!'

'And sign it in blood,' Vanya added.

Mo's dad glared at her.

'Joking.'

'Oh, right,' he said, flustered. 'Got it. I didn't realise vampires made jokes.'

'Maybe there are lots of things you don't realise about vampires, Dad. Your emphasis has been on killing them, not getting to know them. You were involved in the purges, weren't you?'

He looked shocked.

'I worked it all out from talking to the vampires. That last vampire you killed, the one that hid in the rafters . . . ?'

'What about him?'

'He was the uncle of three of my subjects. In fact, all my vampires have lost friends and family at your hands. Anyway, I'm trying to improve their lives now but I can only get them so far. I can sort out their clothes, get them online, listen to their problems, but the thing they really need is for you, the last remaining vampire hunter, to put away your stakes.'

'Give up the job?'

'Yes. You can keep going with carpets, but promise not to kill any more vampires.'

'Impossible!' he shouted, pushing his chair back. 'If the vampires found out, they would seize their chance and come for me straight away. I'd be dead within days.'

'He's right,' Vanya said. 'You can't ask your dad to do this, Mo. It makes him too vulnerable.'

Mo stood up and went over to the window. She gripped the edge of the sink, thinking hard. The others stared at her back until, finally, she turned around.

'Then I must get them to agree to a truce,' she said.

'What do you mean?' Dad asked.

'You promise not to kill any vampires, and they promise not to kill you.'

'They'll never agree to it,' her dad shot back.

'They will. I'll make them,' Mo said, 'but I need you to back me up, Dad, and you, Vanya. If we can live as a family – a vampire, a vampire hunter and the human Vampire Queen – then surely the vampires of Great Britain and the last vampire hunter can live in peace alongside each other.'

Mo's dad let out a long breath. 'You're serious, aren't you?'

'Deadly,' Mo said.

'Pun intended?' Vanya murmured.

'This is the only way for my subjects to ever live well. They constantly fear vampire hunters, but if you can make peace, then their lives will be transformed. Your life too. Wouldn't you like to live free from the vampire threat? Instead of carrying stakes everywhere, you could trust that any vampires out there mean you no harm. Think of that.'

'Mo, this is crazy!' Her dad stood up now. 'Take away the threat of vampire hunters and it's like giving the vampires permission to go on the rampage. It would turn Britain into an all-you-can-eat buffet. No! I cannot agree to this.'

'But you said yourself you can never get rid of them completely, they always come back, so your work is never done. Plus, you've just found out I'm up to my eyebrows in vampires, so hunting them hasn't worked and neither has trying to keep me safe.'

Mo's dad winced. He turned his back to her now, his arms folded, head down. The silence fell thickly over the room. The tick of the wall clock, counting out the seconds, seemed loud as fireworks. Finally he turned around.

'Could it work?'

He wasn't looking at Mo. He was looking at Vanya. She cleared her throat.

'I don't know,' she said. 'Sorry, Mo. Honestly, I don't know if they would accept a treaty –'

'I knew it!' he exploded.

'But . . . !' Vanya said, loud and firmly. 'They *might* . . . and if anyone can persuade them to do it, it's Mo.'

Mo flashed a smile at her.

'It is brave idea. It's original and exciting and just the kind of thing Mo would come up with and, as she says, everyone will benefit from it. So why not?'

'But the blood!' Mo's dad said, clenching one fist in front of him. 'Vampires feed on the blood of humans – their diet means they have to kill. How can I be OK with that?'

'We'll work on other diets for them. Food substitutes, replacement blood – vegetarians and vegans have eaten meat alternatives and plant-based substitutes for years. Why not the vampires?'

'I don't know, I just don't know. This is all so . . .' He ran out of words.

'Look, come with me to Bogdan's funeral. We walk in, this united, diverse family made up of the human Vampire Queen and her non-biological dad who's also a vampire hunter *and* her vampire sister, and wow! You know? We're walking it like we talk it. We will be living proof that the kind of tolerance and equality I'm shooting for can work.'

'Let me think about it,' Mo's dad said. 'I need to go and sit on the comfy chairs now.'

He walked off into the living room. Mo's mum followed.

'Where the hell did that come from?' Vanya asked Mo. 'The whole peace-and-love plan?'

'I just thought of it, by the sink.'

'The sink, of course. Source of so much inspiration. Who hasn't been inspired when standing by a sink?'

'You said yourself they may go for it.'

'They may also rip his throat out, Mo – have you thought of that? Plus he will have revealed his identity. You've seen how furious they get when vampire hunters or the purges are even mentioned, let alone when a slayer is standing right in front of them.'

'I know, but that's also why it has to happen.'

'And you want to do it at Bogdan's funeral.' Vanya whistled. 'This is super high stakes, sis. The Vampire King's emissary will be there. He or she will report all this back.'

'Crap, I'd forgotten about that,' Mo said, frowning, 'but I can't organise a truce between the vampires and the last remaining vampire hunter over Zoom. It has to be face to face, and it has to be soon, before any more killings or lying or threats. Bogdan's funeral is the perfect time. Plus, the vampire hunter showing up at the funeral of the vampire he staked is a bold move.'

'It's a weird one.'

'I think it's powerful. It sends out a strong message of reconciliation. It has to happen.'

'Wow, you're pretty forceful when you're all fired up and leading.'

'I know, right?' Mo said.

'OK, if you insist on your dad going, I'll take care of the emissary. Feed him some dodgy blood or take him on tour of the castle so he misses the action.'

'Cool, thanks,' Mo said. 'That reminds me, I haven't even planned Bogdan's funeral yet.'

'That's the least of your worries,' Vanya said. 'Get the other vampires to do it.'

Mo's parents filed back in now.

They sat down, her dad rubbing his forehead. Mo reached across the table to him and he took her hand.

'Please come with me to Bogdan's funeral, Dad. It's on Saturday.'

'Murderers don't typically go to the funerals of their victims,' he said.

'That's what I said,' Vanya chipped in.

'It's a chance to meet and resolve things once and for all. Plus, can I just say, it's nice to see you identifying yourself as a murderer, Dad, rather than an expunger. That shows real growth.' She squeezed his hand.

'Come and pay your respects. Meet the other vampires. I will explain that Vanya is my sister and that you, Mike Merrydrew, are my dad *and* a vampire hunter, a soon to be ex-vampire-hunter, and we will offer them a truce. It's time to end centuries of feuding and violence. It's time to make peace.'

44

'You look like a zombie, not a vampire,' Lou said when Mo got on the bus the next morning. 'Are you OK?'

'I've made up with mum and dad and Vanya. I got them all together. All four of us, round the table, drinking tea until late last night. Well, three of us drinking tea; Vanya wasn't, she's a vampire so –'

'I get the idea, Mo.'

'Sorry. I'm really tired, but also excited. I've got my sister in my life – still can't believe that. A sister! And I've asked Dad to make peace with the vampires, call a truce. This could be big. Game-changing. My legacy!'

'Peace breaking out everywhere. Wow, they will be writing musicals about you in the future.'

'Hope so,' said Mo.

'What does Luca say about it? Does he know?'

Mo's heart skipped.

'Oh, your face,' Lou said, pointing. 'You're not talking, are you?'

'It's been an overwhelming few days. He's been a bit squeezed out. Maybe I should message him.'

'You think? Come on, Mo, you don't want Luca to get away.'

Mo nodded and took out her phone.

Great news. I made up with Vanya last night. She met M&D too. Peace and love all round!

She kept the phone in her hand, hoping for a reply to ping back immediately, but nothing came. On the way home from school, she tried again.

Setting up a Zoom for tonight to plan Bogdan's funeral. Look out for your invite.

Still no response. He'll be on the Zoom, she told herself, he'll show up for that, but later that evening as the faces appeared on-screen, she realised Luca's wasn't there. No time to think about that, Mo decided, and plunged in.

'Lots to discuss, so let's not waste time,' she said. 'First, Bogdan's funeral. It's on Saturday, today is Tuesday, we need to plan it. If everyone takes on a duty, we can be sure to make the funeral go smoothly.'

'Can I just ask, Your Majesty,' Derek said, 'have you killed Vanya yet?'

'Thanks for your question, Derek. I have neutralised her.'

'What does that mean?' Pat spat.

'She is no longer a threat. The target has been eradicated from the equation.'

'I'm sure I've not a single tiny clue what the queen is actually chatting on about.'

'I'll explain more when I see you, at Bogdan's funeral,' Mo said. 'I will also be bringing two very special guests who I want you to welcome.'

'If it's the Vampire King and a plus-one, they can expect a very not warm welcome from me,' Pat said, baring her fangs.

'It's not him, but his emissary will be there, watching. So best behaviour all round, please. Now, let's move on to details. The funeral needs to be held somewhere grand but also out of the way, to avoid unwanted attention, and by that I mean Wales. Pat and Richard, let's have it at your castle.'

'Really? It's a bit untidy right now,' Pat said. Richard nodded in stern agreement.

'Doesn't matter. Now, as it's your castle, you two can be site managers. Derek, you're interior design. Sven, security. The Tartan Fangs, you're on fireworks. Natasha, cleaning. Girls, hair and make-up.'

'Could we do something else too?' Olga asked.

'Help with your speech writing maybe?' Lenka suggested.

'We've been reading Michelle Obama's autobiography, Queen Mo. We're feeling very inspired about the important contribution we, as young women, can make.'

'That's wonderful,' Mo said. 'Well, if I write a speech, you will be the first vampires I consult for input.'

The girls beamed.

'OK. Where was I? Ah yes, Francis the Mountaineer, you can shimmy up the battlements and hang out banners but not bunting, OK? The rest of you, work with Pat on making the castle look fantastic, and if you can find any peacocks, bring them.'

The vampires nodded.

'Great, everybody clear on their jobs?' Mo paused for a very brief beat. 'Excellent. See you on Saturday.'

She hit the Leave Meeting button before anyone could ask any questions and flipped her laptop closed. Then she texted Luca.

Missed you at the meeting. Everything OK?

She waited, then messaged again.

Vamps on it with organising Bogdan's funeral for Saturday. Looking good so far. I am also planning something BIG!!! It could be a new ear for vampire-human relations. Exciting!

Then,

*era

Then ☺

Still Luca didn't reply. Mo checked her phone every few minutes. Maybe he's asleep. Maybe he's out having dinner. Maybe he's got a headache or lost his phone or has an eye infection so he can't see the screen. (Oh please not that, not his eyes, his beautiful, beautiful eyes . . .) Finally, just before she turned out her light to sleep, he messaged back. A single thumbs up. Nothing else.

School took up the days leading up to Bogdan's funeral, but whenever Mo got the chance she pinged chatty messages to Luca and received disappointing replies hours later: a single thumbs up, a like, an OK.

Never mind, she told herself, I'll see him on Saturday. We have the whole journey to Wales together, plenty of time to talk. What would she say though? Mo wasn't sure. She had ended the relationship and been swallowed up by her family revelations, but she was ready to see him now and wanted him there by her side as her familiar and more . . . It was obvious she was sorry, right? Obvious she'd just been throwing her toys out of the pram when she said they should split? And of course she hadn't ever really been going to kill Vanya. Since then she had had so much to cope with. Surely he understood. Finding out about her parents, and Vanya. It was huge. She knew he'd get it, so why wasn't he responding?

That question never got answered. It was bumped from her brain over and over, by vampire emails flooding in, updating her on preparations, and by Vanya, who spent each evening at her house, hanging out with Mo and her parents, and by her dad, who spent a lot of that time quizzing Vanya ('Ever drained a hamster? Ripped the head off a lizard? Juggled with kittens?'). He showed her his collection of stakes. She politely complimented him on each one, but it wasn't until she fixed the windscreen wipers on his car that Mo suspected he was really coming round to her.

On Thursday, with just forty-eight hours to go, Derek emailed: 'I have had black and red flags made, Majesty. So dramatic! Francis the Mountaineer has put them up. Natasha has been cleaning – you wouldn't believe how many corpses she discovered in the basement. Pat is definitely not a domestic goddess LOL. We have banners up and the grass has been cut. This castle is hardly recognisable from the damp pile of rubble I saw when I got here two days ago.'

And then Pat.

'Did Derek slag me off, saying I don't clean my bloody castle? The cheek of it. I didn't even know about those corpses. Richard must have left them there back in his massacring days. Probably didn't want to admit to it. Bit like that time I bought a new velvet three-piece riding suit which cost an absolute through-the-roof fortune. I told him it was Primark.'

By Friday, Mo still hadn't heard from the Vampire King about when his emissary would arrive. Perhaps he'd forgotten to send one, too distracted by the latest uprising. That would be great, Mo thought, and very like him. He didn't seem to care that Bogdan had been staked, after all.

When she got home from school her dad was standing in the kitchen sipping a mug of tea. He was wearing a new black suit, a crisp white shirt and a black tie. His hair had been trimmed into a smaller, neater version of his usual shaggy do.

'Wow, you look smart.'

'I am ready for the funeral,' he said.

'Really? Are you sure? You'll call a truce too?'

He nodded. 'I have to be there with you, and if this is the only way, then let's do it.'

'I can take care of myself, I promise, Dad, but I do believe this is right.'

'I know,' he said, hugging her. 'And I believe in you.'

45

Mo spent the rest of Friday evening calling Luca, but he didn't pick up. She slipped from feeling hurt and miserable to angry. At eleven o'clock she fired off a chippy text.

You're obviously screening my calls. Why won't you speak to me?

No reply. Mo's rage began to surge through her body. Her thumbs danced across her phone, punching out the words without thinking.

You can't still be angry about us breaking up? Can't we move beyond that? I've had so much going on. I thought you'd understand.

I am amazed you can be so selfish.

Then she hit send. Within seconds her phone sprang to life, the ringtone so loud and shocking Mo almost dropped it. A single name appeared on the screen: Luca.

'*I'm* selfish?' There was no mistaking the fury in his voice.

Mo felt herself shrink. 'I just wondered why you weren't getting back to me, that's all,' she said. 'It's not like you.'

'You mean because I'm normally there, the second you call, with a smile on my face.'

'Yes!' said Mo, glad he'd understood, catching the bitterness too late.

'Mo, we broke up, remember?' Luca said.

'But I've organised Bogdan's funeral and Vanya is now in my life, and I didn't stake her and I've got something really big planned for tomorrow, with Dad involved – Dad! – and all the vampires . . . I thought you'd be pleased about it all. Proud even. I've been working so hard.'

'Good for you,' Luca replied, his voice flat.

'You're coming tomorrow, right? It's your job to bring Bogdan too. What time shall we leave?'

'Yeah, about that . . .'

Mo felt herself tense, sensing danger.

'I'm not coming.'

'What do you mean? Bogdan was your master. I can help dig him up if that is what's putting you off.'

'It's not about Bogdan,' Luca said. 'It's about us.'

Silence.

'Mo, like I said, we broke up, remember? You ended it.'

'I know, I know, but I was stressed and unhappy when I said that. I just chucked it out there. I thought you'd understand. I didn't realise you'd take it so badly.'

'How was I supposed to take it?'

'Look, I'm sorry about that, OK? I wasn't in a good place, Luca. I don't think you understand how difficult it can be as Vampire Queen sometimes.'

'I do understand, Mo, but what am I meant to do with that? Just keep on being patient? Keep on smiling?'

Mo didn't reply. Her hand was shaking as she gripped the phone.

'You don't know how to do relationships, Mo. You flung yourself into vampire work the moment you met them, just like you used to fling yourself into schoolwork, even though you said all along you'd make time for me. Then you were jealous of my friendship with Vanya, but you weren't able to talk about that, and when I challenged your plan to kill her and told you how shocked I was, your only solution was to break up with me.'

'But I said sorry,' Mo stammered.

'What took you so long?'

'Luca, please! I've just found out I'm adopted and Vanya is my sister! Cut me a break.'

'And I could have helped you through that, if you had asked me to be there, but you can only seem to manage having a boyfriend when all the other stuff in your life is going OK. The second it's not, I get chucked out.'

They were both silent for a while. Then Luca began talking again, more calmly now. 'Mo, I care about you, I do, but I can't just be the easy-going sidekick all the time, while you get pulled around in all directions by the vampires and schoolwork and your parents and whatever. We've been here too many times before. You treat me badly or do something odd, and I just smile and say it's OK. It's getting old. I have feelings too.'

Mo nodded but couldn't speak. Her throat had closed over and tears were blurring her vision.

'I want to be with someone who really trusts me and who's as committed to a relationship as I am.'

'I am committed,' Mo protested in a little-girl voice.

'Someone available, serious about us, prioritising us.'

'But it's hard being queen and going to school and seeing you, and then I find out I'm adopted, it's all so much. I am trying, Luca, I really am.'

'I understand it's a lot. That's why I want to take one thing out of the equation for you, to simplify it.'

'What one thing?'

'Me.'

Mo threw the phone away from her like it had burned her, and clutched her sides.

'Mo, are you there?' she could hear Luca saying. 'Good luck with the funeral. I'm sure whatever you're planning will be great. You'll be great. I'm heading home for a while. I want to be with my family. Let's catch up in a week or two.'

Mo reached for the phone, but she was too late. The line went dead. She stared at it for a while, her thoughts swinging violently like a pendulum, between 'How could he abandon me?' to 'He's completely right, I'm terrible at relationships.'

Should I call him back, apologise, grovel, beg him to reconsider? How would I know? Mo thought. I'm terrible at relationships. She gripped the phone to her chest. She crawled under the duvet. She curled into a ball. The pendulum had stopped swinging now and come to rest on a sensation of such intense shame and regret that Mo couldn't speak, couldn't reach out to Lou, could only lie there, very small and very still, until morning.

46

'Mo, we're leaving at three. Oh, still in bed? You OK?'

Mo's dad had put his head round the door and was frowning.

'Three is fine,' she said.

'We'll pick up Vanya just as it gets dark and then should arrive at the castle by seven. Is Luca coming?'

'No.'

Her dad went to speak, but then seemed to gulp the words back. He nodded and shut the door.

Lou texted later.

Good luck with the funeral. I can come and do your hair?

Mo texted back.

I'm good, but thanks. Love you.

It would have been good to have Lou there, fixing her hair, but she would ask about Luca and Mo didn't feel ready to talk about it. She was bruised, embarrassed even, her feelings raw and messy, not yet organised into thoughts she could speak out loud.

Around two o'clock, Mo showered and washed and dried her hair, brushing it into straight black curtains on either side of her face. She pulled on her black dress and embroidered robe, shoved her golden bangles onto her wrist and the jewelled hair slide into her hair. She doused herself in vampire-repelling perfume, stuck her fangs in her pocket and went down to the kitchen.

'I'm ready,' Mo said, feeling suddenly self-conscious at being the Vampire Queen in front of her vampire-hunting dad.

'You look nice,' he said.

'You too.' She flicked his jacket pocket open.

'No stakes there,' her dad said.

He patted her arm and didn't comment on her pale face, the dark rings under her eyes, the raw eyelids.

Vanya did though.

'Very gothy look,' she said as soon as she saw her. 'Loving the red eyeliner.'

'It's not eyeliner. I've been crying. Luca dumped me. It's OK. I deserved it. I don't want to talk about it.'

Vanya nodded, and once they were all in the car – Vanya: 'You have to invite me in.' Dad: 'It's a car not a building. Oh, all right then' – they drove in silence until Dad parked up by the gates of Pat and Richard's home at around 7 p.m. They walked up the drive, the ancient castle looming into view on the hill above.

'Wow,' Vanya said. 'Looks amazing.'

The vampires had decorated its solid grey walls with streamers. Black and red flags fluttered in the winter breeze and there seemed to be fires burning everywhere. Flaming torches lined the drive and, on the lawn, a huge bonfire crackled. At the entrance, two braziers heaped with burning logs flanked the enormous solid-oak door. Mo noticed Richard's cannon there too, last seen at her first meeting with the vampires. What a long time ago *that* seemed.

'Are you certain they're not going to attack us – the traitor and the vampire hunter?' Vanya asked.

'They won't,' Mo said.

'Sure?' Vanya asked. 'You don't sound very sure.'

'Look, they like me, they're loyal and I'm about to offer them peace and prosperity. I know I didn't kill you, Vanya, as they wanted . . .'

'Yeah, what a loser,' Vanya murmured.

'And, Dad, you killed Bogdan, and they're not going to love either of those two facts . . .'

'Understatement,' Vanya added.

'But I also think they have enough sense to see that a lasting truce is the only real solution.'

Mo paused and looked at the sky, a wild look creeping over her face.

'It's all I've got anyway,' she said, flinging out her hands. 'I have to bring everything together, all the strands of my life, all the bits of me. I can't be just Vampire Queen or just Mo or just a daughter or student or sister. I'm all those things, and you both have to be in there too. My vampire-hunting dad and my vampire sister. My family.'

Dad and Vanya nodded.

'I know it's risky, but not trying this feels riskier,' Mo said.

'You've got this, sis,' Vanya said. 'Now go in there and kick some vampire ass. Go full regal. I know you can do it. I've seen you do it before. Channel all your strength and get those suckers to agree to truce. Then we can all get on with our lives.'

Mo nodded. 'I *can* do this,' she said, hugging Vanya and then her dad. 'Wait out here. I'll come and get you soon.' Then she pushed open the heavy door and stepped into the castle.

There was a fire burning in the vast stone grate of the entrance chamber. It made the glass eyes of the stags' heads mounted on the walls seem to flicker with life. Mo could see a further set of doors opposite, and could hear the vampires beyond it. She walked softly across the flagstone floor and peeped inside. It was a huge room – the great hall – with a soaring roof and more flaming torches fixed to the walls. The tall arched windows were draped with black and red swags. Another enormous fireplace dominated one whole side of the room, and opposite was a long rectangular table dressed with red and black tablecloths, pewter goblets and animal skulls.

'Your Majesty, you're here,' Derek said, noticing Mo in the doorway and rushing over. 'Do you like the goat skulls? We found them in one of Pat's spare rooms. I thought spray-painting them fluoro green was kind of funky.'

Mo nodded and smiled. All the vampires were gathering round now.

'This is truly impressive,' she said. 'Thank you all for your hard work. You all look lovely too. The athleisure is so versatile, isn't it? Even right for a funeral.'

The vampires beamed.

'Are you alone, Your Majesty?' Pat asked. 'No familiar tonight? And what about the Vampire King's emissary?'

'Luca is on annual leave,' Mo said, 'and I have heard nothing of the emissary. Perhaps he's decided not to come. I have brought my guests though, as I said I would. Before I introduce them, you must swear not to attack them.'

'Why would we do that? Unless it's a vampire hunter,' Malcolm said.

'Or that traitor Vanya,' Derek added.

'Or that terrible waste of precious oxygen the Vampire King,' Pat threw in.

Great, Mo thought. Two out of three. This could be a hard sell.

'Listen to me! These two individuals matter more than anyone else you may ever meet. If you can agree to get along with them, if you can accept them into our vampire family and if you are willing to forget the past, then I truly believe that a golden future awaits – for all of us.'

'I love golden futures,' Olga whispered to Lenka, who nodded eagerly.

'It will take courage, it will take generosity, but if we can all come together, you, me and the two people waiting outside, then all of us – every last one of us – will benefit. I promise you that.'

'Who is it? Who is it?' Derek cried, hopping on the spot and clapping his hands.

'Is it the Obamas?' Olga blurted. Lenka gasped with excitement.

'I will fetch one of them now. You may be shocked when you see her.'

'Has she got warts?' Pat asked. 'I can never look at a wart.'

'Please remember your promise to be peaceful. I will explain everything.'

Olga gripped Lenka's arm eagerly and Derek's eyes glittered.

Mo dashed outside. 'It's time,' she said. 'Dad, wait here – I'll be back for you in a sec.'

He nodded and, arm in arm, Mo and Vanya walked back into the castle and through the doors to the great hall.

The screeching and hisses hit them like a blast of cold wind. Mo gripped her sister's arm more tightly and walked her forward.

'That's bloody Vanya!' Pat roared, stepping towards them. 'The bloody cheat. I thought you said she'd been neutered or extricated or something?'

'Why did you not kill her?' Derek asked, sounding sulky. 'Queen Mo, you promised!'

'And what has she got to do with our golden future?' Natasha mumbled.

'Traitor!' the Tartan Fangs shouted as one.

Vanya jutted her chin out and stared straight ahead. Mo felt a wave of anxiety sweep through her like nausea. That same fury and violence she had seen on the Zoom meeting was here again. She had to contain it or things could unravel.

'Quiet, all of you. I asked you to hear me out, so hear me out. Vanya does not work for a vampire hunter. She is honest. You can trust her.'

'Horse manure!' Pat shouted. 'She's a snake who deserves to die.'

'Snake, snake, snake,' the vampires chanted out loud.

Oh god, oh god, oh god, Mo chanted in her head.

'I order you to listen to me,' Mo shouted. 'She is not a snake *or* a traitor. She is my sister. She is family.'

Mo expected a pause, some surprise, a change of pace, but Pat launched in without skipping a beat.

'You can still kill your family you know,' she said.

'No!' Mo said. 'We are vampires, not rabid animals. We behave with decency and compassion.'

The vampires finally fell silent, their faces confused.

'I don't understand. How can Vanya be your sister?' Derek asked.

'Did you know all along?' Malcolm said.

'Yes, were you in on this together?' Pat put in, her eyes blazing. 'Are you both traitors? Oh, please don't say it. Don't say we've been betrayed and taken for total, stupid fools.'

The vampires hissed and screamed now, panic rippling through the room like electricity. Mo pulled Vanya to her.

'Traitors, liars, cheats!' the vampires roared.

They're totally triggered, Mo thought bleakly, I'll never get through to them.

'We trusted you, and you deceived us, Queen Mo,' Pat screamed as the vampires' roars grew louder and sharpened into a screech, high-pitched and worse than a thousand fingernails down a blackboard.

Mo threw her hands over her ears and watched, eyes wide, as the vampires bared their fangs and leaned towards her and Vanya. Mo couldn't think through the sound, couldn't work out what to do next, she only wanted it to stop. The noise engulfed her, pinning her to the spot. She tried to speak, but her voice was drowned out when, suddenly, the screaming turned to a collective gasp. The vampires leaped backwards, their arms up, defending themselves. Oh thank God, Mo thought, but then she glanced behind her. Her dad was standing there, holding a stake.

47

'Dad! For god's sake,' Mo hissed at him. 'You promised you weren't armed.'

'I always carry one in my sock, Mo. Force of habit.'

'I told you to wait outside.'

'But all the screaming! I thought you needed help.'

The vampires were all showing their fangs now, trembling like leopards preparing to pounce, fury and fear in their dark eyes.

'Queen Mo!' Pat stepped nearer, shaking with rage. 'Do you know this vampire hunter? Did I actually hear you say this murderous stain on the armpit of the world is your *father*?'

'He is my father, yes.'

Pat hissed so hard her face seemed to stretch. Natasha wailed and clutched the girls to her. Sven beat his chest like a silverback gorilla.

'By all the coffins of hell!' Pat screamed. 'You bring this . . . this *devil* here!'

'He has an important message for you,' Mo said, her voice barely emerging from her tight throat, constricted with fear.

'He better drop that stake right now. *Right* now! Or I will be forced to rip his actual human head off.'

'I'll drop it if you step away from Mo and Vanya,' he said. 'They are my daughters. Well, Mo is, and Vanya sort of is by association or like a stepdaughter or . . . Anyway. *Step back!* Do it! Or one of you gets this nasty sharp stake right in their heart.'

'Vampire-hunter scum,' Pat hissed, flashing her fangs but retreating a few centimetres.

'Bloodsucking filth,' Mo's dad snarled, raising his stake higher.

'That's enough!' Mo shouted. 'Dad, you were supposed to be unarmed. Pat, you promised not to attack.'

But neither seemed to hear. Mo's plan for peace and reconciliation was going up like a tissue in a bin fire. Pat and her dad were locked into a staring competition, eyes boring into each other, bodies poised and trembling until, with absolutely no warning, Pat launched herself – fast – at Mo's dad, her hands out in front of her, furiously clawing the air. His vampire-hunting reflexes kicked in immediately and he thrust his stake at her with a roar, missing her chest but piercing her hand.

'Look! Look what he's done!' Pat roared, staggering backwards. She was holding her palm out in front of her, staring with horror at the stake that had skewered it.

There was blood oozing from the wound, but Pat seemed more outraged than in pain. Snarling like an angry wolf, she rushed at Mo's dad and swiped at him again with her un-staked hand. He ducked, crouching on the floor and, Mo realised, reaching for the stake hidden in his other sock. Without thinking, she threw herself in front of him, shoved Pat backwards and yelled:

'Stop it! This minute! Now!'

Everybody froze.

Mo stood still, eyeing them all, panting a little.

'You both promised not to fight,' Mo said, her voice powerfully angry. 'Do your promises mean nothing?'

She turned to her dad. 'Give me that stake.'

He passed it to her.

'Is that the last one?'

He nodded.

'Promise?'

'Promise,' he mumbled.

Next Mo marched up to Pat, grabbed hold of the stake sticking out of her hand and yanked it out forcefully. Pat winced, but didn't cry out; she only watched with stony eyes as Mo tossed both pieces of wood into the fire.

'Right, let's get back on track, shall we?' Mo said. Nobody spoke. 'I'll take that for a yes.'

She smoothed her robes and looked at all the vampires, standing in their athleisure leggings and tracksuit tops, their dark, suspicious eyes on her.

'You said you wanted to live among humans and have better lives. That sounded great, but I have come to realise that a good life is only possible if we resolve the oldest conflict of all. Remember what that is, Pat? Remember when you said the Vampire King had ignored it all along?'

'The conflict between humans and vampire hunters, yes, yes, I know,' Pat said testily. 'But we could end it here, couldn't we? By killing this fool. Look at him, in his cheap clothes and silly little lace-up shoes, like a teenager who's borrowed his dad's suit to go to a job interview. Pathetic. I say we kill him and drink every last drop of his murderous blood.'

'But there could always be more hunters,' Mo said urgently. 'He has been training one, so you end nothing by killing him, and he achieves nothing by killing you. You can turn more humans into vampires, the hunter he trained can train yet more hunters, and those hunters can train more hunters and those train more, and on and on it goes. It's a cycle of violence unless you stop it, unless you take a stand and choose peace.'

'There can never be peace between vampires and vampire hunters!' Pat roared, stamping her foot like a frustrated child.

'Why not?'

'Because . . . because that's how it's always been.'

'That's not a good enough reason.'

'But, but . . .' Pat spluttered into silence.

The other vampires were listening keenly now.

Mo dropped her voice. 'Don't you see the opportunity that is right in front of you? It's here, in this room. It's between us and only us: the vampires of Great Britain and the last remaining fully trained, super-experienced vampire hunter. If we all, together, commit to a truce, it's done. No more fear, no more violence, no more suspicion, no more purges. Change for the good, for all of us. Don't you want that? Isn't that *exciting*? You all have the power to do this. Forget ripping heads off, this is *real* power. A decision to live together in harmony. An end to the war. A lasting peace.'

Mo's eyes blazed as she scanned the vampires' faces. She didn't notice her dad looking proudly at her, or Vanya's warm gaze.

'Maybe Queen Mo is right,' Derek said quietly. 'I mean, none of us expected this today, but maybe she's right.'

'What would Michelle Obama do?' Olga asked.

'I think she'd back Mo,' Lenka said.

'Well, Michelle is right, whoever she is,' Natasha said. 'I wasn't prepared for this, but I find that I agree.'

'Aye, we three also,' said Malcolm. Donald and Duncan nodded.

'I select an armistice also,' said Sven.

Other vampires nodded their agreement in an atmosphere that seemed hushed and serious. It's happening, Mo thought quickly. They're choosing a truce. I've done it, I've actually gone and done it. My rule, my way, *finally*!

Then Pat threw up her hands.

'What are you all doing? I don't understand. I just don't see how this can happen. The fear and hatred runs too deep. How can we ever trust one another?'

'You trust me,' Mo said, 'and I'm a human.'

Oops. It just fell out of her mouth.

'Yes, but you're not a vampire hunter,' said Pat.

'No, but you get the idea, we can work across the divide and . . . Wait a minute, I just told you I'm a human.'

Pat tutted dismissively. 'We all know *that*.'

Mo's mouth fell open.

'We spotted it the first day we met you at the hotel,' Derek explained, smiling.

'But I was wearing special perfume to mask my human smell. I still am!'

'Yeah, that stinks, but we still guessed.'

'I had my fake fangs in for a bit too,' Mo added.

'But they *were* clearly fake.'

'They cost a lot of money!'

He shrugged.

'Well, why didn't you kill me?' Mo asked, annoyed now.

'Pat wanted to.'

'I did not! Derek, you little peanut brain, why don't you shut your foolish silly mouth. Look, Your Majesty, I just decided to give you a try. We all did.'

'We loved your look,' Olga said.

'We call it sleek geek,' Lenka added.

'You seemed keen and you had strong ideas for how to rule,' Derek added. 'You were taking an interest, which is way more than the Vampire King ever did.'

'At least *he* believes I'm a vampire!' Mo said, still annoyed.

'He also believes he's brilliant and handsome and really popular, so you know . . .' Pat pointed out.

Mo looked from one to the other, and then let out a tiny, 'Huh!'. Her shoulders dropped. She slowly removed the sparkly slide from her hair and tousled her long black tresses roughly with her fingertips. She pulled her embroidered robe off and let it fall in a heap. She eased off the golden bangles and they hit the stone floor with a metallic tinkling sound.

'Here I am then,' she said, spreading her arms wide. 'A fifteen-year-old human as your leader. You never believed I was a vampire. I'm disappointed about that, I've got to say – I was *really* trying – but you gave me a chance anyway, even though you knew I hadn't been turned. So, you *can* adapt. You can open up your life to different people, *human* people. You've done it already.'

The vampires murmured between themselves.

'Think about it. I'm your queen but I'm a human. Vanya is my sister but she's a vampire. My dad is my dad but he isn't my biological father. What does it matter? If we get along, find common ground, show each other respect, we can be family. Don't you want that? No more hiding, no more constantly glancing over your shoulder for vampire hunters. Equality, tolerance, peace.'

The vampires were silent. The only sound was the rain falling outside and the fire crackling.

'Dad, what do you say?' Mo turned to him. 'Do you promise to quit being a vampire hunter, once and for all?'

'I do.'

'Pat?'

'I suppose so,' she said, eyeing Mo's dad like he was something she'd stepped in.

'The rest of you?'

They all nodded.

'Shall we stake on it? *Shake* on it, I mean? Sorry!' Mo blushed quickly then carried on. 'Vampires, you will no longer kill vampire hunters. And by that I mean, don't murder my dad. Vampire hunters – Dad – you will no longer kill vampires. That's the deal. Yes?'

There was silence for a few moments, then Pat held out her hand, now red with the blood that had oozed from her wound. Mo's dad slowly extended his and, keen to avoid the wound, held onto her fingertips.

'Truce?' Mo said.

Pat and her dad stared into each other's eyes. For a second Mo feared they would attack one another again, but then they both nodded.

'Truce,' they said.

The other vampires burst into applause. Vanya pulled Mo into a hug. 'Congratulations,' she whispered into her ear. 'My sister is badass. I'm proud to be related to you.' Mo hugged her back, enjoying the cheers that echoed up into the high roof of the hall. Unnoticed by anyone, Pat leaned in towards Mo's dad.

'I'll rip your head off if you break this truce,' she whispered.

'I'll stake you first,' he replied.

Finally, the cheering died down and Mo beamed at all the vampires.

'This is a brave new chapter in British vampire history,' she said. 'There are always choices in this life, and today we have all chosen peace, security and . . .'

A blast from a hollering horn silenced her. The castle's oak entrance doors were flung open. A chill wind whistled in and ruffled the black and red banners. Footsteps could be heard approaching and then a figure appeared in the doorway.

'Greetings, suckers!' he said. 'Guess who's come to play funerals?'

48

The Vampire King, Matislav Rosstistavich – Steve to his friends – was standing in front of them all, framed by the great arched door and peeling off his black leather gloves.

Mo felt her mouth go dry. What was he doing here? What the absolute hell was *he* doing *here*? He was supposed to be crushing uprisings, his favourite pastime. He was supposed to have sent an emissary in his place. He was *not* supposed to be at Bogdan's funeral in all his medallion-wearing glory. Her mind racing, Mo bowed. The other vampires followed. She held the bow for a few seconds as she struggled to arrange her panicked face into something more delighted.

'Great Lord,' she said, once she was upright again.

'Surprise!' he yelled, tossing his gloves to one side and taking off his hat. It had three corners and a giant red feather. Mo was getting strong pirate vibes from it. Underneath, the Vampire King's hair looked different to the first time she had seen him. He had shaved the sides, but the rest was still long, blond and straggly, spilling down over his black satin jacket complete with silver epaulettes and huge shiny buttons. There were medallions – of course there were – jangling against his pale, bare chest, and a silver sash around his waist. He tipped his head back and tousled his hair, his eyes closed for a few seconds, like he was in a shampoo ad.

Mo glanced nervously behind her. Where was Dad? Not there. Thank God. Then she turned back.

'It is an honour to have you here, Your Majesty,' Mo said. She heard Pat snarl quietly.

'Of course it is,' he said. 'I decided I simply couldn't miss Bogdan's funeral. He would have wanted me here. I sensed his death so powerfully when he was killed, like a shudder in my guts.' He slapped his belly. 'It was almost like I cared about him, you know? So I had to come.'

'And the uprisings?'

'Crushed,' said the Vampire King, clicking his fingers and then walking up to Mo. He tilted her chin with his fingernail and studied her face for a few seconds. Then he moved over to Vanya.

'Who's your friend, Mo?'

'This is Vanya, my sister.'

'How sweet, you have your family around you,' he said.

My dad's here somewhere too, Mo thought, but then froze as the Vampire King put his hands around Vanya's waist, tipped her backwards and planted a huge kiss on her lips. Mo saw Vanya's hands fly up, clenching the air and only just stopping short of shoving him away.

'Delicious,' the Vampire King said, standing upright again and wiping his mouth on the back of his hand.

Mo searched Vanya's face but her expression was numb. Was she OK? No time to find out. The Vampire King was striding around the great hall.

'Now this is a place fit for a funeral. Loving the gothy decor. Fluoro skulls, inspired idea.'

'That was me, Your Mightiness,' Derek said, putting his hand up and blushing.

'Ah!' said the Vampire King, as if he'd ordered the steak but been brought the salad. 'You are . . . ?'

'Derek, Your Tremendousness.'

'And the rest of you?' He eyed the other vampires, his lip curling. They were standing like timid Victorian orphans lined up before their despotic matron. 'Actually, don't bother, I'll never remember your names. Just call me *Lord* or *Hero* or something and we'll leave it at that, yes?'

Then he beckoned Mo over to one side and spoke in a stage whisper.

'Queen Mo, I thought these guys were supposed to be thriving, but they look kind of pathetic to me. What are they wearing?'

'It's athleisure,' Mo said. 'Comfortable, modern . . .'

'Hideous, but then you were wearing disgusting jeans when we first met. Good to see you've made a tiny bit of effort today. That black dress is a little spinsterish, but whatever. You do you, Mo. I'll do me. At least I got dressed up for this special occasion,' he said. Then he burst out laughing, making everyone flinch. 'Only kidding! I always dress like this. So flamboyant, don't you think? The ladies love it.' He winked at Natasha, who seemed to shrink a little.

'Right, shall we get this party started? I'll say a few words.'

The Vampire King cleared his throat.

'Dear Bogdan, sorry you got staked. That was lame. You were a loyal emissary, you worked hard, you always dressed smartly, but not as exquisitely as me, as we have just discussed. What else? You were old. Like, really old! So, rest well and hopefully you're draining all the humans you can get your properly dead hands on up in vampire heaven right now. Ciao, baby.'

He raised his eyes to the sky for a few seconds, then clapped his hands together.

'Done! Right, time for the cremation. Where is he?'

'Who, Your Majesty?' Mo asked.

'Bogdan, of course,' he said, looking at her like she was stupid.

'Oh yes, Bogdan,' Mo said, her stomach lurching. Bogdan, who was still buried in her garden. She wiped her forehead quickly with her fingertips. The roaring fire was making her sweat. Or maybe it was the situation. 'Luca, my familiar, was supposed to bring him, but he's off today. Did anyone else bring Bogdan?' she called out.

Everyone looked around. Pat shook her head. Natasha shrugged. Malcolm patted his pockets, like he was checking for his keys, not for the corpse of a murdered six-hundred-year-old vampire. The girls smiled nervously.

The Vampire King watched with his arms folded. 'Well, I've got to say, I am very disappointed. I came here in my special carriage – my super fancy black one that I reserve for state occasions – pulled by vampire horses. Only the animist shaman vampires of the Ropoli Mountains have the power to turn animals of that size. These horses have fangs like swords. They feed on the blood of pigs and bison.'

He opened his mouth and rubbed one long black thumbnail across his bottom lip, staring at Mo as he did it, his fangs clearly visible. 'And now there's no Bogdan. Bogdan has bogged off! Ha! What a disaster. I'm surprised you didn't make absolutely sure he was here, Queen Mo. Sloppy ruling there.'

'I, er . . .'

'How come you didn't transport him here?'

Mo shifted a little. The other vampires around her were still and tense.

'Well, I . . . Luca was, er . . .' Mo heard how flustered she sounded.

The Vampire King came close. 'I know! You could have materialised here with him in your arms. The dead body of Bogdan, clutched to your breast, appearing before us all like a vampire angel. Wow! So dramatic!'

'Sorry, I didn't think to . . .' Mo shrugged and smiled.

'No, you didn't think. Bogdan's funeral and no Bogdan. Duh. What are you, stupid?'

'Don't speak to the queen like that.'

The Vampire King turned sharply to face the speaker.

Mo gulped. She knew that voice, so clear, so strong, so often complaining about what Mo was doing, but now leaping to her defence.

'What was that, grandma?' He shot across the floor and stood in front of Pat.

'You should speak to Queen Mo with respect,' Pat replied, staring coolly back. Mo held her breath. 'And my name is Pat, by the way. A pleasure to meet you, *finally*.'

She bobbed an ironic curtsy.

The Vampire King's eyes narrowed.

'What are you saying, Pat?' he asked, ending her name with a very crisp *t*. 'I sense a teensy bit of aggression there.'

'I was referring to the purges.'

'I don't think we need to talk about those, do we?' Mo said, moving towards the Vampire King, but he held up one hand in a stop sign.

'Remember those?' Pat went on. 'About twenty years ago? No, how could you. You just ignored them.'

'Purges, purges . . .' He was drumming his fingers on his lips, looking up into the rafters, as if racking his memory. 'Ah yes, they *do* ring a bell,' he said finally, smiling benignly at Pat. 'Nasty business with a vampire hunter, is that right?'

'Many vampire hunters,' Pat hissed. 'Killing many vampires.'

'Well, you made it through OK,' the Vampire King said, looking her up and down, then regarding the other vampires as if to ask, What is she moaning about? 'And who's this guy? Your big giant husband? What's his name?'

'Richard.'

'I'll call him Rick. He survived too. Does he speak or is he the strong silent type?'

He poked Richard's colossal chest with his forefinger. Richard continued to stare ahead of him, his face closed, but Pat was vibrating with rage.

'Don't touch my husband.'

'I will touch who I like, Pat, and I would also remind you, Pat, that I am the Vampire King.'

'And I would remind *you* that I am loyal to Queen Mo. She's a better ruler than you ever were.'

There was a general gasp. Mo felt the heat drain from her face.

The Vampire King stared at her with a look drenched in hatred. 'Interesting,' he said finally, 'but also wrong. Mo simply runs stuff here on my behalf because I have better things to do, but I am the lord, the king, the one true ruler of all vampires in these lands and far beyond. Capeesh?'

'But you've never wanted to do it, have you? Never cared about us. Not like Queen Mo does.'

Mo felt herself shrink inside her robes. Being bigged-up had never felt so life-threatening.

She watched the Vampire King draw himself up to his full height. 'Careful, Pat, this is all sounding rather disloyal. You'd better swear allegiance to me, or I might have to rip your head off.'

There was silence. No one breathed. Pat stared into the Vampire King's eyes, he stared back, and then she dropped her single-syllable bomb.

'No.'

Oh Pat, Pat, Pat . . . Mo found herself pleading. What are you *doing*?

'I am loyal to Queen Mo.'

'Me too,' said Vanya, stepping over to stand next to Pat.

Vanya! Not you as well.

'And if you dare touch a hair of my daughter's head, I will stake your heart so hard it explodes into a thousand million pieces.'

Dad!

He had been hiding behind Richard and now stepped forward. Mo felt her knees weaken with terror when she saw him. His face was hard and fearless and in his right hand he brandished one of Derek's fluoro-painted antlers.

49

The three of them stood in a tight line, with Richard behind, glaring at the Vampire King. Mo wanted to say something, but she felt too weak. Her father, her sister and Pat, the feistiest of all the vampires but, it seemed, also her biggest fan, standing together for her. They were so brave, so united, so *stupid*. They hadn't seen the Vampire King in Lower Donny village hall, chucking Bogdan across the room with a flick of his wrist or hypnotising Luca faster than you can say, 'You are feeling very sleepy.' Dad had warned her that vampires were strong and sneaky, but the Vampire King? He was in another league. They did not understand what they were messing with.

The Vampire King looked shocked and then suddenly scared. Genuinely freaked out. He stepped backwards on shaky legs. Mo saw her dad swap a delighted glance with Pat. They think they've got him, Mo thought, feeling faint with misery – because they hadn't. Of course they hadn't. The Vampire King was playing with them, like a cat toying with a mouse before biting its head off.

'Oh no, I'm so sorry,' the Vampire King said, putting his hands up defensively. 'Listen, guys, please don't hurt me. Pat, Vanya, you look so scary. You could, I don't know, scratch me really badly. As for that tiny man who's just shown up out of nowhere, Mr Scary Human, please, *please* don't hit me with your little toy antler thing.'

He pretended to shake with fear, he whimpered and cowered, he crouched down in a trembling ball. Confusion rippled over Pat's face, Mo's dad gripped the antler harder and glowered, and then the Vampire King suddenly sprang upright, his eyes electrified with rage.

'You fools!' he roared. His voice blasted all the air from the room. Mo felt as if she was suffocating. 'You dare to take me on? When I can do this!'

He slashed at the air, scooping up the first vampire he could. It was Francis the Mountaineer, who soon found himself flung against one wall and then another, with every sweep of the Vampire King's arm, and then hurled out over the battlements and into the darkness below.

The vampires wailed and cried out. They were shaking now, huddled together.

'Psychokinesis, baby! Whoa!' the Vampire King whooped. 'Who's next?'

He raised his hand and pointed at Pat.

'Patricia.' He dragged her name out. 'So eager to speak up but now less happy to step forward, perhaps.'

'I'm not afraid of you,' she said, marching towards him.

'Well, you should be,' he said, sounding bored and flicking his wrist. He threw her across the room without even touching her. Richard roared and ran at him like a bull, but the Vampire King waved him away, blasting him into the table. It broke in two and the pewter goblets clanged against the stone floor.

'Two stupid disloyal idiots left,' he said, smiling at Dad and Vanya.

'Please leave them,' Mo said.

'But why, when I'm having so much fun? Really, Queen Mo, this is quite the funeral. I had no idea you would lay on entertainment like this. Rebellious vampires and a very misguided human, questioning my authority. I'm having an absolute riot!'

'That man is my father,' Mo said.

'What, him? The one I'm about to throw against the castle wall, smashing every bone in his mortal body?'

'Yes,' Mo stammered.

'Really?' the Vampire King laughed. 'Your sister and your dad. Little Queen Mo, can't leave home without her family. I thought you were the strong and independent type. That's what you said to me. I even suggested we get married, but you said you preferred to rule alone.'

'I was wrong,' Mo said, suddenly holding his gaze. 'I'm not independent. Not like I thought.'

And it was true, Mo realised suddenly. She glanced at Vanya and her dad, but then she turned back to face the Vampire King. She began to smile, a wide and radiant smile, as if she had seen a vision. She stepped softly towards him. She felt her father and sister watching her, and their gaze seem to lift her up, make her limbs loose and her voice golden.

'I am weary of ruling alone, great king,' Mo said.

'Meaning?'

Mo clutched the Vampire King's hands. 'Marry me, dread lord,' she said, gazing adoringly into his dark eyes.

'Don't do this!' Vanya shouted, but Mo didn't seem to hear. She raised the Vampire King's hands to her lips and kissed first one, then the other.

'Marry me, oh great master. I am the Chosen One. I am ready now. Together we can rule with unlimited power. Pick me. Choose me. Take me as your bride!'

The Vampire King looked intrigued. 'Mo, what *is* going on? You've gone even weirder than usual. First time I met you, you insisted you were human; today you're more like . . .'

'A vampire saint,' said Mo, beaming up at him and spreading her arms out wide. 'No longer just a queen, but a saint, destined to give holy power to your reign.'

'Ha!' said the Vampire King, clapping his hands. 'I *love* this. What a turn-up. So full of surprises, Mo. You had said you wanted to rule alone, but now you've changed your mind. Well, it's a lady's prerogative, I suppose.'

'Have you hypnotised her?' Vanya called.

'This is my true desire,' Mo said. 'Leave these two behind. Do not waste your god-like power on them.

Look to me, only me. I am the one that will secure your rule. All vampires will quake before us.'

'Which means no more uprisings! Excellent. They were getting a bit tedious, you know?'

'Mo, stop, please,' Vanya said, rushing up and grabbing her arm. Mo shook her off, as if in a trance.

'Get back, Vanya, or I *will* kill you,' the Vampire King hissed. 'And actually Mo, baby, I really do want to kill that dumb idiot father of yours. He's massively annoying me.'

He raised his hand towards him, but Mo seized it again and brought it to her lips.

'I want only to kiss these hands,' she said. 'Do not raise them against mortal cowards like him. A great leader does not squander his power on swine.'

'Hmmm,' he said, mulling it over. 'You are so right. Oh, this is good, this is excellent. I can already see how this is going to work out, babe. All right, let's do this.'

Then he snatched Mo's hand and flung it up in the air, like the referee declaring the winner of a boxing match. 'It's wedding time, everybody! Whoo!'

He pointed at Derek. 'You. Perform the marriage rites.'

Derek hurried over. 'But I, er, don't know what they are.'

'Doesn't matter. Make something up. I'm the king, boy. I make the law. I *am* the law. If I say Mo and I are married, we're married. Stop looking so terrified. This is a happy occasion. Anyone who doesn't agree can have their head ripped off.'

Mo felt Vanya's eyes on her and heard her dad utter a low moan, but she refused to look at them.

Derek cleared his throat. 'Do you, Queen Mo, take . . .' he stuttered, his hands trembling.

'Get on with it,' the Vampire King barked.

'Do you, Mo Merrydrew, Vampire Queen of Great Britain, take you, Matislav Ross . . . Rosstits –'

'Rosstistavich!' the Vampire King roared. 'Why can't anyone pronounce my name?'

Derek quaked.

'Carry on.'

'The Vampire King of the East, to be your wedded husband?'

There was a pause. No one spoke. Mo seemed to be lost in a dream, but then she smiled woozily at the Vampire King. 'I do,' she said in a voice that was deep, treacly and nothing like her usual girlish tones.

'Goody!' said the Vampire King. 'Me too!' And then he pulled Mo roughly into him, planting a huge kiss on her lips.

Mo barely felt it. His thin, chill lips, the pressure of his teeth behind them, the weird smell coming from his long blond hair, like a damp towel. It barely registered. Then it was over, and he was shouting triumphantly at the other vampires.

'Now this is what I call a power couple. You lot better hang on. No more nicey-nicey stuff from Mo any more. She's ruling with me, my way. We will be *soooo* ruthless together! It's going to be wild.'

Pat had dragged herself up and was crouched next to Richard now. She hissed at the Vampire King but stayed where she was. Olga and Lenka stared at Mo, their faces full of shock. Derek rushed up to Mo and kissed her hand. 'Forgive me,' he said, but Mo's oddly glazed eyes were staring ahead, like a sleepwalker's.

As the two of them walked towards the door, Mo's dad rushed forward, his antler raised, but without even turning round the Vampire King flicked his hand dismissively and sent him shooting through the air. Mo heard him hit the ground but didn't turn to look. She glided through the door like a ghost, holding her new husband's hand.

On the threshold he stopped and glared at them all. 'I can read your tiny minds, by the way. I know what you're thinking.' He put on a whining voice. '*Oh no, our lovely queen, taken away to the East, but we want her to stay.* I can see how much you all worship her. Well, you better start worshipping me too. She's mine now. We rule as one, don't we?'

Mo gazed blankly ahead.

'Don't try to stop us,' he threatened, waving his finger like a metronome. 'You saw what I did to big tough Richard over there, and that other puny guy who went out the window and Vanya and silly, silly Pat. I'll do the same to all of you. Then I'll rip your heads off. *And* I'll enjoy it. Got it?'

The vampires said nothing. The Vampire King spun on his heel and led Mo away.

50

The cold outside seemed to revive Mo. Her beatific daydream slipped from her grasp, like a silk scarf through a magician's fingers. She landed back in her body. The Vampire King was still gripping her hand, leading her quickly towards his carriage.

'Let's get out of this dump and back to my palace. You're going to love your new home, Mo. I've just had a new gold-plated hot tub installed.'

Mo felt the freezing rain lash against her face, felt the cold wind tug at her hair.

The Vampire King was now striding ahead of her, dragging her along behind him, and when they reached the carriage he climbed inside, but Mo snapped her hand out of his grip.

'Let me inspect the horses,' she said.

'What? Why?'

'I have never seen vampire horses before.'

The Vampire King sighed heavily. 'If you must.'

The rain had drenched their coal-dark coats. Their

long black manes were dripping. They fidgeted and snorted, eager to get moving.

'Shh,' Mo said, stroking the glistening neck and powerful shoulder of one. It twitched its head, giving Mo a tiny flash of its huge fangs, like sharpened tusks. She gently unbuckled its harness from the carriage shaft, then moved quietly round to the other one and did the same, all the time whispering soothingly.

Then she returned to the carriage, careful to compose her face in a dreamy daze before speaking to the Vampire King.

'I changed my mind,' she said. 'I wish to claim that human who was once my father. A snack for the journey.'

'Yes!' said the Vampire King, eyes twinkling. 'Now you're talking. What better gift for a new bride than a bellyful of paternal blood. Yummo!'

'Exactly,' Mo said, squashing down a grimace, and then she ducked away from the window. She walked slowly at first, but as soon as she was sure the Vampire King couldn't see her, she broke into a run.

Olga and Lenka, watching from the battlements, gasped. 'What's she doing?' Olga said.

'Oh wow,' Lenka said.

They ran back inside.

'Queen Mo has got out of the carriage and she's grabbed one of the flaming torches!' they shouted. 'Come and see!'

All the vampires crowded onto the battlements.

'Is she going to set light to the castle?' Derek asked. 'Destroy us all? She looked like she had lost her mind back there.'

'No, look, she's going over to Richard's cannon,' Natasha said. 'She's put the torch down and now she's trying to move the cannon, but it's too heavy. Oh, careful, Queen Mo, you could put your back out.'

Then, suddenly, a shape appeared at her side. A huge figure.

Pat gasped. 'It's Richard!'

He had run on legs still shaky from being thrown by the Vampire King and now laid his great shovel hands over Mo's. Pat raced down to him too, Vanya following. Together they heaved the cannon around so it was pointing straight down the drive. Now Richard picked up the flaming torch and handed it to Mo.

'Ready?' he said. It was the first time Mo had ever heard his voice. It was deep and soft.

'Wait, I want to see this.' Mo's dad had limped outside, supported by Sven. Mo nodded at him over her shoulder, he nodded back, then Mo held the torch up.

'Let's do this together,' Pat said, laying her hands over Mo's. Vanya joined them, Richard's mighty paws covering them all. Mo stared at the flickering flames for a second, then muttered softly, 'Three . . . two . . . one!' and they lowered the torch onto the cannon's fuse.

The explosion hurled Mo backwards. When she opened her eyes a few seconds later, she was lying on her back on the wet grass. She sat up slowly. Her ears were ringing, so she could barely hear the terrified whinnies of the vampire horses as they bolted away or the roar of triumph from the ramparts as the vampires cheered and hugged and whooped.

Vanya helped her up and they stared in silence at the devastation on the drive. The carriage was smashed, smoke was rising from the shattered pieces of wood and broken wheels. Nothing moved.

Mo hugged Vanya then ran to her dad, still being supported by Sven.

'OK?'

'I think I might have broken my ankle,' he said. 'Could have been worse though.'

'He's wearing body armour,' Vanya said. 'Can you believe that? It's like he knew he was going to do something stupid like challenge Vampire King.'

Mo laughed, then let out a sob of relief.

'Come here,' said Vanya, pulling Mo into her shoulder, where she stayed for several minutes.

'Excuse me, Queen Mo?'

Mo broke out of the hug suddenly. She didn't recognise the voice.

'Oh, Richard, hi,' she said. 'Sorry, I can't get used to hearing you speak.'

He smiled. 'I've checked the wreckage,' he said. 'This is all that is left of Matislav Rosstistavich, the mighty Vampire King of the East.' He dropped a few tangled and dented medallions, like remnants of a Saxon hoard, into Mo's hand.

'Is there any way he could have survived?' she asked.

Richard shook his head.

'I know vampires traditionally can only be killed by staking, decapitating or sunlight, but being exploded by an actual ruddy cannon is also up there!' Pat was by Mo's side now, hooting with laughter and clapping her hands. 'I absolutely knew that cannon had a purpose other than just to annoy the gloves off me. The Vampire King, vanquished once and for all. He's toast.' She punched the air.

'All my dreams have come true, Queen Mo. The Vampire King is dead and I've got my husband back – he hasn't said this much in years!' Then she rushed up to Richard and, on tiptoe, planted an enthusiastic kiss on his lips. He lifted her off the ground and whirled her around, her legs flying out behind her while she whooped like a child.

'And we have a truce, between vampires and vampire hunters, don't forget,' Mo said.

'Yes, we do. Ring-a-ding-ding! It's all change. Looking at you, Mr Mo's Dad,' Pat said, saluting him. 'We stood up to that nasty piece of vampire work, didn't we? Standing together as one. It was totally actually marvellous!'

Mo's dad smiled back and then winced.

'Better get you inside,' Pat said. 'Let me see about that ankle. I was quite handy with a bandage back in my mortal days.'

Sven helped Mo's dad back inside, with Pat and Richard following. Mo heard her dad asking Pat if she'd ever amputated a toe, operated on a donkey, given a hamster mouth-to-mouth resuscitation.

'Look at that – vampires and the last vampire hunter united. You did it, sis,' said Vanya. 'You got the truce.'

'But I killed the Vampire King,' Mo said quietly. 'I said I'd never be ruthless like he was. I wanted to do things differently . . .'

'*You* killed the Vampire King? Excuse me, it wasn't just you, it was you, me, Pat and Richard, with your dad cheering us on. Team effort. You don't need to shoulder this one on your own.'

'But the cycle of violence?'

'It ends here, with him gone.'

'Won't his subjects come after me?'

'Are you kidding? They hate him even more than we do. You have done them favour.'

Vanya hooked her arm through Mo's and they stood quietly. The rain had stopped and the cannon seemed to have blown a hole right through the clouds. A huge full moon now shone through it. It meant they could see the other vampires, and Sven emerging from the trees with the body of Francis the Mountaineer.

'Is he killed?' Mo called out.

Sven nodded. 'Regrettably, he dropped at velocity onto a fence post and was crudely skewered.'

'See!' Vanya said. 'The Vampire King could have killed all of us, not just Francis. He was menace, Mo. He served only himself. That's no way to lead. We're free of him now. You can get on and rule just exactly as you want to.'

Mo nodded.

'Was it all an act, that weird saintly bride thing?' Vanya asked.

'Yes,' Mo said, 'but also no. Hard to say. I was acting, but sort of not too. I just suddenly knew what to do to get him away from you and Dad and Pat.'

They began walking towards the door.

'He is terrible kisser, isn't he?' Vanya said, nudging Mo gently in the ribs.

'The worst!'

'See, that's why I could never be with a man.'

'Not all of them kiss like that,' Mo said, thinking of Luca.

'I don't believe you, and I hope I never find out.'

Mo smiled at Vanya, then paused at the door. 'Look, you go on in. I'll follow you. I need to make a call.'

Vanya nodded and stepped inside.

Mo took out her phone, tapped on Luca's name, heard it ring and ring.

Then . . .

'Hi, this is Luca, leave a message.'

Beep.

'Hey, it's me. Mo. I just wondered how you were.'

She paused, bit her lip. 'So, we just killed the Vampire King. With a cannon. Richard's cannon. Remember that?'

She laughed faintly.

'Everyone's celebrating, so I'd better go.'

She paused again.

'Anyway, vampires and vampire hunters have agreed a truce and with lovely old Steve dead, I'll have a lot more time for, you know, a relationship?'

She stared at the ground.

'I guess I'm too late though, aren't I? Yeah, I think I probably am. Stupid Mo. Can kill the vampire overlord, but can't do relationships. Sorry, Luca. I'm really sorry. I hope you're OK. I, er . . . I really hope you're OK.'

Then she hung up and hugged her arms around herself. It was cold. Her dress was soaked and she realised she was starving. She shivered.

'Mo, come in, you'll freeze out there.' Vanya was standing in the doorway, beckoning her inside. 'Richard has chucked some of the carriage wood on the fire and it's really blazing, and everyone's dancing. Get in here. Now!'

Mo smiled at Vanya. 'Coming,' she said. She glanced at her phone one more time, looked up at the moon and took a deep breath. Then she ran inside to find her sister and join the celebrations.

To be continued . . .

HOT KEY BOOKS

Thank you for choosing a Hot Key book.

If you want to know more about our authors
and what we publish, you can find us online.

You can start at our website

www.hotkeybooks.com

And you can also find us on:

We hope to see you soon!